Redefining Never

Redefining Never

Bethany A. Orlando

Order this book online at www.trafford.com
or email orders@trafford.com

Most Trafford titles are also available at major online book retailers.

Note for Librarians: A cataloguing record for this book is available from Library
and Archives Canada at www.collectionscanada.ca/amicus/index-e.html

Printed in Victoria, BC, Canada.

ISBN: 978-1-4269-0176-8 (Soft)

*Our mission is to efficiently provide the world's finest, most comprehensive
book publishing service, enabling every author to experience success.
To find out how to publish your book, your way, and have it available
worldwide, visit us online at www.trafford.com*

Trafford rev. 10/14/2009

 www.trafford.com

North America & international
toll-free: 1 888 232 4444 (USA & Canada)
phone: 250 383 6864 ♦ fax: 812 355 4082

For my Family

"Honour all men.
Love the brotherhood.
Fear God.
Honour the king."
1 Peter 2:17

Contents

Preface

"To the victor go the spoils." We've all heard the expression, and when we think of the "spoils," we generally think of lands, moneys, treasures, power, and so on. However, the victor wins much more: namely the entitlement to write the history books. Not surprisingly, there are often holes, misquotes, misinformation, and occasionally, lies in the retelling of their tales.

On the part of the victor, mistakes are covered and atrocities buried, so as to make their own history more virtuous and appealing. Conversely, those same actions committed by the "enemy" are blown up and pushed to the forefront, making certain that history remembers our "righteous might," as one former president phrased it.

If the British had won the American War for Independence, how might history have been written? Men like George Washington, Thomas Jefferson, Francis Marion, and Thomas Sumter would be merely a smudge in our otherwise glorious history as Britons. Generals Lord Cornwallis and Clinton, and even Benedict Arnold would be heroes memorialized throughout the colonies for their brave efforts and commendable actions that saved us from anarchy. It's an interesting twist.

This being the case, am I proud of my citizenship and heritage? Without question. I love my country. I respect the leadership in place, even though I don't always agree (a right I am proud we have earned). And I believe there have been many moments in our history when we have indeed displayed a "righteous might."

Still, my pride for my country grows, not in spite of our history, but because of it. The fact is our great heritage was not always won with honour. We're taught in school about how the armies of Great Britain abused much of their privilege and power in the colonies: occupying the homes of private citizens, stealing goods from local farms, and even attacking women and children. But to pretend the Continentals and patriot militia were not guilty of the same crimes against Loyalists and others is careless and naïve.

It is the rediscovering of this truth which inspired me to right this story. It is based on the life and character of one Lieutenant Colonel (later General Sir) Banastre Tarleton: a story less often told because he fought for the "enemy." When his legend is recanted in American history, it is done so with disdain and disrespect. He has been painted one of history's most perfect villains.

My occupation is not to elevate this man to sainthood. Goodness knows he had his faults. Tarleton was a reckless gambler, something of a womanizer, and loved a good party—probably a little too much. Most of his victories, and nearly all of his escapes were won because of a self-inflated, "bullets only hit other people" attitude (as the good people at Oatmeal for the Foxhounds say it). On the other hand, it's important to remember; when he landed in the colonies, Tarleton was twenty-one years-old. If the war took place today, he would be just old enough to have a drink at the local bar.

If you were to research Tarleton in any American text, one of the first things you'd find would be the chapter on the Waxhaw Massacre. There are lists of violent statistics and plenty of ugly remarks about Tarleton's behaviour and ability to command; when in fact, what led to the patriot loss was more the fault of their own commander than the actions of a young dragoon.

By all rights, Tarleton and his troops shouldn't have been able to beat the enemy troupe. Their regiment, which included infantry and light artillery, had covered a distance of more than 100 miles in just over two days. They had done so in suffocating heat and suffered the loss of many of their cavalry mounts along the way, causing the necessity for horses to bear two riders. Several of the men had also collapsed during the arduous march. Not to mention, they were outnumbered two to one.

The patriots had the head-start and the advantage of position and numbers, among other benefits; yet their commander yielded them all. Rather than form ranks when an attack was threatened, he continued to march. Instead of moving his artillery to cover his rear guard, he kept it at the front of the column, rendering it useless in the onslaught. He ordered his men to hold their fire until the enemy was within ten yards–and closing–offering a worthless volley. Perhaps his greatest error was in refusing the initial terms of surrender offered by Tarleton before the fray began.

Then there's the matter of the controversial white flag–a story I will not tell here because of bias. I would prefer the reader find detail himself and form his own opinion.

The result of the skirmish was a tarnished reputation for Tarleton and a new battle cry for the patriots: "Tarleton's Quarter," meaning take no prisoners. The rumour was Tarleton ordered the slaughter of all men on the battlefield–wounded, captured, or otherwise. Reported statistics tell a different story.

While the number of patriot dead was most certainly great, at least 150 wounded were paroled on the field and taken to a nearby church for medical attention. Another 53 were reported to have been imprisoned at the jail in Camden. Many more escaped, including those at the head of the column who may not have seen any action at all, continuing the march and leaving their fellow-soldiers instead.

In retrospect, this battle was as much an important loss for the patriots as it was a victory for the British. The supposed "atrocities" committed that day, revived the rebel militia and the southern arm of the Continental Army, which had been all but completely dispersed after the capture of Charles Town. In point of fact, it's my feeling Americans owe men like Tarleton a debt of gratitude for fuelling the fire. It was these sorts of events throughout the war that kept military recruitment possible for the Continentals and the militia alike. No one wants to be on the losing side of a war, but many find the will to fight, if they can be convinced their actions are avenging their fallen friends and brothers.

It is for this reason–to tell the other side of the tale–that I relate the following story. The characters and their relationships are pure fiction, though within the realm of possibility for the day and time. The battles and other events of the war are told with the greatest care for accuracy, details having been gathered from multiple sources to ensure an unbiased point of view.

Nevertheless, as I mentioned earlier, stories are often full of holes. Mine is no exception. I told only one side of the story. I would not only invite, but sincerely implore the reader to further pursue information on these matters.

If the reader seeks more information on Tarleton or the primary subjects mentioned in this book, the best place to start, in my opinion, would be with Oatmeal for the Foxhounds (www.banastretarleton.org). They have a website dedicated to his memory and his story–and to refuting the damaging image portrayed in film and fiction (my particular favourite being the comparison of Tarleton to Tavington). It's also more fun than reading a history book.

In the end, we all know the good guys don't wear white hats to distinguish themselves from the black-hat-wearing bad guys. Even if they did, the good guys would have to occasionally trade in their white hats while performing certain duties that outsiders wouldn't understand and would probably deem inappropriate at best.

So, before history is written–before the good guys and bad guys are determined–on which side of the war do you find yourself? Do you stand by your King and country and endure the prodigious taxes and misrepresentation; because it's the right thing to do? After all, to do otherwise would be breaking the law at the least, and treason at the worst. The French are beheading people for less.

Is rebellion worth losing your livelihood? Surely sustaining the ability to pay heavy taxes is better than having no income at all. What about your home, your family? The Redcoats could imprison the whole lot, if given reason. Rumour has it, as many people die in their prisons as by the end of their swords.

What if the rebellion fails? Where would you go? Certainly, rebels would be exiled if not imprisoned or executed. The King's territory stretches from Canada to the Caribbean. I suppose you'd have to go west, but I can only imagine the resistance you would meet against the Indians.

Choose carefully. It's not a decision easily undone. Besides, what are the odds of this small group of malcontents actually affecting any change, let alone winning independence from the most fearsome military in the world?

1

The sun had not quite set, and the lanterns posted about carried flames that seemed to dance for the approaching nightfall. The soft light caught the women's jewellery and the brass buttons of the men's coats. They looked like beautiful, tiny stars. Standing out above the rest, Aislin had to admit the soldiers were the most finely dressed. The reds, greens, and blues were impossibly brilliant against the dim twilight.

She stepped out of the carriage looking like a vision faintly remembered from a dream. The cool evening breeze gently moved the edges of the silk indigo dress she wore, but it sent a cruel shiver down Aislin's spine. To her, every event was a test–an examination of how well she had prepared herself.

Anxiously, she eyed the castle-like structure before her. The estate sprawled in every direction, alive with the milling crowd of New Jersey's elite.

Madam Andrews stepped up behind her.

"Mind your fidgeting, dear," her teacher reminded her.

Aislin awoke from her day dream, becoming aware that her hands were entangled in the delicate purse she carried. She ceased the nervous habit immediately.

The two ladies approached the large brick house. When they reached the door, the pair was greeted with bows and nods from gentlemen standing by. Aislin's head reeled from all of the sights and sounds that fought for her attention all at once. Only her mentor perceived her unease, for in most everything Aislin exuded the utmost confidence.

They had moved deeply into the crowd, and Aislin felt as if the whole world was watching her. It made her feel all the more defensive which in turn brought a wild look to her dark eyes and made her appear even more attractive. Aislin couldn't recall exactly when Madam left her side but was startled at the realization that she was alone. It was about this time that she caught the attention of a certain British officer.

"Who is that?" the major asked, slowly and eloquently.

"I'm not sure," replied the lieutenant to his left. "I don't recognize the girl, but the woman who came in with her is Elizabeth Andrews. Her husband was General Frederick Andrews-"

The major interrupted, "I am familiar with the family, but I do not recall them having any children."

The lieutenant continued as though no interruption had occurred. "I had heard that Mrs. Andrews had taken on somewhat of a protégé several years ago-the daughter of a wealthy widower."

It was at this point that the captain on the major's right chose to speak up. "Leave it to Dear Mrs. Andrews to take on such a project." He paused for a moment, then continued. "She certainly is fetching. I wonder if she's spoken for."

Even if she was, the major wasn't about to be scared off such a prize.

"I suppose she'd make a suitable dancing partner," he said, a bit smugly.

The others laughed.

The major began to move in her direction, pausing only a moment as he noticed a young man already taking the lady's hand. Never one to accept defeat, he continued his advance as though the other man didn't exist. Though he'd never admit it, the major was captivated, feeling almost covetous of this beautiful creature.

Making their way toward the other couples already paired for the dance, Aislin and her escort unexpectedly found their way barred by a tall, dark figure. The gentleman in her path introduced himself as he politely nodded in greeting.

"Good evening, Miss. I am Major William Garnett of His Majesty's Army. Might I inquire as to your name?"

"Aislin Laraway," she said returning his bow. She thought it unnecessary for him to recite his hire, seeing as his bright uniform spoke for itself.

"Aislin—unusual. Undoubtedly a family name."

"Yes, it is."

"Hm, how droll," he said with a tilt of his head, his silvery blue eyes wandering over her features.

Aislin felt her face get hot. Her first instinct was to be offended and snap at the major for making such uncouth remarks, but her memory rapidly caught her attention. His name-Garnett-she'd heard it before. It came to her in a rush. The stories she'd heard from General Andrews-stories she wasn't meant to hear, being so young as she was. The general had held no esteem for the man, but everyone who knew better feared him-respect or no.

All of this ran through her mind in an instant, and before she'd gathered her thoughts, the major interrupted her inward turmoil.

"Would you care to dance?" he asked, holding out his hand.

Aislin felt herself step backwards.

"Mr. Carter has already requested this dance," she answered firmly.

"Oh, I'm certain Mr. Carter wouldn't mind."

With this, the major gave a look to his competitor that expressed his insistence. The gentleman forced a tight smile along with his glower as he yielded his partner.

Presently, as she found her hand reaching for Garnett's, Aislin was grateful Madam had insisted on her wearing gloves. She would have flatly turned him away except that Madam had taught her that a refusal is always impolite and thus unacceptable. The fact that he was an officer in the British Army only made things worse, and if the truth were told, she was afraid of him. She hoped to peaceably get through their dance and then be done with him.

They were both exceptional dancers and quite a vision to behold. While Garnett sailed along, enjoying himself and making polite conversation-weather, politics, and the like-Aislin said as little as possible.

"You hardly speak. I find it hard to believe you have nothing at all to say." The major cornered her.

"Keeping silent prevents me from saying things that I shouldn't."

The curtness of her response caught Garnett off-guard, but Aislin would never know. Instead, he continued on.

"Better to be thought a fool and keep silent, than to open your mouth and prove it."

Aislin was shocked. Her demure façade was beginning to crumble.

"Am I to understand you think me a fool, Major?"

Garnett had grown frustrated with her lack of engagement. Not to mention, he did love to hear her speak. Even if it meant an argument, it would suffice. So he did not lament his instigation much.

"I don't believe I've drawn any conclusions, but you haven't given me much on which to base my opinion. I would rather know the extent of your foolishness than continue on in silence."

"I never! The unmitigated arrogance." Aislin felt the urge to slap him dead in the mouth. Fortunately, her self-control had improved greatly due to Madam's lessons.

"Arrogant, am I?" he questioned coolly, "By what criteria do you judge me arrogant?"

"In but the very few moments since our introduction, every word you've spoken to me has been dripping with condescension. What else am I to infer except that you see yourself superior to me?"

"Superior–"

Aislin cut him short. "You Redcoats are all alike." She said it partly under her breath but loud enough for Garnett to hear. Somehow her fear of him had all but slipped her mind.

"Which is it that bothers you most, Miss: that I am military or that I am not a colonial?" His tone was patronizing.

"I couldn't possibly decide, but the combination is unbearable." She was equally as patronizing and twice as sarcastic.

Garnett responded out of somewhat genuine curiosity, "And why is that?"

"You and your kind act as if you know everything, but somehow you find no contradiction in blindly following the orders of someone half the world away. You're hypocritical and self-absorbed, and–"

The major stopped her there. "Well, no wonder you didn't want to speak to me. I suppose you might consider yourself among those they're calling 'Patriots?'"

"I would prefer not to be reduced to categorizing myself."

Aislin caught her tone and swiftly remembered to whom she was speaking. She was glad the major had stopped dancing just then, because she had completely frozen in his icy gaze. The still whirling crowd around them was beginning to make her feel dizzy.

"I see." The thought hadn't occurred to him that she might actually be a sympathizer.

Garnett saw this conversation going no where he wanted to follow. He was impressed by this young woman's vigour. She spoke, not only as one properly educated, but also with passion and pride-traits the major felt were missing from most women. This was the first conversation he could remember having at a ball wherein he wasn't disinterested or utterly bored. He decided it would be best to let the lady part before one of them was truly insulted. Arrogant, maybe. Rude, at times, perhaps. But his timing was rarely questionable.

"Well," he said, "I suppose the best course of action would be for me to bid you good evening and excuse myself."

Aislin gave no response. That was the one action for which she was unprepared.

"Good evening, Miss Laraway." The major bowed his final bow and walked away.

For a moment, Aislin stood, stunned. She was relieved at his absence, but taken aback as well.

Finally, she turned and walked toward the edge of the room. Madam joined her.

"What's the matter, dear?"

"I think I've made a horrible mistake."

"Oh, Aislin."

"I know I should apologize, but I feel if I must speak to that man again, I will only make things worse."

"To whom are you referring, dear?"

Aislin gestured in his direction. It was obvious who she meant. Garnett had just managed a glance at her, still looking just as unrelenting as he did unforgiving.

"Major Garnett?" Madam's speech broke with a snicker. "My, not just a soldier but an officer! What on earth..." Her voice trailed off.

Aislin felt she would be sick. She knew well who and how important Garnett was. Seeing Aislin's sinking expression, Madam tried to put her at ease.

"My dear girl, throughout all of your encounters with men, it is certain that you will say hundreds of things you do not mean and hundreds more that you know you shouldn't."

"Yes, but the problem is that I did mean them, and what's more, he knows it. I'm not sure what I should do."

"Don't worry. I shall speak with your good major."

With that, Madam began to make her way through the crowd. The bag in Aislin's hands was not fairing very well at all.

"Good evening, Major Garnett," Madam opened.

"Mrs. Andrews, wonderful to see you again."

"Likewise, Major. By the way, I do congratulate you on your promotion. I'm sure you've worked very hard to earn it." Though Mrs. Andrews held the major in less regard than her late husband, it was simply not in her nature to be discourteous.

"How very kind of you, Mrs. Andrews."

Aislin watched them from across the room. She noticed Madam's intimidating posture, but could tell by the way her hands were folded that Madam was speaking politely. Aislin also noticed Garnett's prim and proper manner, but the thing about him that most caught her attention was his nonchalant smile. His look of a lack of concern was nearly a death sentence for Aislin's little purse.

"Incidentally," the major continued, "I've just met your Miss Laraway. She's quite a charming young lady, if I may say."

"I'm afraid she's rather embarrassed over whatever exchange the two of you may have had."

"Completely unnecessary. Youth does often lend itself to fewer inhibitions, in spite of what or by whom one has been taught. She was merely voicing an honest opinion." At his

6

remark, Madam better understood Aislin's condition. "However, I do hope that no offence was taken."

"No, of course not." Madam was an excellent bluff. "And might I convey the same of you?"

"Certainly. Tell me, Mrs. Andrews, how is it Miss Laraway came to you?"

"I met the girl in our church when she was quite young. She was such a beautiful child. Her mother was gone, and she was being raised by her father and three elder brothers. Her father is a lawyer in Camden and certainly does well for his family, but it was no life for a young girl: living with four men and receiving no tutelage in those things with which a lady ought to concern herself. So I approached her father and offered my services: to give her a proper education in schooling and etiquette. She stays with me for a few weeks at a time, and she's been a lovely student."

"I am impressed, and you must be pleased. She seems a wonderful young woman."

"And speaking of whom, I really shouldn't keep her waiting. Please excuse me, Major."

"Have a pleasant evening, Mrs. Andrews."

"And you as well."

Madam caught Aislin's attention and walked to the nearest door leading to the terrace. This was Aislin's cue to follow her outside, chased all the way by the major's cool stare. She was dying to know what Garnett had said to Madam but knew it would be rude to pry.

Madam only added to her curiosity. "We'll talk about it later. For now, rest assured it's been taken care of."

"Yes, Madam."

They both had their reasons for disliking those in the military. Madam felt a bit cheated, in that her husband had lived and died in their services. Also, she and Aislin felt strongly about the misrepresentations of the colonies in Parliament. Aislin, unfortunately, had never had a positive interaction with the soldiers. From her perceptions, they looked down on all the colonists and felt their work there was an unnecessary chore, until the fighting had begun, that is.

"The two of you did dance nicely together. I couldn't help but notice." Madam smiled. She knew it was a devilish thing to say. "You could make a lovely couple."

Aislin had to laugh. "Never! Ugh," she moaned, "If you could have heard the way he spoke to me. He was so rude and arrogant. He's positively revolting!"

"You know, dear, some of the greatest storied lovers have grown together out of adversities." Madam was just egging her on now.

"Yes, and most of them ended up dead!"

"What about the ones who lived 'happily ever after'?"

"Shakespeare's Juliet stabbed herself to death after finding her Romeo had poisoned himself."

Both women giggled.

"Well that's a rather cynical take on the subject, don't you think?"

"They can keep their great romances, just the same."

The two ladies stood quietly in the evening air only for a minute before the next interruption presented himself. This one, however, was far more welcome than the last.

The young man's hair was a golden colour, and his eyes were a deep, rich brown–much nicer than Garnett's crystal, blue glare. Aislin had noticed him earlier in the evening and had hoped for a chance to meet him. He was very handsome.

"Pardon me, Miss Laraway, isn't it?" he asked quietly.

"It is."

"My name is Benjamin Ashby."

"I'm please to meet you, Mr. Ashby."

"Likewise," he stammered.

Aislin thought it was sweet.

"I was wondering if, perhaps, you would you like to dance."

"I'd love to." She turned and gave Madam a smile as they left.

Arm in arm, they strolled inside to join the other couples. Benjamin was a bit awkward and clearly had not had much formal training, but all in all their dance was rather enjoyable. Aislin spoke easily with him and he with her. She wasn't even

8

aware that she had the major's attention the entire time. They danced at every opportunity for the rest of the evening.

Benjamin asked her about her family and about what sorts of things she enjoyed in her leisure. Although their conversations weren't all together exciting, Aislin loved that he seemed so interested in her. It wasn't that she was self-centred, quite the opposite. It's just that she wasn't accustomed to so much attention.

In between dances, they took their conversations to some quiet corner of the room, and on occasion, Madam joined them as well. Aislin could tell that the gentleman had Madam's approval.

Benjamin was a banker. He had just concluded an apprenticeship and had only recently taken on himself a business there in Trenton. He was very smart, and his confidence emerged when he spoke about his trade. It was in speaking of more personal matters that he became cumbersome. Aislin found him incredibly charming.

The night drew to a close far too soon. Aislin found herself bidding good night to Mr. Ashby, it seemed, just moments after she'd met him. Though she regretted their parting, she took comfort in Benjamin's promise to call on her when next she visited Madam Andrews.

As they returned home from the ball, Madam related to Aislin everything that Garnett had said in their earlier conversation. It all came rushing back to Aislin's mind, and she partly wished Madam had not brought it up. Madam said all these things meaning them to be a compliment to Aislin. Aislin, however, did not see it that way. She imagined the major said what he had either to poke fun at her, or to impress Madam.

Besides, Aislin thought, *even if he was sincere, what sort of woman would want anything to do with a man like him?*

Seeing the change in Aislin's formerly pleasing demeanour, Madam changed the subject.

"And what about Mr. Ashby? The two of you seemed to be getting on well."

"Yes," she said, a little wistfully but with question in the depths of her tone.

"Don't you like him? You spent practically the whole evening together."

"Oh, he was delightful," Aislin replied, her voice grasping for some excitement it never reached. "I enjoyed talking with him and all, and he was a perfect gentleman. He's the sort of man every girl hopes to marry." She spoke with more conviction that time.

"Then what's the matter, dear?"

Aislin sighed, "I don't know. There just seems to be something missing."

"Perhaps a dagger and vile of poison?" Madam suggested with a smile.

A bit of humour was just what Aislin needed.

2

Benjamin was true to his word. He visited Aislin each time she ventured to Madam's estate. He would take her riding, or the pair would go for walks. When the weather was nice, they'd sit on the porch, and Aislin would read aloud to him. Their time together flew by.

A few short months later, Aislin still thought about the ball and thought often about Benjamin, but only rarely did she have time to linger on either subject. Everything in her life was changing. The British had turned their sights on nearby Philadelphia, and the skirmishes to the north were becoming worse and more frequent.

It wasn't long before Aislin found herself forced to choose sides, and a muddled, confusing time it was for her. As head of the household, Daniel Laraway had made his opinions crystal clear. The taxes had hurt the surrounding businesses and made regular necessities nearly unattainable for those less fortunate. With the stamp taxes threatening his own business, and the growing losses accrued by those on whose dealings he depended, Laraway determined his loyalties ought to lie with the colonies. He was a decided patriot and wholly supported his eldest son in Thomas's decision to join the militia.

Aislin, however, found such resolution hard to come by. She'd heard her father's arguments and knew where her family stood, but she'd heard the talk in Trenton as well. The subject was at the forefront of every conversation, including those had in Madam Andrews's parlour.

Where the patriots referred to themselves as such, those in opposition called them traitors, and Aislin couldn't ignore their reasoning. These "rebels," as they were also called, were refusing to follow the letter of the law set down by the government. Whether the taxations were right or wrong, she couldn't understand the right course of action being to break the law.

She'd been brought up to obey those in authority over her, even if she didn't always agree with their actions and decisions. In this case, she heartily disagreed with the mandates passed from Parliament, and she felt they were abusing the resources of the colonists. Aislin was torn.

Then again, this was not the only dilemma presenting itself.

Benjamin had approached her father to request her hand. Aislin was surprised at how conflicted she felt about the impending proposal. So she turned to the only mother she'd ever known.

"This shouldn't be so difficult," she cried.

"First of all, do stop pacing about and sit down. You're making me dizzy."

"Sorry, Madam." She flopped rather than sat on the sofa.

"Do you love him?" Madam bluntly asked.

"Yes, I do." Aislin was sure of that.

"Then what's to be confused about? You do want to marry the boy, don't you?"

"I know I should at least want to."

"*Should* is never a good reason in matters of love, my dear, and this is no exception. Perhaps you're just not ready."

Aislin was eighteen, quickly approaching nineteen. She knew she should be ready, and she felt like a bit of a failure at the thought.

"Well that's a much better reason than simply not wanting to get married, I suppose. I'd rather it be my fault than Benjamin's."

"Mm, but I don't think that's it. There's something else isn't there."

Aislin took her time, as if she hadn't yet decided what the answer should be. "The war perhaps. I can't help but think of all the men who've been killed. Maybe I'll feel differently about the whole thing when it's all over."

Madam had become very free-thinking since her husband had passed, and in such a frame of mind, offered very practical advice. "If you're unsure, best to wait. Better to give it time than to rush in unprepared and then regret it."

Aislin knew she was right, but it wouldn't make what she had to do any easier.

The next time Benjamin came to see her, she tried to explain her feelings. She thought it would be better to say something before he proposed rather than simply refuse him. Benjamin did his best to hide his disappointment, which was mostly unsuccessful. Aislin hated to hurt him but would have done worse if things had progressed. Of that she was sure. She did her best to convince him (and herself) that she might feel differently after the war was over.

She cried a bit through their conversation; Benjamin held her hand and told her it would be all right.

"It actually makes my news a little easier to tell," he said quietly.

"What's that?"

"I've decided to join the Continentals." He couldn't look at her as the words left his mouth, mostly because he feared his own choice.

Aislin knew he'd been considering it, but was still slightly shaken by his resolution. She was well aware of what was happening just north of their small colony-that the British were making short order of the regulars as well as the militia. She was concerned for Benjamin.

Aislin would have rather he stayed and talked with her a while, but under the circumstances, Benjamin wanted to get home. He craved her forgiveness for such a brief visit and asked for permission to write her while he was away. She was glad for this and was already looking forward to his first letter as she followed him to the door.

Madam met her on the porch and stood with her arm around Aislin's shoulders as they watched the young man ride away.

*   *   *

The battles crept slowly southward, until it was no longer safe for Aislin to travel the roads from Camden to Madam's estate. It wasn't long before the Laraway house became wholly enveloped in the ordeal.

Her family's small involvements in the effort made Aislin feel nervous but a little excited to be on the side of the would-be fledgling nation. She didn't fully understand what their allegiance meant, but she knew she would support her family. She listened intently to any conversations regarding the war or the Continental Congress, and when she spoke on the subject of her brother's and Benjamin's military actions, she did so proudly. While Thomas had gone off to do his part in the effort, the two younger, John and Clayton, were still home helping to keep the household and the business running. At home or abroad, however, one always seemed to find himself in the thick of things.

Colonial soldiers were constantly passing through the area, and the Laraway house became somewhat of a haven for them. The wounded would receive care, the weary would receive rest, and the hunted would receive shelter. Aislin didn't mind these little invasions, although at first, they made her think of Benjamin. She worried about him and wondered if anyone would extend him the same courtesies.

Somewhere along the way, though, Aislin realized the first letter she'd received from Benjamin had also been the last. All she knew was that he'd been sent somewhere in New York. She did her best to put it from her mind but carried constantly the shadow of their last conversation.

*   *   *

The gun fire rang in Benjamin's ears as he knelt to reload. The shock of his first real battle was almost too much for him. Up until now, he'd been safely behind the walls of Fort Ticonderoga, but a clever move on the part of British reconnaissance had put an end to that. Benjamin found himself surrounded by chilling screams as his comrades attempted to defend their compromised rear guard. Benjamin wondered whether the bullets or the bayonets would be the first to take him. He hadn't long to think about it. It was time to fire the next round.

He watched the men opposite the field from him. It occurred to him that those men were in the same position as he–perhaps just as scared, but certainly just as convicted in their cause as he and his companions. The difference was, to his eyes, far fewer Redcoats fell at each Continental command to fire, in comparison to all the rebels that dropped at each shot of British artillery.

It was beginning to overwhelm Benjamin. He wondered why the colonies ever went to war with Great Britain in the first place. He questioned why he would have given up a life–any life –with Aislin to come and fight in a war that could never be won.

The thought of Aislin stuck with him. What would she say to him if she heard these thoughts now? She'd be ashamed of him; call him a coward. He shook his head, realizing she'd never be so unkind. Aislin would remind him of his commitment. She'd remind him for what he was fighting; talk of how great it would be to become citizens of a newly born country; anything to encourage him. But now these thoughts were far-off dreams. They felt cold and unreal. Her voice faded from his mind, and he lost his momentary comfort with the next thunderous boom from the British firing lines.

Benjamin saw men fall across the field, seemingly simultaneously with those sinking to the ground all around him. It was madness. He stood to his feet to fire… one last time.

3

She was heartbroken when she realized what must have happened. Aislin couldn't help but wonder if she could have changed Benjamin's mind if she had agreed to marry him. Maybe he would have stayed–felt a sense of duty to her–if they'd been married. Madam would have told her that one could build a whole life upon *if's*, but a miserable life it would be at best.

Aislin busied herself with the work of their home, taking care of the soldiers being their first priority. Even under the chaotic circumstances of the war, Aislin found herself content in these daily tasks. As she was the youngest Laraway and unmarried, she'd never been the lady of the house as this opportunity afforded her. Even though she missed Benjamin, she felt a sense of purpose in caring for the soldiers.

The Laraways carried on for months this way, and they became very good at their smuggling. But even the best made their mistakes.

It happened to the Laraways one fresh, summer day. They'd been keeping a few wounded and one spy hidden within the house. In the blink of an eye, they found their home surrounded.

Aislin and Clayton had been in the cellar talking with the spy when they heard the pounding of footsteps on the floor above. John hadn't had time to conceal the hatch leading to his now trapped siblings. Light spilled into the dark cellar as the hatch flew open with a deafening crack. Aislin felt sheer panic as she was snatched violently by the arm and thrust into the yard along with her family and the rebel stowaways.

The soldiers bound each of the four Laraways, preparing to take them away to be held (perhaps, even hung) for treason. Just as they were finishing, a second unit of British soldiers arrived.

The slightest glimmer of hope presented itself. Mounted at the head of the cavalry was a familiar face: Major Garnett. Aislin prayed that if the major held her in any regard, as Madam had said, that he might find some way to help.

"What's going on here?" Garnett asked approaching the captain.

"These people were harbouring spies, sir."

Catching sight of Aislin, the major continued. "Is this any way to treat a lady, Captain?"

"Uh, sir–we were–" the Captain stuttered. He was nearly grateful for Garnett's interruption.

"We are gentlemen, Captain, representing the His Majesty's army; and as such, we must conduct ourselves accordingly, even if they are only rebels," he sneered.

Aislin was furious, and distraught. It seemed Garnett was only taking the opportunity to degrade her further. She felt absolutely lost.

The major spoke again. "Before you take them, I'd like to question them myself."

"But sir, we've–"

A sharp glance quieted the Captain.

Garnett mock-surveyed the family until his gaze fell upon Aislin. He dismounted and walked to where she stood, wrists bound in front of her waist.

"Lieutenant Danvers," he called. "Ladies first," he said to Aislin as the lieutenant came to escort her.

Aislin and her captor followed the major into the house. Once they'd reached one of the inner rooms, where he was sure they couldn't be heard, Garnett dismissed the lieutenant to return out of doors with the rest. When the major turned to face Aislin again, any sign of confidence or pride had vanished. Instead, the face that met her had gone white.

"Tell me it isn't true," he said, almost breathless. "You couldn't really be so foolish."

Aislin, although startled by the major's shaken disposition, spoke with the smoothest tone she could manage, "Everything they've said is true."

The major heaved a sighed and turned away.

"I thought you were going to interrogate me."

"Interrogate–no. Please, Miss Laraway, I must have a moment to think."

He took his time, milling about the room. He looked deeply concerned–scared, Aislin would have said if she didn't know better. Finally, Garnett moved to stand face to face with her.

"I can save your family," he began slowly, "if you come with me."

"What do you mean?"

Aislin backed away from him. She'd never been quite so frightened of him as she was then. His pale eyes looked different, kinder somehow, but it brought her no comfort.

"I can't save all of you. Someone has to play the guilty party."

"So if I go as your prisoner, you'll let my family go free?" Aislin thought for a moment. She couldn't believe she was actually considering it, but she knew she'd never forgive herself if she lost the opportunity to save her father and brothers. "What will happen to me?" she murmured.

"I'll see that you're looked after. I promise I'll do everything in my power to keep you safe."

"But won't I be…" Aislin didn't finish the thought. It was too horrifying.

"It isn't likely they'll hang a woman or even jail one. Although I'm afraid I can't predict the exact outcome." His statement wasn't entirely true.

She spoke again with more force and confidence, "I have your word that my family will be freed?"

"You have my word," the major replied stoically.

"I suppose that'll have to do then." She couldn't believe she had actually said it.

Garnett called for the lieutenant, giving him orders to escort Aislin outside. She glanced at her father as she passed by.

"I'm sorry," she said, trying not to sound fearful.

It all moved rather quickly. The order came to cut the men loose as Garnett stepped forward.

"The woman acted alone. She is solely responsible for the rebel soldiers. The men only discovered them this morning."

Aislin's brothers were dumbfounded. Slowly beginning to realize what was happening, her father tried to lunge away from the soldiers still restraining him.

"No, Aislin! Don't!"

"Untie the lady's hands and see her to the wagon," came the major's final command.

Aislin's heart skipped a beat. She tried her best to hold back her tears–to show her father confidence so that he would think everything was all right. It wasn't working, and as she climbed into the wagon she broke completely.

In the struggle between soldiers and Laraways, Garnett looked back and caught her father's eye. It wasn't the look he expected from the man whose daughter he'd stolen. He was nearly in tears as his sons shouted and cursed at Garnett.

The major remounted, and the party began to move from sight. As the wagon rolled roughly along, Aislin wondered what lie in store for her. What were Garnett's intentions? Why even offer to save her family? He didn't know them. He barely knew her.

Knowing him, she thought, *he must have some selfish motivation. What could he possibly want with me?* The idea made Aislin shiver.

She looked back in the direction of their house, but instead of finding her family, she found Garnett, who had insisted on participating in the transport. Such a job was none for a major or the cavalry. The captain and his men just assumed that Garnett intended to take credit for the raid on the Laraway house.

Aislin turned her gaze forward. There she saw the rebel soldiers, still bound and even the sorely wounded forced to trudge along with the rest. She felt great pity for them. Even if she did manage to elude the gallows, there was no hope for those poor men.

Aislin gradually got her emotions under control, but her mind still swam with the thought of things to come.

4

It would be nice to say their journey was uneventful, but it wouldn't be true. They were dodging rebel attacks all along the way. Aislin hid in the wagon at each onslaught, with a few of Garnett's men posted to protect supplies more so than her. All the blood shed was very hard for her to take in. Still, after each engagement, it somehow made her feel better to see the major's face over the wagon, asking her if she was all right. She supposed this small comfort came because as long as Garnett lived, there was hope for her survival.

The major had indeed been right about taking a woman prisoner. Not only was she not mistreated, it seemed several of the men had taken it upon themselves to look after her, especially Lieutenant Danvers. Aislin questioned their motives at first, but with the personal interest Garnett had taken in her, she surmised that none of them would dare cross a superior officer.

For days the company travelled until Aislin finally lost count. She'd had only the one dress, and after a time, it became unfit to wear-torn from catching in the wagon, among other things. By the time they had gone two weeks into their march, Aislin was dressed in the poorly fitted clothes of a soldier. There were days and instances for which Aislin was glad to be wearing the trousers rather than her dress, but on one particularly humid day, she was not so grateful.

She slouched in the wagon trying to find some position in which she could sit so the uniform wouldn't feel so hot and uncomfortable. She was unsuccessful. Aislin wondered how the soldiers managed to fight, or move at all, dressed this way. Then she realized the comfort of their clothing was probably the last thing on their minds when their lives were in danger.

I'm such a girl, she thought with a hint of a smile.

Out of the clear blue sky came a sound like the sharp snap of thunder. Aislin caught sight of a soldier toward the front of the troop. He had stumbled, once, and then fell like a stone.

"To arms! To Arms!" was the first shout she heard.

Then came the voice of the lieutenant: "Miss Laraway, get down!"

The last thing she saw was the major's horse rearing back and the lieutenant drawing his pistol. She threw herself to the floor of the wagon. The conflict commenced.

Aislin always tried not to listen to the goings on of the battles. It felt like complete insanity to her. Everyone was shouting at everyone else in between ear-piercing gunfire.

The wagon unexpectedly lunged beneath her. The fighting wasn't finished, and she wondered why they'd be moving so rapidly away while still engaged, at the risk of exposing their retreat to the enemy. After a moment, she chanced leaning up on her arm to check her surroundings.

She first noticed that the wagon was moving toward the tree line. Aislin then realized, to her astonishment, the man driving the wagon was none she recognized; and he wasn't wearing a uniform: a militiaman. She'd been captured along with the targeted supplies. She wasn't sure why she'd expected them to, but her Redcoat captors weren't chasing after her.

Aislin then began trying to decide what to do next. If given the chance, she might be able to explain her situation to the rebels; and perhaps, they could help her get back to her family. But what would happen if she did get home? Would they only come after her again? She could run to Madam Andrews, but that would merely put her friend in danger as well. Maybe one of the men knew Thomas, or even Benjamin, and would offer to help.

She hadn't much longer to think about it. The wagon had cleared the path and was well within the woods. She felt them slowing and eventually stopping. Aislin held her breath as the driver disembarked. The sound of men's voices signalled their approach.

Upon reaching the wagon, one man offered his hand and roughly pulled her to stand before him.

"Well boys, I suppose this is the infamous Miss Laraway," he said haughtily.

The men all cheered, evidently very proud of their conquest. Aislin didn't know what to make of her circumstances. She deduced from their conversations that they had been looking for her, apparently intending to rescue her, but she didn't feel the least bit rescued. Rather, she still felt very much in danger.

She was never asked to move. Instead, she was pushed and forced where they wanted her to go: pushed back into the wagon on their way to camp, pulled from the wagon once they'd arrived, forcibly shown where to sit round the fire and offered nothing to eat.

She kept to herself as much as possible and didn't have to worry about speaking to anyone as no one ever addressed her directly. Most talked about her as if she wasn't there at all. Aislin felt like crying but was afraid that any show of weakness might make things worse. She actually missed the British camp.

It had only been a few hours and already she wanted to be far away from these barbaric men. She started planning how best to approach their leader, thinking over what she'd say and how. She knew she'd have to be forceful as it didn't seem they responded to any other sort. She'd demand a horse and to be shown the route to Trenton. There was at least a chance it could work.

Aislin tugged at the end of her sleeve, wadding the excess into her hand. She arduously wiped the sweat from her forehead and the back of her neck. The heat combined with her nerves was making her nauseous.

The talk among the men soon turned to the day's events, and their primary topic drew Aislin's attention. A few of them were talking about Major Garnett specifically, which surprised her. It seemed most had known someone for whose death they blamed Garnett, in one way or another. They all had hateful things to say about him; and the words they used to describe him, she thought, should have shamed a gentleman. She hated to think this was the company Benjamin and her brother had shared.

"Just one honest shot," a man was saying, "that's all it'd take."

The other men were laughing. Aislin detested the conversation: that one man could speak so casually about killing another. But her time amid the group was short-lived.

"Send in our little prisoner," a man jeered from the front of his tent.

Aislin had guessed this to be their leader–a conclusion hard to arrive at as they wore no uniforms. She didn't want to go into his tent. She didn't want to be nearer to any of them than necessary. She hoped the invitation was only to discuss her return home.

This leader dismissed the others still inside and walked toward Aislin. She cringed and retreated as the man approached.

"Easy, love," he said, in his gruff voice. "This won't hurt a bit."

The man leaned in to kiss her. Horrified, Aislin pulled away. The man seemed shocked and was certainly offended. With the back of his hand, he struck her across the face, the force of the blow knocking Aislin to the ground. Tears immediately ran down her cheeks.

"I'd think you could show a little more gratitude for saving your life," he growled.

"Please, don't," she cried.

He paid her no heed. Aislin was cornered. She wanted to scream, but there was no help to call for.

A loud commotion outside temporarily distracted the man. It was followed by gunfire and shouting. Aislin saw her opportunity. She pushed the man off balance and fled.

She ran outside in the confusion but stopped when she realized she had nowhere to go. She spun around in a panic, searching for some way out. Suddenly, he appeared. Slowing just enough to safely collect her, the major reached out his hand, which she gladly took. Before she knew it, she was gathered into the saddle in front of Garnett.

He kept the slower pace long enough for her to take position.

"You'll have to ride astride for balance," he directed.

Aislin mutely moved into place, with the major's free arm holding to both her and the reins. She closed her eyes and held tightly to the horse's mane, just like her father had taught her.

Sword in hand, Garnett fought their way free and broke for the darkened woods before them. Seeing their commander clear and their objective achieved, the rest of the troops followed, pulling their recovered supplies just behind. Aislin caught herself leaning back against the major as they rode, utterly relieved to know she was safe once more.

He whispered softly in her ear as they rode. "Are you all right?"

She sniffed away a tear and nodded. Sufficiently relieved himself, the major spurred the horse on.

It was when they arrived at camp, and Garnett helped Aislin to dismount, that the major saw the damage inflicted on his recovered captive. Her cheek was still red, a thin crimson streak cut from the heavy ring borne on her attacker's middle finger.

Garnett scowled and slowly raised his hand. Aislin winced as she braced herself for the feel of his touch against her cheek. He saw her shrink, and lowered his hand.

The major growled under his breath, "What sort of monster would do this?"

He paused. She'd accidentally caught him in her shadowy gaze. Both quickly looked away.

"Are you sure you're all right?" he asked quietly.

"I'm sure I will be."

Garnett nodded, as she turned to walk away.

Aislin practically crawled into the small tent they'd provided her. The hard cot looked far more inviting than usual, and she'd even managed to forget about the uncomfortable heat.

She had pulled back the tent flap to let the slight breeze into her quarters. Aislin didn't worry about leaving the door open. Her tent was always set right next to the major's (as per his instruction), so if there was any trouble, help was quick to come. If nothing else could be said of him, she had to admit that he had more than honoured his word to keep her safe.

The thought came to an abrupt halt at the sound of voices outside her tent. Two of the watchmen were sitting near the fire. Aislin strained to hear the conversation.

"That was risky business, eh?"

The speaker was reloading and readying his weapon.

The second man huffed in response. "Well, the major knows what he's doing, I suppose."

"I'm not convinced that one prisoner and a few supplies was worth all that," the first groaned.

"It's not your place to question," the sergeant's friend sternly answered.

A third voice broke abruptly. "Suppose we didn't recover what they'd taken."

It was Garnett. He was easier to hear, speaking slowly and articulately. Aislin had been able to clearly see the sergeant's face and that of the other but only had a view of the major's profile. His features were sharp against the firelight, giving him a rather unearthly appearance. In a strange way, she thought he looked rather handsome.

"It may not make much sense to you, Sergeant, but I'll not give the rebels even the slightest inclination that they could get away with such treachery."

The men looked at their feet, like children who had been scolded. Sullenly, they both replied their, "yes, sir," and gathered their weapons to begin their watch.

Aislin could see another man approach Garnett: Lieutenant Danvers.

"Foolish youth, sir," he said. "They'd rather we'd run through the camp and wiped them out rather than achieve any sort of initiative."

The major's authoritative stance shifted as he rubbed the back of his neck. Clearly, there was something weighing on his mind.

"I must admit, the rebels' unexpected strength and strategy is commendable."

"I wonder, sir, if perhaps you give them too much credit."

Garnett smiled. "I wonder myself sometimes."

Danvers laughed a little to himself.

"Still," the major quietly continued, "The rebels' greatest asset in this campaign is their passion. An asset we lack in many ways. Those men fight because they want to. We fight because we're told to, because it's our duty. It could make a difference in the end."

"You don't believe they could succeed, do you?" the lieutenant inquired with a hint of disbelief.

"Of course not," Garnett huffed. "But they could make this much more difficult than we had anticipated. The important thing to remember, and what the younger men tend to forget, is that these colonists are our brothers. When this war is over, our task will be to mend the broken relationships. We must do everything we can to sever as few ties as possible."

"Let it never be said that you underestimated an enemy, sir," Danvers said and patted the major's shoulder.

The voices died away as the men moved toward their quarters. Aislin, lying in her bed, rolled to her back and stared at the tent ceiling, finally succumbing to the weary spirit that gripped her.

5

A few evenings later, when Aislin was convinced that they must be closing in on the coast, the major summoned her to his tent. She was alarmed at his request. Aislin presumed Garnett now intended to collect payment for his favour. Determined to maintain the illusion of strength and confidence, she tried to convince herself that she did, in fact, owe the major something for saving her family. The illusion failed, however; and as she approached the tent her hands began to shake.

She very tentatively entered the small room, yellow with the light of only a few candles.

"Please, sit down," the major addressed her.

Aislin sat in a chair near the middle of the room. Her back was to the entrance, and ahead she faced a table covered in maps and writing utensils, along with other tools she did not recognize.

With a nod, Garnett gestured the lieutenant to leave. Aislin felt her muscles tighten as the major drew closer. Once they were alone, he knelt beside her on the floor. He spoke to her in a very low, barely audible tone so they had to be face to face for her to hear.

"My messenger has just returned with word from my quarters south of Newburgh."

As he spoke, his arm found its way to the back of Aislin's chair, just around her shoulder. Aislin was now very aware of how still she was sitting.

"A rider will arrive tomorrow night. After the lights are out and the men are asleep, I'll lead you to where you'll meet him–just outside the camp. Can you ride?"

"Yes," Aislin answered in a whisper.

"Good. You'll ride a few hours to the north. You should arrive well before dawn."

"Where am I going?"

"To my quarters in New York. Everyone's been alerted to your arrival, but all they know is they're to receive a guest. A cousin, they were told. The only one who knows of our plan is James, the rider. He's my most trusted servant." Garnett could see the question behind her eyes. "I know it's odd, but there's no place you'd be safer. No one would think to look for you there."

Both sat silent and motionless, as if expecting to be caught.

"Is everything all right?" the major asked her at last.

Aislin only nodded. She was terrified. Was this really happening? This meant escape from the camp, from imprisonment. She knew there were questions to ask, but couldn't think of them.

"Best you get to sleep then. You'll have a long night tomorrow."

With that, Garnett stood. Aislin paused, briefly, and then rose from the chair. When she reached her exit, she looked back at the major. He nodded and gave a weak smile. Aislin pushed through the soft barrier and went to her own quarters.

She felt sick. She wanted to feel relieved, knowing she would soon be out of harm's way. The major was risking a great deal to help her escape, but still she wondered why.

Lying down didn't help. The echo of Garnett's words rang in her ears and was only drowned out by the questions her mind finally found.

Could this rider really be trusted?

What about the guards posted?

What would happen when she was discovered missing?

How would the major cover all of this?

What if they were caught?

What would happen after she reached Garnett's estate?

The possibilities of failure, of being caught, seemed to greatly out-weigh the possibilities of success.

Aislin was jarred awake. She didn't remember going to sleep, and was surprised to find herself awaking to the sound of the soldiers breaking camp. She collected herself, still wearing the crude uniform, and stepped outside. She was promptly greeted by Garnett.

"Good morning, Miss Laraway," he said, more cheerful than usual.

"Good morning, Major. Have I missed something?" Aislin gestured to the bustling soldiers.

"No. I thought perhaps you may have had a difficult night. After our discussion, I mean. I told the men to let you sleep. Breakfast was left on the fire."

"Thank you, Major," was all she could manage.

Garnett had correctly deciphered her state. She still felt dizzy from what must have been a restless sleep. She managed to get down some breakfast by the time the company was ready to move, though her stomach wasn't very happy about it.

The day seemed to go more quickly than any she could remember. She was frightened by the prospects brought with the sinking of the sun, and her fear was only fuelled by Time's rapid progression. No one else seemed to care or even notice her distress. No one except Garnett, that is. Every time Aislin so much as glanced in his direction, the major's clear, azure gaze was there to meet her. His seemingly infallible perceptions were unnerving.

Aislin's attention was impulsively drawn forward at the familiar crack of a musket shot. Expecting to see enemy troops in that direction, she was relieved to see the soldiers were only shooting at a deer just off their path. She had a feeling, as she tried to relax, that this wouldn't be the last start she'd experience that day.

Night fell all too soon. Aislin was comforted by the firelight, for as long as they burned she still had time before her escape. She sat upright on her cot in the back of her tent. She had intended to sleep, as she would need all her strength for the ride; but now, she could no sooner lie down than fly. She realized she was shaking. She tried to think of the event positively. She would be out of immediate danger, although Garnett's estate was the last place she wanted to be headed.

Speak of the devil, she thought.

The tent flap was pushed aside, revealing the major's form against the now dark camp. Aislin was so nervous she hadn't noticed the lights going out.

Garnett stepped inside and dowsed her lantern light. He reached out and took Aislin's hands.

"Are you all right? You're shaking," he whispered.

"Just nerves, I suppose," she tried to cover.

The major nodded, and though he was concerned, there wasn't time to press further.

"Be very quiet," was all he said.

Aislin held his hand tightly for fear of losing him in the rush. They moved quickly out of the camp and into the surrounding woods. A pale moon, not quite full, gave them only enough light to see their next step.

It will be impossible to ride this way, she thought.

Ahead, Aislin could barely make out the silhouette of a man and two horses. She and Garnett were nearly beside him before Aislin could see him clearly.

"All right," the major began, but was stopped.

"Wait," came Aislin's wavering voice, "what about the guard? What will you tell them?"

"There isn't time, Miss Laraway. I have to get back before I'm missed. I'll take care of the guard. You must trust me." He spoke soft but firm.

The rider handed Garnett the reigns of the large, reddish horse and then prepared his own mount. Aislin moved into position and took hold of the saddle. She unexpectedly felt the major's hand over her own.

"I've done my best to get you as close to the estate as possible without bringing us too close to the border."

"You were stalling," Aislin said.

"Yes. Hopefully the men haven't noticed. Please, take care tonight. Give James a shout if the pace is too much."

"Thank you, Major."

With this last exchange, Garnett gave her a leg into the saddle and stood for a moment watching them ride away.

What should have been the beginning of the end of this ordeal for Aislin now became only the end of the beginning.

*   *   *

The pair raced on through the woods at a maddening pace. Aislin wondered how either the horses or James could tell where they were going. She was a very good rider and had no trouble keeping up; still, the gentleman looked back over his shoulder from time to time. Aislin tried to determine whether he was checking on her or if he was just making sure she didn't run off.

The thought had entered her mind to run away, but so had the thought of being caught in the woods by soldiers or some wild animal. So she kept to her escort.

The night was so quiet the dull thud of the horses' hooves against the ground sounded more like the rolling of thunder. At what Aislin estimated to be about two hours along, the rider slowed and eventually stopped. He waited for her to pull alongside of him.

"We should be well away from trouble now. Best we give the horses a rest. Been riding pretty hard," said James.

They held the horses to a walk and kept on in silence at first. Uneasily, and much quieter than necessary, Aislin's gentle voice soon broke the stillness.

"How much further?"

"I'd say less than an hour, barring any interference."

James turned toward Aislin to see her looking about the woods as if expecting to be pounced on at any moment.

"Don't worry, Miss," James said calmly. "It's not likely we'll have any problem. With General Howe's capture of New York City last year, this area has become quite securely held by our boys in red. Not to mention the strong Loyalist presence here. There are few Continentals in the region and the militia tends to stay a bit farther south."

Aislin relaxed a little. The more she thought about it, the more she realized James was right. Unless they'd been followed by someone from the camp (which was unlikely), it was probably safe to say that neither the British nor the colonials would bother with two unaffiliated riders.

"How long have you been with Major Garnett?" Aislin liked it better when there was conversation.

James sighed, "About fourteen years or so."

"Are you happy in his service?"

"Yes, I am. And no, I don't think he's as terrible as everyone says."

He smiled in sensing her underlying meaning. Aislin tried to ignore the remark.

"We are more than taken care of. It's a comfortable living."

"How many of you are there at the major's home?"

"Well, even though it's just the major, it's a large estate. There are two indoors, a cook and housekeeper; and there are three outdoors who take care of the gardens and the grounds and all. And then there are the stable hands–two of them. And myself of course. So that's ..." he trailed off, putting the numbers together, "eight."

"Good heavens. All for one person?"

The conversation paused as Aislin thought of the best way to ask her next question. "Are there women at the estate?"

"Yes, of course," he paused, taking stock of her inquiry. "You have a good deal of apprehension about all this don't you?"

Aislin lost her words and began fidgeting with her horse's mane.

"You have nothing to fear, Miss. The major must think a great deal of you to go through all this trouble. You'll be well looked after with him."

Aislin never answered him. She didn't want to think about it any more. It had been a nice enough ride. She just wanted to enjoy what was left of it.

A little further on, they galloped out the rest of the way. When they arrived, a single lantern burned near the door. The only thing Aislin could see was the shadow of the enormous house. It loomed ominously over them as they quietly made their way back to the stables.

James tied the horses outside their stalls and rejoined Aislin.

"I'll tend to the horses once we get you inside. It wouldn't do for anyone to see you dressed that way."

He led her into the house through a back door. Aislin tried to pay attention to where she was going, so as to remember the way later, but was concentrating much harder on not making any noise. Around a corner and up the stairs, they soon came to a door near the end of a hallway.

James stopped before he entered. "That," he whispered, pointing to the last door in the hall, "is the major's room, when he's home." He led Aislin into the door directly before them. "This will be yours," he said, still whispering but a little less timidly. "There's a sitting room just on the other side of that door, and you'll find more appropriate clothing there in the wardrobe. The major sent for some other things for you that should arrive in a day or two. My quarters are at the other end of the hall. Two of the housekeepers share a room downstairs. Don't concern yourself with getting up in the morning. I'll explain to the others that you got in late."

"Thank you for all your help," Aislin softly replied.

"You're welcome, Miss Laraway. Good night."

"Good night."

Aislin was so relieved to be in a real house standing beside a real bed, for a moment, she couldn't have cared less whose house it was.

6

When Aislin woke in the morning, the sun was already high. She sat up in the bed and looked around the room. She hadn't been able to take in all the sights the previous night because of the dark, nor would she have had the energy to do so had it been daylight. The room was very richly furnished. There were two plush chairs beside the fireplace and a lovely vanity set on the adjoining wall to her right. On the opposite wall stood a very ornate wardrobe and to its right was the door James had said led to a sitting room.

It was all so lavishly done, Aislin could hardly wait to see the rest of the house. As she was about to get out of bed, the door to the hall began to open very slowly.

"Hello?" Aislin said quietly.

"Forgive me, Miss. I didn't mean to disturb you," the tiny voice came from a girl who must have been just younger than Aislin. "Mr. Parish asked me to check on you."

"Mr. Parish?"

"James Parish, Miss. The gentleman who saw you in last night."

"Oh, I'm sorry. I only know him as James." Aislin noticed that she had not yet taken her eyes off the ground. "What's your name?"

"I'm Rebecca, Miss." The girl gave a little curtsy.

"I'm pleased to meet you, Rebecca."

The girl quickly glanced up at Aislin and gave a small smile. "Likewise, Miss."

"I suppose I have slept rather late. If you'll excuse me, I'll dress and see myself downstairs shortly."

"Do you require assistance, Miss?"

"No, thank you. That's all right." Aislin was never comfortable with the custom of servants helping her dress.

"I'll see that tea is ready when you arrive."

Before Aislin could say anything else, the girl was gone and the door shut.

When she finally made her exit into the hall, dressed in one of the fine gowns that had been provided for her, she saw James leaving his quarters at the other end of the hall. He looked quite different than he had the night before. Aislin could clearly see flecks of gray through his otherwise dark hair; and he wore spectacles pushed down on the end of his nose, revealing his smart green eyes. He had a kind appearance, she thought. Carrying some papers he was shuffling through and looking rather in a hurry, he stopped sharply when he saw Aislin.

"Miss Laraway. Well I must say, that dress is much more becoming than that awful uniform," he said with a smile.

"Thank you, Mr. Parish," she returned his smile.

"Here now what's this 'Mr. Parish' business? It won't do for the lady of the house to address me as such. It'll be simply 'James,' Miss."

"I'm sorry. I'm not used to addressing men by their given names."

"While I appreciate your being so polite, you're going to give us all away if you continue." James paused to look down the staircase in a rather suspicious manner and spoke more quietly. "If they're to believe you are truly the cousin of Major William Garnett, then you must act like..." he stumbled for a proper description, "nothing short of a lady of the British court."

"Forgive me. I guess I forgot about that part."

"I'm afraid we can't afford for you to forget. Servants talk—in town and in other influential homes. We can't have them spreading rumours about our unusual guest, now can we?"

"No, certainly not." Aislin squared her shoulders a bit.

"Now that's a girl. I'll do my best to keep an eye on you and help when I can."

"I'm obliged for all you've done already, James."

Aislin's lips found a smile once again. James grinned and gestured her down the stairs.

The rest of the house was no disappointment, as she had expected. Aislin had a sudden revelation. It was no longer any wonder that the officers in the British Army behaved the way they did, arrogant and snide. If they were treated like royalty, it made sense that they should act that way.

Aislin tried to gaze in every direction at once; that is, until James stepped up behind her.

"Try not to look quite so impressed."

They both laughed quietly.

James opened and held the door for Aislin to enter the dining room. She saw two women–Rebecca being one–busy setting the table.

James whispered as he helped her to her seat, "I'll stay for a quick bite, but then I must be off."

Aislin wondered if it was that transparent that she didn't want to be left alone just then.

Neither spoke as they ate. James sat away from her toward the opposite end of the table and was again scouring through his papers. Aislin tried very hard not to swallow the small meal all at once. She was very hungry and the food was wonderful–and not just because she'd been eating with soldiers for the last few weeks.

She was just finishing when James rose from the table. Aislin spoke quickly.

"I suppose it would be all right if I saw myself around the estate?"

"Certainly, Miss," James replied. "Let the others know if you need anything."

"Thank you."

James didn't answer. He only bowed a little.

"Can I get anything else for you, Miss?" came a voice just over her shoulder.

It was the older woman working with Rebecca. Aislin was still hungry but thought better of asking for more.

"No, thank you."

"Excuse me, Miss."

The woman left the room, and Aislin sat for a moment. She decided to give herself a tour of the house first.

She traversed from room to room finding each one to be more impressive than the previous. Madam Andrews had a very lavish house, but it paled in comparison.

I wonder if she's heard about what's happened to me. The thought was fleeting.

Aislin found herself fascinated by the artwork: paintings, statues, and tapestries collected about the rooms, each one following a different theme or colour. Most of the floors were covered by beautiful rugs almost as decorative as the tapestries; and she couldn't help but run her fingers over the intricate carvings laced throughout the fireplace mantles.

But her favorite room of all was the library. The ceiling, she gathered, must have reached all the way to the top of the house, rather than being just one floor as the other rooms were. The shelves and all the furniture were dark wood, with a slight reddish tone, making the room feel very warm. The seat cushions and rugs were various hues of greens and blues, complimented by only a few paintings and statues placed in the rare blank spots on the walls and shelves. Here, the books themselves seemed to be the décor.

There was one large window in the centre of the wall opposite the door. It was hung with heavy velvet drapes, dark green, pulled back to let in the light. And in the far left-hand corner stood a lovely spiral staircase leading to a loft that encircled the room.

The staircase and the railings were all iron, and between the breaks in the shelves on this second tier were thick wooden doors that curved at the top, rather than being flat and squared. Most of them only led to shallow closets, but a few led into hallways and rooms upstairs. Aislin elected to continue her investigation through the rest of the house and then come back later to trace these other passages.

She managed to find the small staircase in the back of the house that she and James had used the previous night (the other means of getting upstairs being the large, grand staircase at the front door). She came directly into the wide corridor between the upstairs bedrooms. She saw the door to her room and, though her curiosity nearly won out, resolved she would not go near the major's room.

That left four other doors. One of which was James's room, and she wouldn't bother. Two of the doors preceded only guest rooms–just as elegant as all the others, but not quite as nice or as large as her own.

The last door held within it a type of study. It seemed well-stocked and frequently visited. The centre piece was a desk littered with many of the same articles as she'd seen that night in Garnett's tent. Aislin imagined it might be a place James or the major would use to go over business and paperwork–the sorts over which she'd seen her father frequently working. She wasn't very interested in such things.

Having satisfactorily concluded her tour, she returned to the library. She climbed the spiral staircase in the corner and began a new search. Most of the doors were a disappointment: leading only to the attic or a storage space.

But may be a good place to hide, should the need arise, Aislin thought. She caught herself and considered how a little more than a month ago, she would never have had such a thought.

One of the doors led down a flight of stairs behind the walls. There was almost no light at all, so Aislin walked very carefully. At the end of the staircase was a door. She slowly pushed it open. As she did, light rushed in–so bright Aislin blinked at the harsh invasion. She was at the side of the house looking straight out to the barns. Surprised to be outside (and fortunately so), she had paused before stepping out. Had she not, Aislin would have been in quite a lot of trouble. The stairs had not led her all the way to the foundation. She was a man's shoulder height off the ground with no where to go but back the way she came.

An effective way to escape, she thought, *but quite a jump that would be!*

Back upstairs, Aislin tried another door. This one, at the top of a few stairs, guided her down a long, narrow passage. At the other end was another spiral staircase, much shorter but similar to the one in the library. A door met her at the bottom, latched shut but easily opened. Unsure of where she was, Aislin cautiously entered a small parlour, decorated in soft hues with two windows on the longest wall. She knew she was on the end of the house facing the back of the estate and by looking out the windows could tell she was still upstairs and should be near her room.

She opened the door nearest to her left, right beside the one she'd come in through. On the other side, she recognized her own bedchamber. She was proud of herself for having correctly deciphered where she was. Pulling closed the door to her room, she acknowledged this parlour to be the sitting room James had mentioned (she'd meant to settle here later with a book she'd choose from the library).

There was only one other door in the parlour, and Aislin thought nothing of exploring it. As she opened the door, however, she regretted her hasty decision. It took only a moment for her to realize she had walked right into Garnett's quarters.

She knew she ought to turn and leave, but she couldn't help herself. In she walked, though very tentatively–touching nothing. She'd never be so rude.

From the door, the room bent round to the right. In this corner where she stood was a small desk and chair, neatly kept. To the right she identified the door that would lead to the hall. Directly in front of her was the bed with four large posts but quaint, simple bedding–just the pillows and light summer-time coverings. Her own bedding was much more elaborate.

Beside the bed on the far wall was the fireplace. There were no chairs as in her room. Around the bend, there was a mirror and a few old trunks.

The room was so very curious. There were no paintings on the walls, leaving only the windows and their plain drapes for art work. The empty shell looked barely lived in.

Aside from this, the only piece of furniture in the room was a small table between the bed and the fireplace. A Bible lay alone on the top. This above all surprised Aislin, though she wasn't entirely sure why.

She hadn't the time to think about it. Something about that place told her she was no longer welcome. She left the room and quietly closed the door.

Aislin felt hungry and wondered what time she'd be called for dinner. She left all her mysteries behind her and went downstairs.

When she reached the dining room, the women were moving in and out in preparation. Aislin decided not to get in their way, but as she moved away to find some other way to occupy her time, the older woman called after her.

"I'm sorry, Miss. I suppose we're a bit late."

"Oh, I thought I was early. What time is dinner taken?"

"We serve at six o' clock for the major."

"Then I am early." Aislin realized they were hurrying to accommodate her. "There's no need to rush. Six o' clock will be fine." She tried to be agreeable without sounding like it.

"Are you certain, Miss?"

"Yes, of course."

The woman bowed hastily and turned to leave.

Aislin called as she reached the door, "Has James returned yet?"

"No, Miss, but he's usually home in time for dinner."

"Thank you."

The woman forced a smile and left. Aislin wondered what she'd done to offend her.

James did indeed arrive just in time for dinner, which went much the same as tea had. Afterward, James escorted Aislin to what he again referred to as a sitting room (Aislin remembered it as the yellow room, because the colour was its predominant theme).

She was glad for the company, as James must have guessed. Aislin hadn't spoken to anyone for most of the day.

"How did you enjoy your first afternoon with us?"

"Quite well, really. I only had enough time to explore the house. I'll have to see the grounds tomorrow."

"It is rather large isn't it?"

They both smiled.

"I was impressed with the library. The doors upstairs were fascinating."

"You found the passages then."

"Yes. I do hope that's all right."

"Of course, you're our guest. You're welcome to wander wherever you like. Best leave the major's quarters be, though."

Aislin was glad she hadn't mentioned that portion of her adventure.

"I'm curious," Aislin continued, "why all the passages and funny doorways?"

"Well, as the colonies go, this is somewhat of an older house. There was still a healthy Indian population when it was built, and the owner was a mite paranoid. He built all that, including the doors to the main suites, in case he needed to make a quick getaway. That's why that door on the side of the house opens out to the barns: so he could get to his horse and be quickly away."

"Why is that door so far off the ground?"

"So that it would make a better exit than an entrance. He was worried someone might try to get in that way. Actually, when the military acquired this house (I'm told), they had to add doors. The front entrance was the only way in or out. Peculiar, eh?"

"Indeed."

The two smiled and relaxed in their chairs. They talked a while longer before finally deciding to end the evening. It was late when they parted. Aislin would have to begin her reading another night.

*   *   *

The next morning, Aislin discovered an Eden of gardens outdoors. There were beautiful flowers–every kind, it seemed, that she'd ever seen–blossoming throughout the grounds. Between each row of blooms were sweet cobblestone paths, and tucked away in one corner was a delightful swing–small and simple but very charming. This instantly became one of Aislin's favourite places (one of, as the list was rapidly growing). The lilies surrounding this nook greatly added to its allure. To Aislin, lilies were the most wonderful of all flowers, appealing in both scent and sight. She couldn't get enough of them.

Her next finding was the stable. Garnett, Aislin knew, had involvements with the cavalry. For this reason, he knew a good horse when he saw one. This was evidenced in the immaculate animals kept at the estate. Most of the other horses Aislin had seen were for work. It seemed it would be an atrocity to even lay a saddle on one of these creatures.

That afternoon, and each day after, Aislin made time for a ride, frequently choosing the large, chestnut stallion that'd served her so well the night of her escape. The grounds were expansive, and she had no trouble finding new opportunities for exploration.

Everyone took to Aislin's presence at the estate, even the curt Mrs. Morgan (who worked with Rebecca in the kitchen) came around with time. The stable hands were always ready to tack the horse of her choosing, and one of the groundskeepers regularly brought in fresh flowers for the dining room table.

The achievement with which Aislin was most pleased, however, was her eventual ability to bring Rebecca out of her shell. When James wasn't available to talk, Rebecca became a wonderful substitute. Had Aislin not been forced to maintain a particular appearance–if she'd been able to be herself–she and Rebecca probably would have been great friends. But as it was, the two were grateful for each other's company.

At first, Aislin had wondered if she wasn't too well liked. After all, James had told her to behave like a courtier, and besides Madam Andrews, she couldn't think of any well-to-do individual that she had particularly liked. James assured her that was not the case. She was perfectly mannered, he'd said, just much kinder than most. She came to truly enjoy her time at the estate and nearly forgot the reason why she was there.

7

He arrived early one afternoon without announcement. The major had been granted a short leave of his duties and had returned home. Nearly two months had passed since he had seen his captive safely away.

Garnett met with James briefly in matters of the estate, after which he set out to find Aislin. It didn't take him long.

She was reading, sitting beside the lilies in the garden. The major lost his breath. It had been so long since he'd seen her, he had all but forgotten how strikingly beautiful she was. Not to mention, the last time he'd seen her, she looked more like one of the grubby soldiers in her barrowed uniform than she did any sort of lady. Now, she looked so fair, the major felt he should like to steal away into the house to sit and watch her from a window.

Aislin was startled to find she had an audience.

"Major," she gasped.

"I'm sorry, Miss Laraway," he said softly. "I didn't mean to frighten you."

"Quite all right," she sighed. "I didn't know you'd returned."

"I just arrived."

"I see."

Neither knew what to say for a moment, and their pause was awkward.

"How have things been for you here?" Garnett posed at last. He stood with his arms behind his back, looking very proper, still wearing his uniform.

"Everything's been very nice, thank you."

"Good," he nodded and shifted his gaze as if surveying his grounds.

"And how have you been since I left?" Aislin asked, a bit broken but trying to be polite.

"As well as could be expected, I suppose. The summer was somewhat successful, and we now hold Philadelphia. Though...," he stopped, realizing no woman would want to know anything on the subject, least of all one who'd been arrested for harbouring spies. He tried to smile instead.

"What was said of my escape?" Aislin requested of him after only a short silence.

"Well, I think you'd be pleased with the manner in which it was handled. When the guards asked where you were, their inquiry was easily bypassed by accusing them of falling asleep on duty. If you'd escaped, it would be their responsibility. So when I simply explained that I'd arranged to have you transferred to another company, and they had come for you late that night, it was all the enlightenment they required. The guards insisted they had seen the other troops and just didn't realize their purpose." The major laughed a little.

"And no one was suspicious?"

"Lieutenant Danvers was at first. It's unusual that I would not convey such goings on to him, but it's not unheard of. In the end he too was convinced."

"I must admit, I was nervous as to how you could possibly explain such a disappearance. I am impressed."

"Thank you," he said almost sheepishly. "I assume you found the library." The major pointed to the book in her arms.

"Yes. James said it would be all right if I-"

Garnett put up his hand. "It's fine. This has been your home for months now. It's only natural that you would make yourself comfortable. James tells me that everyone here is quite taken with you. I was glad to hear it."

"Mm." Aislin looked away. She was a little embarrassed.

The major couldn't help but note how attractive she looked when she blushed.

"Well, dinner should be nearly ready. Shall we?" he gestured to allow Aislin passage down the pathway.

Though neither knew it, both were allayed at the idea of a change in scenery and activity. Not to mention, James would be there to assist in conversation. Dinner was frequently a time for the major and his servant to make plans for the following day. Afterward, however, James went his way, and the two were alone again.

They sat together quietly in the parlour; the major with his drink, looking out the window and Aislin (wishing she'd gathered materials to sew), trying not to look at him. She wanted to read–anything to take her mind off of the discomfited silence–but knew it would be rude.

She had thought she'd wait until at least the next evening to bring it up, but now couldn't think of why.

"Major?" she opened quietly.

"Yes." He turned a little in her direction.

"I was wondering, what's to become of me now?"

"How do mean?" He took another drink.

"Well, in general. What happens now?"

"Oh." The major didn't know what to say. "Honestly, I hadn't thought about it. I don't normally make a habit of freeing convicts. I only considered far enough ahead to prevent your imprisonment. I hadn't planned anything further."

"I mean," Aislin wasn't sure where she was taking the conversation, "I suppose it would be impossible for me to return home." She looked directly at the major.

"Well, that's for certain. While we covered the tracks of your escape well enough, there's bound to be talk when it's discovered that no Laraways have been held prisoner. I imagine there'll be a search," he answered quietly, peering at his emptying glass.

"I hadn't thought of that." Her gaze shifted to the window.

"Don't worry," he spoke almost too indifferently, "you're safe here. I only meant that it would be too dangerous for you to travel back." The obvious finally presented itself in the major's mind. "You miss your family."

"My family, Madam Andrews … my life."

"Are you unhappy here?"

"No, no sir. I just–" Aislin sighed, "I'm not unhappy. I don't mean to sound ungrateful, Major. I just asked to satisfy curiosity."

"Uh huh."

"I think I'll retire," she said as she stood to her feet. "Good night, Major."

"Good night," he said, turning to watch her go.

It wasn't at all how either of them wanted to end the evening, but there was nothing good to come of pursuing their discussion. Aislin still couldn't help but think of him in terms of the rude man she'd encountered at the ball, nearly a year ago now. Garnett never could quite say what he meant to–what he knew she wanted to hear. It was always uncomfortable and clumsy, which frustrated them both.

The next morning at breakfast, the major made an effort to smooth everything out. James had quietly mentioned to him Aislin's love of her daily rides; and if she and Garnett shared any common interest, it was a good horse on a clear day. The major asked her over their meal if she would accompany him that afternoon and perhaps let him show her a few new sights. Aislin agreed, knowing she had no legitimate reason to decline.

After he and James briefly attended to a few issues following breakfast, the major met Aislin in the stables. The horses were quickly readied, and the duo was off. Autumn had fallen on New York, promising cooler weather and handsome scenery for their ride.

It seemed this peacefully occupied region was nearly the perfect place to be. The British had just successfully completed their campaigns in Philadelphia and Saratoga and were preparing to settle in for the winter. They now securely held most of New York and New Jersey. There were, of course, the occasional uprisings, and everyone knew the uneasy calm wouldn't last. It couldn't.

The ride was uneventful and enjoyed mutually by the major and his charge. The two spoke very little, except when Garnett was pointing out a feature in the landscape. Aislin was surprised at how refreshing another's perspective was to her view of the countryside.

They'd been gone most of the day before either realized it, and Aislin was beginning to get hungry. But that merely presented an opportunity for her to discover one of the most excellent characteristics of a military man: constant preparedness. He'd had Mrs. Morgan pack them a few provisions.

The couple had come to a small grove and settled under one of the trees to break from the perpetual sunlight. As they sat, Aislin again began the conversation (as seemed to be developing into her role).

"There was something I wanted to ask you last night." She immediately had Garnett's attention. Aislin blurted the question. "Why did you save me?"

"I–I don't know, really." He squinted in thought. "That's not the answer you wanted."

"Well it's certainly not what I expected."

"I'm not sure I could relate it to you properly. Perhaps it would suffice to say that things are not always what they seem."

"You, Major, are living proof of that."

She expected a rebuttal but none came. He only smiled.

"So that's it then. You don't know, and things aren't always what they seem. What exactly am I supposed to gather from that?"

"You're unaccustomed to not getting the answers you want, aren't you," he teased.

"Honestly, I've never dealt with anyone so difficult to follow." Her manner was more distressed than annoyed.

"It's not my intention to be difficult."

"I wonder if perhaps it isn't just your nature," she prodded back at him.

"I say, now really." Though he knew she was joking, the major was amazed she'd be so bold.

"I'm sorry," she said in a very mocking tone, "but you know how youth often lends to fewer inhibitions. I was merely voicing an honest opinion."

"She told you–Mrs. Andrews told you what I said to her about you. Well, that was rude," he said, his smile broadening.

"That was rude? Were you privy to your own remarks, Major? Why, no one's ever spoken to me the way you did in all my life!"

"Then it was high time." Garnett was quite amused at her frustration.

"Uh! You know you really can be rather horrid at times." She wanted to be angry but thought their whole discussion was a little funny.

"I blame a lack of practice. You see, the only people I ordinarily converse with are either servants here at the house or the men in the field."

"That seems to be a fairly pitiful excuse, if you ask me. You know all this began with a moderately simple question. One to which I thought you'd readily share an answer."

"Conceivably, Miss Aislin, you do not know me as well as you thought."

"To that, I concede."

8

Time passed at the estate rather as it had before the major's return. The only difference was he occasionally joined Aislin on her rides, when the weather and his duties permitted, and there was more company at meal times. Often it seemed the entire house forgot there was a war at all, although there were the occasional reminders–usually just the correspondence for the major. But on one fateful day, the war brought Aislin's world crashing down around her.

James had just returned from town, and Garnett was upstairs in the study. James immediately went on the hunt for Aislin, trying not to attract any attention from the major. It was a dank afternoon following a very rainy day, the sort on which Aislin was never hard to find. James nearly startled her as he noiselessly entered the library. He pulled from his coat a bundle of papers.

He spoke as he opened them, "I normally don't pay much attention to these, but something caught my eye."

Aislin recognized the list. It was put out from time to time by both sides in the war: a list of casualties. This one happened to be from the Continentals. Her heart was pounding as she scanned the particular section James had opened for her, and it didn't take her long to see what had caught his eye. There, near the bottom of the page, she read "Laraway, Thomas." Aislin's hand covered her mouth.

"I'm dreadfully sorry, Miss, but I thought you'd want to know."

Tears began streaming down her face. She couldn't take her eyes off the name written on the harsh manuscript.

"Is there anything I can do, Miss?"

"No." She more mouthed the word than spoke it. She swallowed hard, trying to choke back her grief. "I appreciate-" she closed her eyes, trying to gather herself, "your going through the trouble to bring this."

James handed her a handkerchief. When she had composed herself a bit more, Aislin rose from her seat and threw the papers into the fire.

Turning back to James, she implored of him, "Please don't say anything to the major."

"It's just between you and I, Miss." James wrapped an arm around her shoulder and kissed her on the forehead.

"Thank you. I'd like to be alone for a while."

"Certainly, Miss." James nodded and pulled the door shut as he left the room.

Aislin didn't cry for long, but she couldn't shake the devastation that hovered over her. At first, her thoughts centred on her brother: about the last times she'd seen him and what the rest of the family would think when they found out.

These reflections soon turned her memory to Benjamin. She remembered vividly seeing his name on such a list. The war suddenly became very personal to Aislin. And here she was, in the house of a British major. She wanted more than anything to run home and be with her father and brothers. She wanted to see Madam. She wanted to find some way to relieve the pain that was suffocating her. She knew she'd find no such reprieve at Garnett's estate. If only she could speak to Madam, just for a minute. Aislin was sure she'd find the counsel and guidance she needed with her teacher.

She had thought her heart could never again break the way it had the day she found out Benjamin had been killed. Then she was stripped away from her home and family. Now this. It seemed the world was simply lying in wait, thinking up new ways of hurting her.

She knew she couldn't run. Free of the British Army maybe, but she was still a prisoner none the less. That being the fact of things, her first instincts were to lock herself away in her room until the war ended. Now more than ever, she wanted to see the British defeated.

A knock came at the door. James barely cracked it to tell her that dinner was ready and would she be coming. She wanted to say, no, but then she'd have to explain to Garnett why.

She told James she'd be along in a moment.

Aislin straightened herself as much as she could. She knew she wouldn't be able to hide her mood and hoped James would keep the major occupied beyond noticing.

She entered the dining room, followed almost immediately by Rebecca and Mrs. Morgan with dinner in hand. Garnett and James were already present and stood when she entered the room. James gave her a wink and a weak smile.

The men delved into business, but it concluded far sooner than Aislin would have liked. The major soon became conscious of her sullen disposition.

"Miss Aislin, what's the matter?" Curiosity more than concern masked his question.

"I'm fine, Major." She was very short.

James wanted very much to flee the room or stop the major from speaking to her again, but he was never given the opportunity.

"Well clearly that's not true, but if you don't want to talk about it," Garnett left the statement unfinished. He tried to ignore her and go on with his meal, but something in him prevented this. "Come now. You know you're being rather impolite."

Without looking at him (without hardly moving at all), Aislin posed a question: "Were you involved in the fighting at Fort Ticonderoga, near Vermont last summer?"

"No, actually. Why?"

"The man I loved was killed there." Her voice barely rose above a whisper.

The major felt a mite indignant. "Along with many other men, I'm sure."

Aislin faced him now. The tears she'd lost had returned to her hauntingly dark eyes.

"How can you be so cold?"

Garnett sighed, "Miss Aislin, you live in a real world, with real problems–a world that is engulfed in a very real war. Men die at war."

"Major, sir," James tried to step in but was overrun.

"I've heard the stories-" she shot back, her strong sentiments inhibited by her emotions, "from General Andrews, from the Patriot soldiers. I've seen with my own eyes the way you fight. You're brutal and merciless!"

"Now just a moment, Miss Aislin!" the major roared. "I spared you and your family, didn't I?"

"Yes, and I do willingly recognize the debt I owe."

"Well, at least that's something," Garnett was infuriated. "Don't you think you're being awfully naïve about all this?"

Aislin shook her head and then looked him dead in the eyes. "You really are a beast!" She ran from the room, hardly able to get the words out of her trembling lips.

"Why you ungrateful-" he shouted as he jarringly came to his feet.

James was relieved the major hadn't finished what it was he'd meant to say. He wasn't sure he should speak but chanced it anyhow.

"She doesn't understand, sir."

"That doesn't have the slightest thing to do with it, James!" He paced back and forth behind his chair.

"Yes, it does, sir. And you don't understand about her either."

Garnett stopped his pacing and looked at James, who wasn't sure what to say having told Aislin that he'd keep quiet.

"What don't I understand?" The major was quieter but still far from calm as he gripped the back of his chair.

James decided it would be in Aislin's better interest to try to explain to Garnett rather than hide it. "Her brother, sir-with the Continentals-she received word only a few hours ago. He's been killed."

The major dropped his head. "Why didn't you tell me, James?"

"She asked me not to, sir. I didn't want to betray her confidence."

Garnett muttered something under his breath. James was glad he couldn't hear it.

The major drove the chair viciously into the table and stormed out of the house.

Aislin had run straight to her chamber upstairs. She buried her face in her pillow and cried until she thought she'd be sick. She knew the discussion itself was her fault. She had instigated it. But why did he have to say such cruel things? It made her angry that he hadn't tried at all to be civil, and she was too upset to see the failure in her own actions.

She cried until she fell asleep–so soundly that she hadn't heard the major return to his room, after stopping to listen at her door.

Neither of them went down to breakfast in the morning. Aislin slept quite late and awoke with a magnificent headache. She found out from Rebecca (who later brought her tea) that the major had left very early that morning and had not yet come home. A little later, using her passages so as to avoid Garnett had he returned, Aislin visited the library to retrieve a few books and told Rebecca that she would be taking dinner in her quarters as well.

The major didn't return until very late that evening. Aislin heard him as he entered his quarters and shut the door. She then determined that she would not spend another day locked away. She would go down for breakfast and go about her regular routine, and hope Garnett disappeared as he had that day.

At daybreak, Aislin did exactly what she had set in her mind to do. She dressed and went downstairs for breakfast. She was delighted to find James already in the dining room. He was very happy to see her and asked all the questions Aislin had expected. As Rebecca set down her plate, she discretely relayed to Aislin that the major had indeed already left the house, just as he had the day before. This was less of a comfort to Aislin than she thought it would be. Still, she and James had a pleasant meal and parted ways just as they had so many times before; after which, Aislin set out on one of her notorious rides.

Winter was quickly approaching. There had already been a few light snows, in fact, but she hardly noticed the chill. The barren trees reached vainly for one another in their swaying, the cruel winds biting at the face of the unwavering rider. Blaming her pity for the horse on such a cold day, Aislin cut her ride relatively short.

She returned for tea, after which she locked herself away in the library for the rest of the afternoon. She tried to bury herself in the books–to think about anything but him–but of course, it didn't work. She wondered if he'd be home for dinner, when deep down she knew he wouldn't be. Aislin couldn't figure out why it mattered to her. She was still overwhelmingly angry at him. Nonetheless, part of her was terrified at the thought of their next meeting. It turned her stomach to even think of seeing him.

All of her anxiety came to naught in the end. Garnett, as predicted, did not return.

James could practically read her thoughts it seemed. They ate dinner alone together, as they had breakfast. He wanted to comfort her or try to coax out of her all the things she was concealing, but knew the timing wasn't right. Instead, without a word, he sat with her at dinner and silently kept her company afterward until she went to bed.

Again, Aislin's restless spirit kept her awake, just long enough to hear the major return home. It was not, however, the closing of his door that she heard first. There was an exchange between Garnett and his well-meaning, but stranded, servant. The two men must have been near the landing of the stairs, by the sounds of it. Aislin couldn't hear anything they said. Their voices were kept low, probably assuming she was asleep. She could barely pick up the begging in James's words, but couldn't make out the major's responses at all. Eventually, she heard footsteps and the door closing at the opposite end of the hall. She held her breath as she saw a shadow pause just outside her door. It stayed very still for a moment and then moved on with the click of a door handle.

Aislin sighed and closed her eyes.

9

Aislin had never been quite so stunned as she was when the major entered the dining room the next morning. She couldn't take her eyes off of him as he procured his seat to her right, at the head of the table. He caught her for a mere instant in his translucent glance, and thereafter faced only the table before him. With nothing more–not a single utterance–Garnett ate and then left.

Those features, which had been so faithful until then in giving away that which the major kept hidden, had failed Aislin. She couldn't tell if he was angry or upset. Maybe he didn't care at all.

The major went straight to his study. Once it was certain he'd cleared the room, James poured out what he'd obviously been withholding.

"You should talk to him."

"I'm sorry?" Aislin set down her glass.

"You should talk to him," he repeated slowly.

"Me, talk to him? After the horrible things he said?"

"I know your feelings were hurt, Miss Aislin." He leaned forward and folded his hands on the table. "And I know you hate to think of it in these terms, but you probably have a while yet to stay with us–most likely until the end of the war. Do you really want to spend it in enmity with the major?"

Aislin leaned forward and ran her hand over her forehead.

"I don't think I can."

"Look, you two will obviously never have that good a friendship, but it would probably make things easier if you could at least tolerate one another. Otherwise, I shall have to look for other employment," he continued with a touch of sarcasm, "because the climate in this house is rapidly becoming unbearable."

The two shared a smile.

"Well, now we certainly can't have that." Aislin sipped from her glass, and then squinting as if in pain asked, "Are you sure?"

"I am sure, Miss."

She dropped her chin in her palm and exhaled with great effort.

James raised his glass to her: "Good luck."

Aislin stuck out her tongue. Madam would not approve, joking or not.

In somewhat mock-compliance, she decided she'd take the first opportunity to talk to Garnett; but in her obstinacy, refused to immediately allow such occasion. Aislin left the house and set out across the countryside on a mount from the stable.

She wasn't home for tea, and she was not in the dining room when the major arrived for dinner.

"Where's Miss Aislin?" he inquired after his charge.

James shook his head nervously. "She went riding, sir, but I haven't seen her since this morning. It's not like her to be gone so long."

There was only calm in Garnett's voice. "Perhaps she returned, and it merely escaped our attention."

"I suppose it's possible, sir."

"Go and check the library."

"Yes, sir," James answered.

The major stepped out onto the terrace overlooking the gardens. He searched the area, but it was just outside the gardens to where his attention was drawn. A saddled horse paced around the barn, finally being run down by one of the hands.

Garnett ran into the house, immediately confronted by James.

"She isn't there," the servant blurted.

The major hadn't waited for him to speak. "Her horse is loose outside."

He said nothing else as he grabbed his coat and hat and sprinted toward the stables. He quickly gathered his best mount and turned down the trails leading away from the estate.

He knew the most likely paths she'd travel and trusted his tracking skills to guide him where logic would leave off. The major raced down the trail glancing all around him as he went. He wasn't sure exactly where he would find her, or in what condition; and the farther away from the house he travelled, the more concerned he became. There was no telling what had happened to her.

Garnett easily identified her horse's tracks where the path forked, and continued, slowing his pace just enough to accommodate the snowfall that had begun. His heart beat more loudly than the hooves of the animal beneath him. He'd gone well more than a few miles from the house, he knew. If she was injured, the danger would be exponentially compounded. He ran every feasible scenario through his mind, only further wrenching his nerves.

The major then thought of their argument–his last words to Aislin.

"This is my fault," he muttered to himself.

If anything had happened, he wondered how he would ever forgive himself.

A shadow just off the trail ahead caught his eye. He squinted as the snow continued to fly back in his face. He sighed with a groan as he closed the distance. It was Aislin, sitting huddled under a tree.

The major didn't even wait for the horse to stop. He hurriedly dismounted and rushed to her side. He could see the marking beneath her reddened eyes where the tears had been pouring down her cheeks.

Garnett removed his hat and knelt down beside her. Aislin was so relieved to see him, her first instinct was to throw her arms around him. She, of course, did not.

"Are you all right?" The worry he felt showed clearly in his silver eyes.

Aislin took a deep breath and nodded. "I think so," she said, then gesturing toward her feet. "I turned over my ankle."

"I thought the rebels–" he cut himself short, shaking his head, not wanting to imagine what might have happened. "Can you walk at all?" he asked.

"Just barely."

Garnett replaced his hat, got his feet under him, and then reached for Aislin.

"Put your arms round my neck."

She tentatively wrapped herself around the major as he carefully lifted her off the ground. He sat her up in the saddle of his horse and began appraising the damaged ankle.

"I don't think it's broken," he said, and then catching the wince on Aislin's face, added, "Sorry, I imagine it still aches a bit."

She only nodded.

"What on earth happened?" he queried, looking up at her.

Aislin hung her head as she spoke. "A deer ran across the path–nearly ran into us. I was caught off guard and fell." She was clearly embarrassed. "That's when I turned my ankle. The horse ran off. I tried to walk back but couldn't." Her eyes began to well again. "I'm glad you came along. It was getting awfully late."

The major could well envision the hours she'd spent sitting alone, wondering if or when anyone would find her.

He said the only thing that came to his mind. "I'm sorry."

Aislin almost smiled. "It isn't your fault, Major."

"I have to wonder if it isn't, at least somewhat."

She didn't answer.

"I'm sorry you were left here alone, and ..." he continued slowly, "I'm sorry about the other night. I should never have said those things to you."

This was the last thing Aislin had expected, especially under the circumstances. She felt compelled to take some of the responsibility herself.

"I'm...humbled by your apology, Major and grateful; but I feel I should–"

"Don't–please," he gently interrupted. "I know what you're going to say, but what was really nothing more than a misunderstanding, I turned into the brawl that it became." He paused for moment. "And I'm sorry it took us so long to miss you."

Aislin didn't know what to say. She only smiled at him. And he smiled back. Things were set right between them.

*   *   *

Confined to the house while her injury healed, Aislin tried to vary her days. She read in the mornings after breakfast and sewed in the parlour in the afternoons. Knowing how restless the restrictions had made her, the major would frequently move any necessary business downstairs in the afternoon; and the two would talk while Aislin sewed and Garnett worked.

Aislin caught herself, more than once, eagerly watching the clock, waiting for the major to leave his study.

One late morning, an unexpected knock came at the front door. James cordially greeted and invited in a very handsome man, whom Aislin guessed to be a little younger than the major (who was already on his way downstairs to keep his usual place in the parlour for the latter part of the day).

"Good afternoon, Mr. Drake," Garnett greeted, leaving his final stair behind and reaching for the outstretched hand of the guest. The salutation wasn't particularly warm but courteous enough.

"Good afternoon, Major. I hope I'm not intruding."

"Not at all," Garnett replied.

"I was in town and heard a courier mention your name. As I was already heading in this direction, I thought I'd save him the trip," he said, a little nervously, handing the major a letter.

Aislin still had a good deal to learn of exactly how feared and respected Major Garnett was, even off the battlefield.

"Thank you, Mr. Drake."

Just then the visitor spotted Aislin. "Good afternoon, ma'am."

Garnett turned with a start. His brilliant blue eyes widened as he caught her in his sights. Aislin knew they were in trouble. She didn't know why she hadn't hidden when the knock came in the first place.

"Good afternoon, sir." She headed for the door very confidently. She was thinking as fast as she could. "Won't you introduce me to our guest?" she addressed the major.

Aislin imagined Garnett could have killed her himself at that point.

"Ah," he was deliberating quickly also, "this is Isaac Drake. His family lives nearby. Mr. Drake, this is," he paused for barely a second, "my cousin–" and then he froze.

"My, you're being odd," she said to Garnett and presented her hand to Mr. Drake. "Elizabeth Garnett." She turned rapidly back to the major. "I think he might be ill," she gazed ponderously at her phoney relative. "He's been acting strangely all week."

"I'm–pleased to meet you, ma'am," Drake stuttered, unsure of her diverted attentions.

"Likewise." Her cheerful performance seemed to be working.

"Cousins, eh? Well, it's always nice to have family in for the holidays."

Garnett suddenly realized how well that played into their little game.

"Yes, well, I couldn't let our darling major spend Christmas alone, now could I?"

Garnett couldn't help but smile at her exuberant behaviour.

"Indeed," Mr. Drake said with an undertone of laughter. "You're only here for a short visit then?"

"I'm afraid I'm not sure, what with this dreadful war and all. It's made travelling rather inconvenient."

"I can imagine." Drake was thoroughly amused. "Well, I've done what I came for. I look forward to seeing you both again soon."

"Oh, I'm certain we shall," came Aislin's jovial response.

"Good day, ma'am. Major," he nodded.

"Good day," they both replied.

Garnett shut the door and released a breath he didn't realize he'd been holding. Aislin, right beside him with her back against the door, began to show signs of her repressed mirth in her shaking shoulders.

"It's not funny, you know." The major couldn't finish the sentence without smiling, which soon turned into an escaped chuckle.

Catching his expression, Aislin doubled up in her giggling. The major was unable to contain himself any longer. The two of them resigned to absolute hysterics. Aislin pulled herself to the stairs holding her stomach, in pain from laughing; while Garnett braced himself against the doorpost, wiping the tears from his eyes.

James watched the twosome, overwhelmed with relief and laughing himself (though he did so much quieter so as not to disrupt their moment of hilarity).

"Oh," Aislin barely squeezed out, "that must have looked absolutely ridiculous!"

Still not quite under control, the major answered, "You are, by far, the most sensational liar I have ever seen."

"And a good thing," she retorted, "or we'd both be in quite a mess."

The major huffed another laugh and began to pull himself together. James saw it as the perfect time to slip away. The pair eventually settled, and Garnett joined Aislin on the stairs.

"So, Elizabeth now is it?" he jested.

"I couldn't think of anything else."

Shaking his head, but still smiling, the major began instruction, "Next time—"

"I know," Aislin finished his thought, "hide."

*   *   *

The ominous stillness that had taken hold of New York had also settled over Garnett's estate. Aislin and the major existed harmoniously but with the flavour of anticipation floating amongst them—anticipation of the next conflict, which seemed to be inevitable.

Christmas came, and though the thought had crossed both of their minds, it went without discussion. The two did not exchange gifts.

Covertly on Christmas morning, however, James presented Aislin with a small box containing a simple but lovely hair comb (for which she found many occasions to wear), and she in turn gave to James a brilliant blue scarf that she'd made herself. After breakfast, Aislin managed to sneak Rebecca out from under Mrs. Morgan's watchful eye just long enough to give her a small gift as well: a delicate, white handkerchief into which Aislin had sweetly stitched pink flowers around Rebecca's initials. Rebecca, having not gotten Aislin anything (as it had simply never been done in Garnett's home-servants and mistresses exchanging gifts), was only assuaged of her guilt when Aislin insisted that she'd be offended if Rebecca tried to make recompense for the gift.

The day culminated in a wonderful dinner enjoyed by the three usual attendees. They'd been invited to the Drakes' home, but politely excused themselves, claiming it was a family tradition. In truth, they couldn't risk Aislin being seen by too many people. Aislin deeply regretted their necessary refusal. She did so enjoy parties and the like around the holidays. For the past several years, she and her father and brothers had attended Christmas at the Andrews'. Madam always threw the grandest parties. Aislin tried very hard not to think about it. She didn't want to ruin what had been a splendid day.

The major stayed home throughout the entire winter season. Aislin frequently found that she was quite glad for his continued presence. It was a hard winter, the kind her father always dreaded. Aislin thought of him often, on days that it snowed in particular.

On the other hand, Aislin was just as well looked after with Garnett as with her father. The major, being who he was, made sure the estate was well provided for and that everyone was comfortable. This was Aislin's greatest consolation, especially since she was unable to ride in such foreboding weather.

10

Spring took its time arriving. Just after the return of Aislin's favourite flowers, the major received new orders.

"Where are they sending you?" Aislin asked, standing in the doorway as Garnett busied himself with collecting his necessities from the study.

"I'm to meet a detachment of cavalry near New York City and then head south to New Jersey. There have been ongoing negotiations with the rebel congress, and in our interim indolence, Washington has taken it upon himself to put a great deal of pressure on our troops at Philadelphia. That, combined with the fact that the French are on their way, has led the generals to believe that we'd do better to leave Philadelphia and concentrate the army here in New York."

"You don't agree with their course of action?"

"Whether or not I agree makes no difference."

"Do you know when you'll return?"

Her question caught the major off guard. His focus veered swiftly in her direction; Aislin's unvarying gaze met him.

"No," he returned to his gathering just as quickly as he'd left it. "We seldom do. It depends greatly on the forces we encounter, battles that take place, any number of things really."

"I see."

Aislin's time at the estate had been so contented, she hadn't thought about the major leaving. She struggled to figure out why it bothered her so.

Garnett had somehow always had a fairly accurate insight in regard to Aislin's mannerisms, but was only just beginning to correctly translate the appropriate response.

"I suppose there's reason to believe we could return as soon as... the summer. But if this year is anything like last, that would be more than optimistic."

He was close but had faltered. Garnett always had a way of diminishing hope with the realistic.

"Mm," was Aislin's meagre response. She left the room to go downstairs.

The major paused a moment in his packing to watch her leave. He stood with his hands to his waist, staring at his bag; he sighed and shook his head. When everything was finished he met Aislin and James on the front porch.

"James, I trust you'll look after things..."

Aislin didn't hear the rest of what he said to the master-by-proxy. She started thinking about how this might have been the same time Garnett left his estate last year, just before their fateful reunion. It hit her all at once: it had been nearly a year now since she'd seen her family. Her heart sank.

"You'll be all right while I'm away," the major half-stated, half-asked.

Aislin snapped to attention at the address. "I'm sure I will."

Unconvinced, he nodded with a forced smile, "Good bye."

"God Speed, Major!" James called after him.

With one last nod, Garnett rode out of sight.

*   *   *

There isn't much to say of Aislin's time at the estate in the major's absence. She passed this stage in her life in much the same way as she had since she'd first arrived. She was happy for the most part, spending time with James and Rebecca as much as riding and reading in the gardens.

It was at this point, however, that things shifted a bit concerning the war, and so for Garnett as well.

Garnett and his small echelon arrived and camped near Trenton by the end of May, with orders to wait for General Clinton and his soon-to-be evacuating troops from Philadelphia. It was there, while making a short venture into the town, that Garnett made an interesting encounter.

A tall, young man dressed more finely than most, caught the major's attention. The boy looked familiar, but he couldn't place him. What bothered Garnett all the more was that the boy was relentlessly glaring at him. Very casually, the major approached him (casually, but with his hand resting on the hilt of the pistol at his side).

"Forgive me," he said, certain to keep his tone low but stern, "do I know you?"

The stranger gritted his teeth. "No, sir," he rumbled, "but I'm afraid you know my sister."

"Your sister," for an instant, Garnett honestly had no idea who he meant. Then he understood. "You're one of Miss Aislin's brothers."

The boy said nothing; he only persisted in his glower.

"I see I left quite an impression," he said, haughtier than he'd meant to.

"You murdering son of a-" John nearly attacked him right there in the streets.

Garnett stepped back, but more to brace himself than retreat. His stance remained aggressive with one hand up to keep the boy at bay and the other freeing his weapon.

"Now wait. Wait! It's not at all what you think," he said, quickly trying to deescalate the situation. "I saved your family-your sister included."

"Until they hang her!" He pushed Garnett's hand away from him.

"You don't understand."

The major looked around. No one seemed to be paying them any attention. He glanced around him once more.

"Not here. Follow me," he murmured.

John tentatively followed after the major's slight summoning.

There was nowhere to go to be completely out of view, so the major made do with the side of a small building.

"Your sister is safe," he whispered.

"Safe aboard one of your floating dungeons?" He spoke a little louder than Garnett would have liked.

"No!" The major paused to compose himself. "She was taken to my estate. She's been well cared for."

John's eyes widened as his mind turned to another horrendous possibility. "If I find you've laid one hand on her, so help me, I'll gut you myself!"

"Will you please calm down!" Garnett said, sounding rather raspy, trying to remain discrete. "I would never!"

"I'm not so sure."

"Please try to understand. I did the only thing I could do in taking your sister. She's been living very well at my estate with the world at her disposal." He was trying very hard to defuse the boy.

"Then tell me where she is, so that I can bring her home."

"You know I can't do that. It would mean giving us all away. They'd come after you, your brother, father and your sister. I promised her I'd keep her safe, and that's exactly what I intend to do."

"It's no concern of yours–"

Garnett cut him off, "I made it my concern the day she came under my charge, and I'll not let some arrogant youth jeopardize everything!" Garnett broke eye contact and looked at the ground, rubbing his chin. He shifted his bearing trying to appear less oppressive. "Is there anything I can do to put your mind at ease?"

"Humph." John turned away at the major's egotistical assumption.

"If you won't let me," the major tried to speak more congenially, "then there's nothing I can do."

He began to back away.

"Tell me why I shouldn't just turn you over to one of your own generals? It would be treason wouldn't it?"

Garnett put himself face to face with his would-be assailant. "Because after they hang me, the first thing my men will do is raid my home and take your sister–guaranteed to kill her. And a lot of good that would do us all."

If niceties weren't going to work, then the major wouldn't waste anymore of his time.

"Put my mind at ease then," John daringly replied, without backing down. "Deliver to her a message for me."

Garnett yielded, "Write her an entire letter if you like. You have my word she'll receive it as soon as I'm able to return home. It would do her good to hear from you."

"Might I bring you letters from my father and brother as well?" he asked, still suspicious but slowly realizing from Garnett's tone that he meant well.

"They're here nearby?"

"Yes, we left Camden shortly after..." he didn't finish his thought, but he didn't need to.

The major nodded, "I have business to attend. Meet me back here in three hours."

"Three hours then."

The men parted ways, and faithfully returned at the appointed time. John's father had wanted to come along, but John convinced him that it wouldn't be a good idea (justifying this by explaining his earlier meeting with Garnett). The major took the letters with an oath that he'd see to their delivery. Young Laraway took one last opportunity to question the officer, still hesitant in trusting his sister's kidnapper. In the end, they left peacefully.

It would be the major's last visit to this town. Garnett and his men began to make the jaunt toward the bulk of the British troops to assist in their extrication. This brief repositioning was the last moment of peace many of the men would enjoy.

*   *   *

The army had made it to Monmouth. They had hoped to rest their troops, beaten down by the extreme heat, but they knew the Continentals weren't far behind. British reconnaissance had gotten wind that there were several militia groups about the area as well. They couldn't stay, even though so many of the men had already collapsed and several died. They'd have to move and continue their march north to New York.

Garnett and his men would stay behind with the rear guard to ensure that the supply train and the successively retreating group made it safely away. The rebels were in position shortly after most of the British Army had detached, leaving still a sizable unit behind. The fighting immediately ensued.

The guard managed to counter-flank the Continental force just after sundown, and by large groups at a time, the departed British troops began to return to the battlefront. The ordeal was an instantaneous mess.

The commander of the Colonial Regulars seemed to lose his head the second his men encountered the opposition, and he ordered a retreat. The British felt firmly in control, but did not count on the rebel legions being able to reorganize, which they finally managed to do.

The cavalry went about their usual bloody business once the rout was on, but somehow, the enemy held their ground. Up until now, the Continental forces (when comprised mostly of militia, as they were) had never acted so strongly.

Garnett found himself surrounded by a company of opponents he had expected would retreat. Still they pressed him, and there was no available help. The Redcoats were up to their necks in an ocean of foes; fighting, too, the oppressive heat that clung to them, even now in the oncoming darkness.

The major took down yet another rebel soldier with the swing of his sword, but each time one fell, it seemed two rose in his place. This hydra of an army was as relentless as the roasting temperature. Garnett's eyes were stung by the salty sweat that ran down his face.

An attacker came from the major's right, and soon the valiant fool had Garnett's complete and ruthless attention. It was at this same moment, however, that a second militiaman was able to take full advantage of the major's distraction.

He struck true. Garnett folded on top of his horse and then toppled to the ground.

11

Summer was upon New England. The hot, balmy days bore evidence of that. The major had said he could possibly be home by summer. Since the first day of June, Aislin had wondered when Garnett would return. It didn't concern her much at first; but now, nearly August, it consumed her. She didn't question her motivations as she had in the past. She didn't have room for doubt in the chaos that swallowed her. The only sensation she could afford was the anxiety that had overtaken her.

Conversations at the dinner table were all but extinct. The only subject on anyone's mind was one they dreaded discussing.

Aislin found herself wandering around the house, going from room to room as if she were lost. Before she went to her chamber each night, Aislin couldn't help but pause for a moment and stare at the door leading to the major's quarters.

She asked James impossible questions to which he had no answers, and he was running out of consolations. She begged him to find out something the next time he was in town. He was unable to do so, though he did try. With the fray in New Jersey and the troops moving so rapidly out of that area, there wasn't much at all the Newburgh locals could tell him, least of all about one man. Aislin thought she'd worry herself sick over the whole event.

The high temperatures gave way only to the rain. Aislin again became a prisoner. She was unable to leave the house, bringing her more chance to think about Garnett's want of presence. When the rains, too, finally acquiesced, everyone at the estate began preparing themselves for the worst.

The major had not returned. By now, they'd heard of what had happened at Monmouth. They also knew that Garnett was supposed to be with that division. Most everyone was out of New Jersey, and still there was no word.

James had made the decision that he would travel to New York City, where the army had taken up headquarters. If there was any news to be had, it would be found there.

Fear stripped Aislin of every other feeling she'd yet had–a fear like she'd never felt, including the day Garnett had arrested her. She was terrified. She'd feared first for the major, wherever he was. Then another thought captured her. With the major gone, who would protect her? If it was true–if he'd been killed–the servants at the estate would be disbanded, and then what would happen?

Aislin felt guilty for thinking of herself at a time like this, so more often than not, her concern and hope for the major's safety won out in her thoughts. She truly did want him home, and not just because of what might happen. She missed him.

She wanted badly to go to James with these worries but didn't. She knew he had concerns enough without her adding to them. So Aislin suffered silently. There were many nights that she cried herself to sleep–with no one to hear.

$$* \quad * \quad *$$

The preparations were set, and James was leaving just after breakfast. Aislin managed only to eat one bite of the gourmet set before her. James was heartbroken at her distress, and he hated more than anything this necessity to leave her.

Aislin walked him to the door. Here, he put his arm around her shoulders, as he often did, and placed a gentle kiss on her forehead. She was so overcome that she hardly tried at all to hold back her sadness. She watched until James was out of sight and then ran to the library. The once warm room, with its soft hues and gentle lights, felt more like a tomb to the poor girl. She'd never felt so alone.

Aislin didn't know how long she'd been sitting, staring out the window, but her trance was suddenly broken by shouts coming from within as well as all around the outside of the house. She came running from the library upon hearing the noise.

She caught herself as she burst out the front door. There she stopped as a few of the men and one of the stable hands ran out to meet James–who was escorting the major. Aislin felt she'd never been so simultaneously relieved and excited in all her life! She couldn't hold back her smile; in fact, she felt her face hurt from the sheer force of it (tears, of course, still streaming down her cheeks). It seemed every sentiment within her was trying to escape all at once.

Her countenance fell, however, as she watched Garnett dismount. He was overly cautious and wobbled a bit as he gained his bearings on an unstable left leg. She saw him reach back for a makeshift cane that made up for the unclaimed weight. Seemingly outside herself, she hurried toward him.

Before she could say a word, the major calmly assured her, "I'm all right, Miss Aislin. Believe me; it looks worse than it is."

"What on earth happened?" She looked abhorrently at the damage.

The major smirked at her, "Why the war, my dear."

"Oh, you would make jokes." With great effort, she attempted to be stern, but a grin broke away instead. "What happened?" she insisted.

"A bayonet. There were two of them at once. I'll spare you the details. Now if you don't mind, I'd like very much to relax in my chair and have a drink."

After the major was settled into the parlour, he had James bring him a small leather case containing the three letters from Aislin's father and brothers. Tears again welled up in Aislin's russet eyes as Garnett told her of his encounter with John in Trenton. She sat quietly beside him as she read the words written by the family she hadn't seen in more than a year.

John and Clayton's letters were much shorter than her father's and mostly resounded the same sentiments of their concern for her, with a few details of their recent goings-on. Her father wrote much more loving and comforting words. For a moment, Aislin thought she could almost feel him sitting there beside her. She was also delighted to read what he had to say of Madam Andrews. Her father had told Madam the truth of Aislin's disappearance, and he wrote of how Madam cried the day he told her. Madam was very proud of Aislin for having been so brave. It was the greatest comfort of all for Aislin to hear of this.

Garnett watched as she read, absorbing the glow of happiness that emanated from within her soft features.

She shared little bits of her letters with him when she was finished and must have thanked him more than a dozen times for arranging this wonderful surprise. The major smiled, and his blue eyes sparkled at seeing such a beautiful woman so completely overjoyed.

Everyone breathed a sigh of relief at the major's homecoming. Garnett healed quickly, and by the time he'd been home for a little more than a week, he was walking without assistance (albeit with a slight limp). Aislin always snickered a little when he complained of the pain being aggravated on days that it rained. She thought it was silly.

It was a good bit of fortune things worked out the way they did, and as soon as they did. Trouble soon fell once more on the major's quiet estate.

There was a knock at the door, accompanied by the intermittent thudding of several feet on the porch.

"I'm coming, sir," James called from the kitchen.

The major was already at the base of the stairs. "Never mind, James," he replied and reached for the door knob.

James dutifully joined his master at the entry anyway, as Garnett heedlessly opened the door for their easily identifiable visitors: soldiers. At the head of the crowd was Lieutenant Danvers. Garnett was noticeably mortified. James, upon seeing his expression, began to back away from the door so as to remain out of sight and make a quick exit. He stayed only long enough to hear the lieutenant explain the reason for their visit.

"I'm terribly sorry to disturb you, Major. We've been sent here on orders to search the area for an escaped prisoner; specifically, the young lady we were transporting, around this time last year. We've been ordered to search every home as well as the countryside."

James caught the major glancing at him out of the corner of his eye and ran to the library. Aislin had been reading there, waiting for Garnett to conclude his business and join her for a ride.

The major, though he needed no further explanation, pressed for details only so he could try to collect his thoughts as to what he would do. "Escaped? How could that be possible?"

"Well, sir," the lieutenant seemed embarrassed, "the best we can surmise is that the men who were supposed to transport the girl on to New York City must have been rebels in disguise, and they set her free. It wouldn't be the first time they've pulled a stunt like this. And the way we figure it, when they heard we'd arrested a woman, they took it a might personally."

"I suppose that wouldn't surprise me," Garnett quietly responded, "but what makes you think she's somewhere near here?"

"Uh, sir, we were told there was someone in the area who fits her description," he stumbled over his words.

"What's that," he chuckled, "a young woman with brown hair and brown eyes? Of course there is. There must be hundreds! Half of the new brides in the county must be under suspicion."

The lieutenant shifted uneasily and looked away. The major narrowed his gaze.

"They suspect that I've had something to do with this, don't they?" He was very pompous, but his voice rumbled a little. "Preposterous," he said under his breath.

Outwardly, Garnett was portraying the perfect image of a man completely in control, but inside, he felt he might physically shrink from fright.

"I'm very sorry, sir," the lieutenant responded with his own measure of trepidation, "I-I tried to refute the allegations myself, but they wouldn't hear it. They insisted they would only lay to rest the accusation after the premises were searched."

"Then search," Garnett replied, perhaps overly confident. "I have nothing to hide, and the sooner it's done, the sooner we can put this ugly business behind us."

"Yes, sir," Danvers nearly moaned.

He motioned for the men to enter and begin their hunt. Garnett stepped out of their way.

In the library, without much explanation (Aislin needed only to hear there were soldiers looking for her–that was enough), James had rushed Aislin up the stairs and into the doorway leading to the side of the house. Their plan was simple. They would hope the men would only open the doors and take a quick glance around the space. Should the soldiers look further, they'd make a run for the stables. Aislin wondered how the major would get away.

The two huddled quietly on the dark stairway. They could hear movements in various places around the house, and a few in the library, now just adjacent to their hideaway. As violently as her heart was pounding, Aislin feared someone might hear it.

Back at the entry, the major was trying to return to his poised and assertive self, while making pleasantries with Lieutenant Danvers.

"I heard about what happened at Monmouth," Danvers reached for a conversation piece. "I also heard that a commendation was to be granted."

"One does what one can," the major answered coolly.

"Uh, someone mentioned that you had a cousin who'd come to visit. Has she left already?"

"No, she's still here, although we're hard-pressed to keep her home when the weather is good." The major's thoughts slipped to Aislin, wondering if she was all right. "She loves to ride."

"Ah, so the two of you have that in common then."

"Mm." His attentions returned to the present. "All the same, I am expecting her back soon and would like very much for this to be over by the time she returns. I'd hate to have to explain all this to her."

"Certainly, sir. I told the men that this was to be as unobtrusive as possible. Please understand, none of us wanted to be party to this."

"I know, Lieutenant. Necessary evils." Garnett forced a smile.

James and Aislin heard the doors opening and closing above their heads. The turn finally came to search the entrance to their nook. When it opened, they could just make out the light coming from the doorway. It remained open, and there were a few footsteps. The pair silently inched toward the next stair down the way. Then there came a voice.

"We're not here to be snooping in the major's home. These are all just storage. There's no need to pry."

"Bah," was the only reply they heard before the door closed, leaving them again in darkness.

The gratefully concealed pair sighed noiselessly.

The search concluded mercifully soon after it had begun. Lieutenant Danvers made a last apology, which the major now gracefully accepted (having successfully evaded any trouble). Garnett assured Danvers that he understood the subordinate was only doing his duty, and the lieutenant promised Garnett that he would report his findings, or lack thereof, as soon as possible. The major thanked him, and the soldiers went their way.

Garnett waited until they were well away and then ran as fast as he could to the other end of the house.

"James! Miss Aislin!" he shouted as he entered the room. "James!"

The door upstairs opened as the couple revealed their hiding place.

"Thank goodness," the major said breathlessly.

"Are you all right, Major?" came Aislin's wavering voice.

"I'm fine, Miss Aislin, and the two of you?"

"We're fine, sir," James answered as they reached the library floor.

"That was close." Aislin knew it didn't bear saying, but her relief compelled her.

"Too close," said the major, his hands on his waist. "Well, that does it." Garnett turned and left the room.

For a moment, James and Aislin just looked at each other, both searching for some justification for the major's strange behaviour. They chased after him all the way to the study upstairs.

"Major?" Aislin inquired.

It was the only word she uttered before Garnett spilled his explanation.

"That's it. I can't take any more of this."

He wasn't angry. He didn't even seem upset. He sounded perfectly rational; only as if he'd finally made up his mind about something the two of them ought to have been privy to.

"I can't–I won't risk any more of this nonsense," he was shuffling through papers on his desk and reaching for a pen. "I've withstood the fear of being caught by my own subordinate officers, and I've born your accusations of–" he stopped. Garnett leaned his weight on his outstretched arms upon his desk. "I'm sorry. I don't mean to sound as if I'm placing blame. This is all my fault."

Aislin didn't answer.

"I'm the one who insisted on bringing you here. It's not that I regret it. It's just..." he paused, "I suppose I never realized all that this would involve."

No one said anything for a while. Garnett went to scribbling something on the paper he finally found.

"If you don't mind my asking, sir," James imposed, "you seem awfully resolute about whatever it is you're doing. I must confess, I–and probably Miss Aislin, as well–we're a might... concerned."

"I'm writing a letter to General Clinton, or whoever has taken charge at New York City now. I'm requesting a transfer."

"A transfer, sir?"

"The farther we can all get from here, the better off we'll be."

"But will they let you go, with everything now being so centred here in New York?" Aislin stepped in.

The major stopped writing. "I don't know, but it would be our best chance of surviving this war and avoiding the gallows."

The blunt statement startled her, but this time, Garnett didn't apologize.

Aislin and James waited while the major finished writing his letter. As he sealed it, Garnett addressed James.

"I want you to take this to the generals at New York City. Wait there until you have their response." He handed James the letter. "Keep it until the morning. There's no sense in you leaving tonight. You wouldn't get far before dark. For now, I want to enjoy what's left of the evening." He gestured everyone out of the room. "Shall we?"

The trio headed toward the staircase. No one said much at dinner that night. What conversation there was came mostly from James and Aislin. Everyone tried very hard to forget all that had transpired that day.

12

James left early the next morning carrying the major's letter. He had no idea what the correspondence said, but if he had, it would have interested him greatly.

The language of the letter was imploring. Garnett wrote very properly and respectfully, but he was nearly begging for this transfer. He listed, as his reasoning, an important family matter that required his attention and asked for accommodation. Had either James or Aislin read the letter, they would have been shocked at its pleading nature.

Just the same, James ignorantly carried the correspondence to the military headquarters and successfully returned with their reply, travelling by way of the Hudson River to avoid crossing into New Jersey. He arrived back at the estate in less than a week. It was hard to say whether this meant good news or bad.

Garnett eagerly opened the reply to find his answer.

> *Mjr Wlm Garnett,*
> *We are first to commend you on your successes and achievements at Monmouth, New Jersey, last June…*

The major skimmed the letter a bit, deciding he'd read for details after he'd found what he was looking for.

> *You are hereby promoted to the rank of Lieutenant Colonel.*

Though pleased with the news, he continued to glance over the article.

> *In regard to your request for transfer, allow this letter to stand as your official reassignment.*

The major-or now colonel-sighed with relief.

The letter went on to detail his move. He, and all those considered to be of his household, were to depart New York City at the end of the following week. Their new home was to be near the Fort St. Mark in St. Augustine, Florida. The opposite end of the colonies-Garnett couldn't have been happier.

Over dinner, the colonel relayed the good news of his promotion and their upcoming relocation. Both Aislin and James congratulated Garnett, and the three began making their plans.

"But isn't Florida Spanish territory?" Aislin inquired.

"There is still a small Spanish population throughout the colony, but they do not govern the area to which we're travelling," the colonel explained. "After the war, the Spanish surrendered the fort to England in return for lands we had captured in the Caribbean. We've held command ever since."

"I see. So you'll be posted at the fort then."

Garnett nodded with a smile.

"What business is there for the army in Florida?" she continued.

"Well, as you noted, there is the Spanish presence to contend with. There is also the concern of threats from Georgia. Their militia, while having yet to face a real standoff with the army, do frequently harass loyal citizens in the area. Many families, hoping to escape the trouble, have moved to St. Augustine, in point of fact. So we keep a strong presence in Florida to discourage," he said, more emphatically, "any potential problems."

"And if I may say so," James interjected, rising from his seat, "I imagine our boys in the south could use a little leadership from the likes of our colonel."

Garnett laughed under his breath.

Aislin looked at them both. "What makes you say that?"

Garnett answered, "Rumour is, Florida is a mite favoured over the other southern colonies. She never seems to lack for supplies of any kind, even when others lack the most basic provisions; and there are many affluent Loyalists currently residing there. I know of at least one governor who retreated to the area before the war, when he began drawing unwanted attention from the militia."

"So your assumption is they're a bit soft," Aislin surmised.

The colonel huffed again. "Something like that." He leaned back and sighed. "It should be a relished change of scenery."

Everyone felt much more at ease at the notion of leaving New England. The whole house was abuzz preparing for the move. Aislin, however, was a bit unnerved. Though glad to be leaving the danger behind, she'd never been aboard ship before and was not particularly looking forward to it. On the other hand, she had asked Garnett, and he had agreed, to arrange for Rebecca to come with them. The colonel had said it was only fitting for Aislin to have her lady by her side. This became Aislin's greatest comfort as they made their move.

With everything settled, the party began their journey with the trek to New York City. They had been needlessly worried about the possibility of Aislin being recognized, and all were soon safely aboard the vessel heading south.

As they left the northern colonies behind, Aislin was surprised at how quickly the climate changed. In New York, the autumn weather was already considerably cooler. The farther south they moved, the warmer it became. Colonel Garnett told her stories of terrific storms that came along through the southern coasts called hurricanes. It made Aislin nervous at first. A storm at sea was nothing to trifle with. In her limited knowledge, even she knew that. Garnett assured her they had usually subsided by this late in the year.

The ship floated right past the enormous fort upon arrival. Aislin was awestruck. All of the forts she'd seen on her various adventures paled in comparison to this imposing structure. Besides the fact that it was monstrous in size, it was also beautiful. The walls bore domed bastions on each corner, and large cannons and mortars peeked out from between breaks in the walls. Except for the weaponry, it looked more like a seaside castle to Aislin.

To the colonel, it was simply another station in his long military career, and he chuckled at Aislin's lack of prowess.

While the crew unloaded the passengers' effects, Garnett and Aislin, followed by the rest of the household, were escorted to their new residence. It was far greater than Aislin had expected. Though much smaller than the estate in Newburgh, it was very charming.

At the front, on the second floor, was a quaint little balcony looking directly out to the bay; and just down the way, the fort could be plainly seen. In the back, there was a small courtyard with which Aislin immediately fell in love. All the trees and flowers were different, but what most caught her attention was that everything was still green and very much alive. Back in New York, the leaves had already changed and were beginning to fall; and her coveted lilies had left long ago. Here, there were brilliant palms standing beside majestic oaks, all surrounded by pretty little flowers just coming into season. Aislin determined that she'd be very happy here.

The group settled very comfortably into their new little home. The layout tended to be much like it had been. The difference was that all four bedchambers upstairs were occupied by Garnett, Aislin, James and Rebecca. The study, along with the dining room and parlour, were downstairs.

The stables and servants quarters were just beyond the gated courtyard. Two stable hands had come with them from New York, along with Henry, another of Garnett's servants. At residence here already were two groundskeepers and two who kept house and cooked. Aislin found these four to be particularly interesting. They were married couples, the cooks being the wives of the grounds men; and they were Greek. Their English was broken but easily understood. Aislin thought their accents were beautiful.

The space in the new house was ample, but to Aislin, this felt more like a home. Its smaller size was much more inviting and warm, in her opinion.

After she finished reorganizing a few things in her new quarters, she decided to step out onto the balcony to view her surroundings. Aislin leaned on the railing and closed her eyes as the cool sea breeze washed over her.

Garnett had, himself, ventured onto the balcony. He stopped and quietly stood, smiling, as he studied her graceful figure.

Aislin heard his approach behind her. Without opening her eyes, she spoke softly. "It's beautiful here."

"I'm glad you like it." Hands behind his back, he slowly walked toward her.

"I suppose its greatest appeal is the want for wondering when the soldiers will come looking for me."

"This little escapade has been quite a disruption to your otherwise quiet life, hasn't it?"

"To say the least, but I suppose no more of a disruption than I've been to yours," she replied, glancing at him over her shoulder.

"I'm sorry," he said quietly.

"For what?"

"It was my idea."

The colonel shifted his weight, leaning on one side against the rail, looking out across the bay.

"That much is certain," she said a little mockingly. "It's been an adventure I'll not soon forget."

Garnett said nothing. He only gazed at Aislin and smiled.

"I don't believe I've ever actually thanked you for all you've done," she added with a small stutter.

"That isn't necessary, Miss Aislin."

"Just the same, thank you, Major-ah, forgive me-Colonel. I'm not sure how I'll get used to that. I've only ever known you as a major."

"Well… you could call me William."

"Oh, I don't know. It was quite an adjustment for me to call James by his given name. I'm not sure I could."

The colonel huffed a small laugh as he pushed away from the rail. "It's all right, Miss Aislin. It was only a suggestion, but should you change your mind…" he left the statement unfinished. "The cook informs me that dinner will be ready shortly. I'll leave you to your view."

"I'll see you downstairs then," Aislin more asked than stated.

Garnett nodded to her as he backed away and went indoors.

The motion immediately reminded Aislin of how he had bowed and left her the night of their infamous meeting in Trenton. A flush of emotion made her cheeks feel hot. The sensation was not the same as it had been, but it made Aislin squirm a bit.

She remembered, without any trouble, the conversations the two of them had that night. The event felt so far away, yet the words and emotions ran through Aislin's mind as if it had been only yesterday. Some of the things she felt shocked her. It somehow seemed the major she had known and the colonel she now knew were entirely different people. Everything was different now, including their relationship.

Aislin caught herself twiddling her fingers and began to reflect on just how far she, herself, had come since the ball. She'd had to do a lot of growing up all at once. She wondered, would Madam be pleased? Would she be proud?

*   *   *

Life in St. Augustine was rather dissimilar from life in Newburgh, but the changes were for the better. Garnett tried to attend to any business at the fort as early in the morning as possible, so as to free his afternoons. Aislin didn't know it, but that was primarily for her.

In the countryside of Newburgh, it didn't matter if she rode alone, because there was no one to notice. Here in the city, however, it wasn't done–a woman without an escort. James was busy and didn't particularly care to ride anyway; so Garnett tried to make time for her. In truth, Aislin preferred the company. Among other reasons, it was much easier to lose one's bearings here; and there were a great deal more people, some of whom made her a little nervous. By her experiences, Aislin knew she was safe with Garnett.

The market was very near their home; so on days when the colonel was unavailable to ride, Aislin and Rebecca would follow James through the bustling Quarter. They adored all the brightly arrayed shops and wagons and were always eager to see the new wares the traders would bring.

The colonel had arranged for Aislin to bring some of her favourite books from the library at Newburgh, and she still made time for reading on days that it rained.

The one change Aislin really didn't care for was the weather. She thought it was too warm, and most of the others agreed. On the other hand, by evening, it had cooled just enough that everyone looked for a reason to be outdoors. Thus, Aislin's best-loved of their new practices was dinner on the terrace, overlooking the courtyard. Oddly enough, this tradition was initiated by Colonel Garnett.

He had come home late one evening from his duties at the fort. Rather than tired or irritated, as his work often left him, he arrived in unusually good spirits–and with a gift for Aislin.

"Lilies!" she gasped. "Where did you find these?"

"I'm told they grow later here because of the warmer weather." The colonel's gaze danced bashfully. "I remember how much you liked them in the gardens at Newburgh."

"Thank you, Colonel. They're beautiful."

Garnett only smiled.

He asked Aislin how she would feel about taking dinner on the terrace, which she thought was a marvellous idea. They had done so (accompanied by James and Rebecca) every decent evening since.

For Aislin, this all resembled a perpetual holiday. In her mind, she couldn't possibly ask for more.

Late in the fall, the temperatures had begun to shift; but out of nowhere, a remarkably warm day presented itself, holding on to the last remaining threads of the southern summer. The colonel did not go to the fort that day. Instead, over breakfast, he posed Aislin with what seemed like a peculiar question.

"Have you ever seen the shoreline at the beaches?"

"Forgive me, but isn't that a rather silly thing to ask? It lies just beyond our front door."

"No, not the harbour," he chuckled. "Have you ever seen the ocean where the tides meet land with no man-made boundary?"

"Oh," Aislin was now incredibly curious. If she hadn't seen it, she wanted to. "I'm not sure I have."

"Well, this should be a good day for such a venture. James, have our horses readied and have the cooks prepare a small meal." He addressed Aislin again, "Dress comfortably. The sand and water tend to be a might...," he searched for the word, "intrusive."

Aislin wasn't certain what that meant, but she didn't care. She was too excited. She knew exactly what she'd wear. On the colonel's bidding, she and Rebecca had gone and purchased a few new articles of clothing, one of which was a lovely linen dress. Aislin had also bought, to accompany the dress, a sharp blue apron which covered front and back but left visible the dress's sleeves and intricately embroidered hemline. It wasn't nearly as fancy as her other dresses, but this outing was just the occasion she needed to wear it.

After the two were dressed and packed, they headed off in a direction Aislin had not yet been. As they left civilization behind, she felt a little anxious. The roads soon ended; and beneath the horses' feet, instead of dirt (or any earth that Aislin recognized), was a soft, nearly white powder. If not for the heat, she might have mistaken it for snow. With a slight eastward turn, the pair presently reached their destination.

Garnett brought his mount to a walk, and Aislin followed suit. The horses trudged up a small hill. Near the crest, Garnett looked over at Aislin and smiled broadly. Rather than return the smile, she looked at him quizzically but for hardly a moment. A muffled roar erupted just in front of her. Aislin couldn't move- couldn't think. Nothing could have prepared her for the sight.

The flat sand stretched brilliantly out before them, and just beyond was the sea. It sparkled like millions of diamonds dancing in the sunlight. Two simple features could never have looked so amazing. Gazing to the left or to the right, it didn't matter. The beach, as the colonel had called it, swept as far as she could see in either direction. It was in this sideward glance that Aislin realized she, not the scenery, was the focus of Garnett's interest. His sharp blue eyes peered right back into hers.

"So," he began, "what do you think?"

"I'm not sure what to think," she sighed.

Garnett smiled. "Come on." He headed his mount toward the churning waters.

Near the sands' end, he dismounted and, after removing his boots and stockings, walked to Aislin's side. The whole event was so extraordinary that she thought nothing of the colonel's odd behaviour. He took her by the hand and helped her down. Aislin had already taken off her gloves, and it was only then she realized Garnett had done the same. His touch made her blush.

She had only a moment to note the sensation before another captured her awareness. The sand shifted beneath her feet as she tried to gain her bearing. Her grip tightened on the colonel's hands.

"It's all right," he smiled. "It's perfectly safe, but you'd might as well remove your shoes. You'll get just as much sand on your feet-maybe more-with them on as off."

Very unsure of the general affair, Aislin did as he said. The warm sand seemed to penetrate through her feet, carrying the feeling over her whole body. She looked up, and she smiled at Garnett. He turned and offered her his arm, and as she gladly accepted it, felt his other hand reach over hers.

The pair carefully walked the rest of the distance to the water's edge. Aislin gasped as the cool water splashed against the bottom of her legs, but as the sea retreated, so did the sand underneath her. She felt she was sinking and quickly reached her free hand to the colonel's arm. The motion hadn't surprised him-not until she didn't let go, even when she realized she was safe.

They walked a short while up and down the shoreline, but fighting the pull of the sand and tide was tiring. They soon stopped to enjoy their provisions.

"So now that you've had time to take stock of your surroundings, what do you think?" the colonel asked.

"I think I could never have imagined such a place. It's absolutely amazing. Thank you for bringing me here."

"You're most welcome, Miss Aislin."

"How did you know it?" she inquired.

"A few of the gents at the fort were talking about it the other day. They come here to swim in the summer."

"Swim in the ocean? Wouldn't that be dangerous?"

"No," Garnett smiled, "it's safe in the shallows."

"Do you swim, Colonel?"

"Only if the ship I'm on is sinking."

They both laughed.

"I swim a little, but not very well. I learned when I was young, at my family's home in England. There's a lake at the edge of the estate–perfect for swimming, fishing. I believe you'd like it there."

"It sounds lovely." Aislin decided to take the opportunity to pry a little. "Do you still consider England to be your home–not here in the colonies?"

"Yes, of course. I make my living at the bidding of the King's Army, but England is certainly my home. My estate–most of all I've ever known is there."

"Then you'll return when the war is over?" Aislin was surprisingly disheartened.

The colonel spoke very gently. "Yes, I suppose so."

He could sense the emotion in Aislin's questions but was unable to determine their exact nature. Though he hated the idea of her being unhappy, Garnett couldn't help but hope some small measure of her feeling was disappointment at the thought of his absence. He had learned a few things, however, in his dealings with Aislin.

Jokingly, he added, "But at the rate we're going, that may be a hundred years from now. And if the search for you continues, we may be forced to flee the colonies never to return to either continent!"

Aislin smiled. The colonel had achieved his desired result.

They finished their meal, cleaned their rather dirty feet, and packed for the trip home.

13

Warm weather or cold, Christmas came all the same. The temperatures had dropped, but the whole house lamented the lack of snow that usually accompanied the holiday.

On the afternoon two days before Christmas, the colonel came home uncommonly early and seemed rather flustered. He called for James the moment he walked through the door. Aislin, hearing the commotion, followed shortly behind.

"Good, you're both here," Garnett blurted out, as he removed his hat.

"What's the matter?" Aislin asked. She'd never seen him so out of sorts.

The colonel stood still for the first time since his entrance, and took a moment to collect himself. "We've been invited to the general's home for a Christmas Eve ball. He insists on meeting you," he said, referring to Aislin.

"Oh, no," she gasped.

"No, no, Miss Aislin. It's a good thing. He knows nothing of our ordeal. It's merely an invitation."

"It's a very great honour, Miss," James added.

"Indeed," Garnett grinned.

"Oh," Aislin replied, "well in that case, I'm very happy for you, Colonel."

"This means good things for all of us," the colonel said, sounding very enlivened.

The atmosphere of the colonel's home filled with excitement all at once. Everyone was in wonderful spirits after Garnett's good tidings from the general. Dinner was splendid, and afterward, Rebecca played carols on the piano for everyone. Aislin couldn't remember a time when she'd been happier. She still thought of her family in the holiday season, but for the first time, felt these people with whom she spent her every day were also becoming family to her.

As she prepared for bed that night, a soft knock came at her door. Aislin reached for her shawl and opened the door, supposing it to be Rebecca. It was Garnett, however, who was revealed at its opening.

"Colonel. Is something the matter?"

"No. I'm sorry if I disturbed you."

"Not at all."

Aislin stepped aside to allow him entrance. They passed through her room into the sitting room which connected their quarters as it had in the Newburgh estate. It was then Aislin noticed the small package under the colonel's arm.

"I had meant to give you this for Christmas but thought it might do for tomorrow." He awkwardly handed her the box.

Aislin looked at him quizzically. "What is it?"

"Open it," he smiled broadly.

She did so. Resting gently within was a spectacular necklace, Aislin would have supposed, made for a queen. Her jaw dropped, and her eyes widened. It was adorned with glistening red and white gems that caught a different point of light at every direction they were turned.

She finally found her voice. "Diamonds?" she asked breathlessly.

Garnett nodded nervously, "And rubies."

"Colonel, it's just too extravagant. I can't accept this."

"Nonsense." He was so pleased she liked it, and his ever-growing smile was proof. "And I shall be terribly offended if you don't."

"I don't know what to say."

"Well that's mildly refreshing," he teased.

Aislin looked back at her sparkling gift. Garnett didn't know it, but she was preparing for her next statement.

"Thank you, William."

It was partly spouted, partly whispered. Either way, he couldn't have been more surprised.

Aislin could tell. She gazed up at him and gave a crooked grin.

"I suppose if I'm to pretend to be your cousin for an entire evening, I'd better practice."

The colonel accepted this farce of an explanation with a nod. "Well, I won't keep you any longer. Good night, Miss Aislin."

"Good night."

*　　*　　*

The next evening came all too quickly for Aislin. The last ball she had attended was the tumultuous night at which she'd met Benjamin and the colonel, so not surprisingly, she was not very excited about this one. Then again, she was unexpectedly calm as the sunset advanced. Perhaps it was because she knew better what to expect this time. Perhaps it was because there was little to no possibility of her encountering any unwanted company at Garnett's side. At any rate, Aislin sat placidly as Rebecca helped her prepare.

"It's an honour to be sure, Miss," Rebecca said wistfully, adding Aislin's hair pin. "I imagine every head in the room will turn when you walk in on the colonel's arm."

Aislin sighed, "I thought I'd be more nervous."

"Don't worry, Miss. I'm sure your nerves will catch you at a most inconvenient moment."

The girls giggled.

As the finishing touch, Rebecca carefully fastened the gleaming bobble around Aislin's neck.

"It really is something, Miss."

"Mm." Aislin's lips turned a slight smile as she gently touched the shining stones. "I suppose I'd better get downstairs. The colonel will be waiting."

Garnett knew he was staring as Aislin descended the staircase, but he couldn't help himself. At that moment, nothing in the world could have made him take his eyes off of her.

Aislin's vision was also locked. She so rarely saw the colonel in anything but his uniform and couldn't help but notice how striking he looked in his sharp, black jacket. The deep colours and his otherwise dark features caused his arresting, blue eyes to stand out as brilliantly as the gems in her necklace.

Garnett had just managed to eek out, "You look lovely," and Aislin thanked him, when James cleared his throat to catch their attention. The carriage was ready.

Once they had arrived at the general's home, things seemed remarkably familiar; that is, until Aislin found herself once again on Garnett's arm. She had a thought: *Rebecca was right*. She felt at any moment her heart might leap straight into her throat, especially when he laid his hand over hers and smiled.

Aislin composed herself as they approached their hosts. The colonel introduced her, while she accepted a few compliments. The general and his wife were delightful people, but Aislin still felt intimidated. She was glad to be one of many coming through the room. Garnett led her away from the crowd after they'd gotten inside. He was just about to say something when two gentlemen approached.

"Good evening, Colonel," a red-haired man addressed Garnett.

"Good evening, Mr. Hollingsworth," he returned. "Captain Turner," he directed to the second man.

"Sir," he replied shortly.

"This is my cousin," the colonel turned, "Aislin."

Both men bowed as Aislin gave a small curtsy.

"How could such a lovely creature be related to a brute like you?" Mr. Hollingsworth jested.

The other two men huffed at his statement, which Aislin did not acknowledge. It was overly outspoken in her opinion.

"Would the lady care to dance?" The proposal came from the Captain. "Perhaps I might save you from any more of Mr. Hollingsworth's jokes."

Unsure of herself, Aislin looked to Garnett. He nodded. Knowing he'd never put her in jeopardy, Aislin accepted the young man's hand.

"I'm surprised we've never met before," Turner conversed as they danced.

"We've only been in the south for a few months," Aislin replied.

"Ah, yes. Well we're happy to have your colonel amongst our ranks. A man of his experience and reputation is just what we needed here."

Aislin said nothing. She wasn't sure exactly what the captain meant.

"Do you attend many parties with the colonel?"

"No, Captain. Not many."

"How terribly unfortunate. And call me Charles."

Aislin dropped her eyes and tried to hide her grin. She felt more than a little uncomfortable.

"I don't consider it to be so unfortunate, Charles. I don't fancy these parties much at all." She'd learned her ability to bluff as well as her manners from Madam.

"What a shame. Such beauty must have been bred for these affairs."

She tried very hard to ignore him. Even if only in pretence, Aislin had to be careful in her dealings with the colonel's acquaintances. In any case, the music was beginning to wind down, and their dance would soon end.

She wondered if she'd fair better to run to some quiet corner afterward or just return to the colonel. If she went to Garnett he might offer some measure of defence. The same could not be said for the corner, so she did return to her escort. The colonel seemed to note her unease and immediately took her in arm. Turner was right behind.

"Thank you for the dance, Miss Aislin," he bowed.

"You're most welcome, Captain," she maintained her ruse.

Conversations ensued, about which things Aislin was not interested. Thus, she paid little attention unless she herself was addressed. Garnett soon became aware of her boredom.

The conversation lulled as the musicians began a new tune. It was to this which the colonel asked Aislin to dance. The strings plucked along in music box fashion as they moved gracefully with the crowd. They had shared only the one other dance, so very long ago, but somehow dancing with Garnett felt almost second nature.

"How are you enjoying yourself?" he asked.

"Agreeably enough, I suppose."

He'd expected a much different answer.

"Well, this evening does seem to be progressing more amiably than the last ball we both attended."

"Considerably," Aislin agreed with a smile.

"I am compelled to apologize for the behaviour of the men in our company. I know they're a bit... rough."

"You owe no apology. And I suppose they're not that bad."

"That's kind of you to say but a terrible falsehood."

Both laughed.

When their dancing ended, they were again joined by Mr. Hollingsworth and Captain Turner. There was also a third gentleman, about the colonel's age, who entered the group.

"Major Allen, how good of you to join us."

Aislin recognized the colonel's tone. It wasn't friendly, although there was effort. The others didn't notice.

"Hello, Colonel Garnett. And you must be Miss Aislin."

He made a gesture like he would reach for her hand. To prevent the manoeuvre, Aislin took hold of Garnett's arm and only nodded to the stranger.

Not seemingly the least bit affected, the major continued, "I see rumours of your beauty are vastly understated."

"You're too kind, sir," she respectfully returned.

"Why should you be so fortunate to have such a relative?" he turned to Garnett. His manner was teasing, but something in his voice upset Aislin. "You couldn't possibly merit such a treasure."

The colonel had prepared a response, but Aislin beat him to it.

"On the contrary, Major. William is a tremendous gentleman, and he's provided a wonderful living for our household." Aislin was amazed at her own assertion.

Garnett smiled at his valiant defender.

"Well, it would appear I'm not acquainted with *your* dear colonel. Why, his actions at Monmouth alone could disqualify such a statement." The man chuckled a little.

"It seems to me, you're telling stories out of school, Major," Aislin retorted.

His mirth was ended.

"Gentlemen," Aislin made clear her address, "please excuse me." She caught the colonel's eye and smiled as she left the gathering.

She stepped outside to a landing that overlooked the gardens and the bay beyond. She was alone for only a moment. Garnett had stayed behind with the company of gentlemen just long enough to avoid being rude.

"Miss Aislin, are you all right?" Those familiar words startled her.

"Yes. I'm sorry I ran off," she said softly.

"Think nothing of it," he smiled. "It was completely understandable."

Aislin smiled back.

"By the way," he spoke slowly, "thank you, for those things you said."

"You're welcome."

"I imagine your opinion of our company has changed somewhat," the colonel teased.

Aislin laughed. "That it has."

"I must admit, I thought you'd spend the entire evening dancing; or having learned from previous experience, have you refused all of the young men?"

"I'm afraid there haven't been any to refuse," Aislin answered, playing to the joke.

"You mean no one's asked you?" Garnett was genuinely surprised.

"No one except the Captain," she said, and then added slyly, "Perhaps they're all afraid of my cousin."

The colonel laughed. "Well, if your boredom is my fault, then I ought to be the one to relieve you of it."

He took Aislin by the hand, ready to lead the way indoors, when they were approached by a young man in uniform.

"Colonel Garnett, sir," he said with a bow.

"Yes." Frustration enveloped the word.

"The general and his wife would like to have a word with you and the lady."

"Certainly."

As Aislin took his arm, she whispered, "It seems my boredom must be prolonged."

The colonel laughed again, pulling her closer to him.

The meeting with the general was pleasant. His wife was very kind and spoke sweetly with Aislin as the men discussed other matters.

The rest of the evening passed in a flash. Garnett monopolized most of Aislin's time either in dancing or in walks through the gardens or along the waterfront.

It was very late when they returned home from the ball. Aislin and the colonel were both unsure of exactly how to end the evening. Garnett thanked her for her company and made some excuse about needing to see James. They said good night, and Aislin went upstairs.

Once alone, her thoughts were immediately absorbed in the night's events. She'd had such a wonderful time at the party, and there was only one person to whom the credit belonged. Aislin formed a plan.

She anticipated the colonel would wait until after he'd assumed she was asleep before returning to his chamber. Aislin then determined to be awake when she heard his door.

It played out just how she'd imagined. The colonel paused briefly outside her door and then entered his quarters. Aislin gathered herself and went, by way of their small sitting room, to Garnett's door. She knocked without hesitation.

Caught entirely off guard, the colonel quickly answered. "Miss Aislin, what's wrong?"

"Oh nothing, nothing," she answered nervously. "I just wanted to-to thank you."

"Thank me?"

She felt her fingers entangling themselves in one another. "For tonight-I had a very nice time at the party, and I just wanted to thank you." The words were impatient and rushed.

"Oh... well you're welcome. I'm glad you enjoyed yourself."

Aislin's confidence returned as a question arose. "Why was tonight so different from the last time?"

Garnett's weight shifted, denoting his unease. "You mean the ball in Trenton."

She nodded and began more assertively, "Your behaviour in Trenton–"

"I know. I know." The colonel laughed awkwardly. "For that, Miss Aislin, I must apologize, which I'd meant to do long ago."

"I see." Aislin grinned.

"I'm not sure you do," he replied mysteriously. "The man you were with, you called him Mr. Carter."

She vaguely remembered. "Yes?"

"Had he been in uniform, you might have known him as Lieutenant Carter. We were stationed together in Trenton and had been in Philadelphia together before that."

Aislin's interest was peaked. "And?" she prodded him.

"That man," Garnett shook his head, "well, he frequently left only broken hearts and shattered reputations in his wake. I can't speak to his intentions that night, but I have to imagine they weren't all that honourable."

"Oh," Aislin sighed.

"I'm sorry." The colonel couldn't help but smile as he spoke. "I hate to be so blunt, but I suppose it's high time I explain my conduct. You see, I'd been assigned as somewhat of the lieutenant's keeper that night. When I saw the two of you in arm, I had to do something."

"But that still doesn't explain why you said the things you did."

"Oh, it does," he continued, casually. "You see, Carter rarely preyed on women of any...great intellect," he chuckled. "I simply assumed you were like all the others. It was too late when I realized..." Garnett stopped and rubbed his head. "Well, you're right. It still doesn't excuse what I said"

Aislin laughed at the colonel. "Maybe I do owe you some debt of gratitude for rescuing me then. Perhaps we could just call a truce."

"That would be very generous of you," he said, laughing a little at himself.

She could have resumed her goading and very much wanted to do so; but judging by his posture, Aislin was sure Garnett was ready to see the conversation ended.

"Well, it's late."

"Yes," the colonel hurriedly responded.

"Good night."

As Aislin turned to go, the clock in the hall began to chime the hour.

Garnett called after her, "Miss Aislin."

She stopped. "Yes?"

"It's morning." He said with a smile, "Merry Christmas."

"Merry Christmas, Colonel," she gently returned.

Garnett leaned against his closed chamber door with arms folded. "Colonel"… he had hoped to hear his name.

14

Although the night before had been a long one, Aislin had no trouble waking in the morning, and her anticipation must have been contagious. James and the colonel were already in the dining room when she arrived for breakfast. As the gentlemen rose from their seats, they greeted Aislin with a chorus of "Merry Christmases." Rebecca joined them the very next moment.

Breakfast was simple and delicious, but everyone tried not to fill themselves as they'd be having an early dinner. They were expecting company a little later–a small gathering to celebrate the holiday. Aislin had not met one of the couples–Major and Mrs. Lawrence. The other guests were the Russells, whom Aislin was eager to see. Anna Russell, the colonel's wife, was a brilliant woman (if not overly exuberant at times), and Aislin greatly admired her.

There would be only a few brief hours before the guests started to arrive. Thus, Aislin was taken aback when Garnett asked her to join him for a ride, though she happily accepted the invitation. She changed quickly and came back down stairs with a bundle in hand: the colonel's gift. She had wrestled with the idea, but after the incredible gift the colonel had given her, she was glad she'd done it. She found Garnett in the parlour.

Grinning wildly, she handed him the package. "Merry Christmas, Colonel."

"What's this?" he asked, not waiting for her response to begin unravelling the parcel.

"I wasn't sure if I should, but–well, I hope it's all right."

"Oh, I'm sure it is."

He stopped as he carefully pulled loose from the wrapping a radiant green coat. There were black and gold accents and braiding throughout the cloth, finished off with the traditional brass buttons. The material was rich and soft, not nearly as abrasive as the average uniform coat. It was a masterpiece fit for a general. Aislin was very proud of it and had worried, night and day since its completion, over whether or not Garnett would like it.

"Did you make this?" he finally asked.

"Yes. I do hope it's right. I had James to borrow one of your others to match the size."

"It's perfect," the colonel sighed, as he put it on. "I'll be the envy of every man in the army." He took her hands and placed a small kiss on her cheek (a more formal custom among British elite, Aislin knew). "Thank you, Miss Aislin."

"You're welcome, Colonel," she answered bashfully.

Garnett added, with a rather sly expression on his face, "I must be getting to you."

"I beg your pardon."

"Outfitting a British officer? The Aislin Laraway I met in New Jersey would never have done such a thing."

"For shame, indeed," she said sarcastically. "If my father or Madam knew what I'd done, they'd probably die of embarrassment."

The pair shared a laugh.

"We've come quite a long way, haven't we?" the colonel posed.

"I expect we have. You know, James once told me he thought it was unlikely you and I would ever be friends."

"Yes, well, what does he know?" Garnett jested.

Aislin chuckled, and then spoke more seriously, "He was nearly right."

"Mm. On more than one occasion, we almost ruined everything."

Aislin huffed in response, but still smiled.

"Well, we'd better be off if we're going to be home in time," the colonel said, motioning to allow her to lead the way outdoors.

Their trek was brief but exhilarating. The weather was cool and the sky was clear. For two who so loved to ride as they did, it was perfect.

As they reached the city gates on their return, the riders brought their mounts to a walk and conversation ensued.

"So it seems you've had a lot to say about me at the fort," said Aislin, in a very mischievous tone.

"What?" The question caught the colonel completely unprepared.

"Well, everyone seems to know who I am, and many have already made a great deal of assumptions long before they meet me. A few have even gone so far as to say they've heard all about me."

Aislin knew she was putting Garnett in an awkward position, but she did so to tease rather than in an effort to be mean.

"Ah–well I," he stammered through his words, laughed, cleared his throat, and then began again. "Um... people talk. Some of them asked about you, and I merely answered their questions. I suppose I was just unnecessarily thorough."

He was endeavouring to sound nonchalant but was clearly fighting for a way to wiggle out of the conversation.

Aislin giggled and nodded. "Oh, I see. I was just wondering."

She grinned at the colonel, who was trying very hard to hide his own smile as he looked away and shook his head. He knew he'd been caught.

The cold weather had reddened their cheeks, and both were keen to warm by the fire upon their return.

Aislin was barely finished dressing and come downstairs when all four guests arrived together. The house immediately erupted with greetings and laughter as introductions were made and drinks were announced in the parlour. Aislin stayed just a moment behind. She gave James a smile, and he in turn, as was tradition, took her under his arm and kissed her forehead.

Anna Russell pulled Aislin aside the moment she entered the parlour, and Maggie Lawrence followed.

"I see the colonel liked his gift," Anna said, noticing Garnett still wearing the coat.

"Yes, I think he did," Aislin humbly replied.

"Did you make that?" the new member inquired.

"With Anna's help."

"Oh, bah," Anna exclaimed. "I showed her the stitch to make the braids, that's all. Miss Aislin is a great talent."

"It certainly is impressive, I must say," Maggie said, quietly.

"Speaking of impressive," Anna's eyes fixed on Aislin's necklace (she'd worn the colonel's gift to compliment her red gown), "where on earth did you get that?"

"From William. He gave it to me to wear for the general's ball last night."

"My, my," Anna resumed, "I'd wager you turned more than a few heads."

Aislin only giggled in response. She thought about making some silly comment about the attention she'd drawn, and how the necklace had little to do with it; but she thought better of it.

"I do hope I'm not speaking out of turn," Maggie began again, "but I dare say you, Miss Aislin, are the envy of every woman in this city."

"Truer words were never spoken," Anna added.

"Well what, pray tell, would give either of you that impression? I was just about to ask what it was I'd done to make the ladies in this fair city so unhappy with me."

"The answer is one and the same, my dear," the lead explained. "They're all jealous. And why shouldn't they be?"

"I certainly can't see any reason for them to be so."

"Then, darling, you are blind. You're beautiful for starters. That combined with your being the lady of Colonel Garnett's home-well it speaks for itself. He's handsome, brilliant, and powerful; and worst of all, he's yours. Of course you're envied."

"But I'm only his cousin."

"In word alone, Aislin. Mr. Russell's parents were friends of the Garnetts in Liverpool. We all know the colonel's parents had no siblings." (They knew, but somehow it had escaped Aislin.) "To tell the truth, we all eagerly await the news of your engagement."

Aislin nearly gasped. How could Garnett have allowed such a flaw to slip into their design? Unless, this is what he'd intended all along.

"I'm afraid you may be in for a disappointment then, Mrs. Russell. There are no such arrangements on the horizon for the Garnett household." Aislin did her best to cover the situation.

"We'll see," Anna responded. "I suppose it's also escaped your attention that you've had the colonel's eye since you walked into the room."

Aislin knew she was blushing. All she could do was try to ignore the comment, which, under the colonel's watchful gaze, was very difficult.

"Very well. A change in subject then," Anna snickered.

The ladies talked and giggled together while the men conversed over more serious matters, interjected with jokes from time to time.

The evening was spectacular. Everyone had a terrific time and said so over and over again. The Russells had brought the colonel and Aislin a beautiful holly wreath, and the Lawrences brought a magnificent bottle of wine. At evening's end, both visiting couples received baskets filled with all sorts of sweets. The women mock-fussed over ruining their figures (as they were expected to do), and the men vowed to have the baskets emptied by sunset tomorrow.

The party was so grand, Aislin hated to see it end. She and Garnett closed the door after their friends and were left alone.

The colonel laughed under his breath, "Quite an evening."

"It certainly was," Aislin sighed.

"Did you enjoy yourself?"

"Very much. Everyone was wonderful."

"Mm. Well, I'm going to see to James one last time. Merry Christmas, Miss Aislin."

"Merry Christmas, Colonel."

Aislin went straight upstairs to bed. She was utterly, but pleasantly, exhausted. She decided not to say anything to Garnett about her discussions with Anna and the 'cousin' issue.

15

The two women came bursting through the door in a fit of laughter, Rebecca and Aislin nearly falling over each other. James had no idea what had spurred this behaviour, but he smiled all the same. The inspiration for their merriment turned out to be only the misfortune of a poor merchant whose mule had decided he'd pulled the cart far enough. It normally wouldn't have been so amusing, but something had taken hold of the Garnett home.

Everyone blamed the weather, and the cool, late January temperatures were invigorating. Then again, they all knew, deep down, there was some other force at work within the household. The air itself seemed sickly sweet with liveliness.

"This came for you while you were out, Miss," James said, handing Aislin a letter. "The young man will be back shortly to collect you response."

Gaining her composure, she opened the correspondence.

"Oh, it's from Anna. Her Colonel Russell has had to go north for a week or two, poor dear."

"Will you be going to visit, Miss?" James inquired.

"Not tonight. Tomorrow perhaps," she replied, reading on.

James and Rebecca looked at each other. They knew the reason for the response. At breakfast, the colonel had asked Aislin to accompany him on a walk that evening. Walking, rather than riding, usually denoted more conversation.

"Very good, Miss," James noted.

Aislin gave James a look to let him know she caught his mischievous tone. "If you'll excuse me," she said smartly, "I'll prepare my letter to Mrs. Russell."

Everyone, including Aislin, muffled their laughter as she left the room.

After dinner, the colonel and Aislin left for their walk. The twilight was very still, feeling more like a New England spring evening than a southern winter night.

As custom dictated, Aislin began their conversation. "I've heard rumours of all that's going on in Georgia and in the north. Do you think we'll be here much longer with all that's happened?"

Garnett sighed, "That's difficult to say. The battles here in the south have certainly been to our advantage. With such victories, I see no reason for my superiors to consider my relocation. Although, they do frequently make decisions I don't fully understand. I suppose it's too soon to tell what could happen on this new front."

Aislin did not respond.

"You do like it here, don't you?"

"Oh, yes. I didn't mean to give the impression that I'm unhappy. I was just curious."

"Mm." The colonel smiled to himself. "I have spent far too much time with you."

"I'm sorry?" came Aislin's exasperated reply. His sarcasm had escaped her.

"I can tell when you're lying," he said coolly.

Aislin huffed a small laugh. "Oh."

"Why are you really asking?"

"I received a letter from Anna Russell today."

"About David being sent north."

"Yes. I guess–I was just wondering–when I should expect similar news about you."

"Are you so anxious to be rid of me?" he mocked.

"No, of course not." Aislin jumped to defend herself, even though she knew he was only taunting her. She took a deep breath, but there wasn't time for her to speak.

A deafening bellow erupted from the harbour. The colonel caught Aislin in his grasp and watched to see exactly what sort of danger they were in.

"Pirates," he growled, "or a weak attempt by the Spanish. We'd better get to the fort."

"But won't they attack the fort?" Aislin was panicked.

"Most likely, but it's still far safer than the house."

Garnett took her hand, and the pair fled to the stronghold's defence. The ship's guns continued to fire as the mortars from the fort began to sound in return. Aislin was terrified, trying her best to keep up with the colonel. They rushed in just as the citadel's doors were closed.

The explosions persisted on both sides. Aislin clung tightly to Garnett's hand as he led the way through the chaos.

"Colonel Garnett!" The voice came from a man much older than the colonel. "What are you doing here?" It was the general, but barely recognizable.

"Wrong place, wrong time, sir," he had to shout to be heard.

"Get somewhere safe. We'll soon have this mess under control, and it's just unnecessary for both of us to be out here."

"Are you certain, General?"

Aislin looked around her. It had been a good while since she'd seen such combat, but it was all remarkably fresh in her mind. She found her empty hand now reaching for the colonel's arm. He turned at her touch.

"You just look after the lady," the general insisted, noticing Aislin's obvious fright. "Take her to my quarters. I'll send for you, if you're needed."

"Sir." Garnett quickly nodded and turned to direct Aislin.

For some reason, she had expected all the noise to quiet once they were inside the general's room. Needless to say, it did not.

The colonel sat her on the bed against the wall and knelt before her.

"Are you all right?" The words were rushed and breathless.

She didn't answer, only nodded absently.

He stood.

Aislin could tell Garnett was having a hard time staying put. It wasn't in his nature to hide in the heat of battle. He paced around the room and occasionally glanced at her. She hid her face in her hands.

The colonel wanted badly to comfort her, but couldn't. He didn't know how. His unease was compounded by a feeling of uselessness-unable to help his men, unable to help Aislin.

The blasts grew louder and stronger. The bandits would not sail quietly into the night, no matter what the opposition sent their way. The walls trembled as enemy arsenal pounded away at the unwavering structure, and dust from above floated gently to the ground as the volley was returned by the fort's own rounds.

The colonel had withstood all he was able.

He groaned, "I should go and see what I can do to help."

Desperation saturated Aislin's eyes as she watched him reach for the door. She couldn't bear the thought of being without him.

She pushed herself to her feet. "William!" she cried, tears flooding her cheeks.

He turned quickly, startled to hear her call.

"Please don't leave me," she whimpered and then covered her quivering lips as if trying to stop the escaping words.

It took the colonel only two steps to cross the room to her. He wrapped his arms around her as tightly as he could, and Aislin returned the embrace, her head resting against his chest.

"I won't leave," he whispered. "I promise. I won't leave."

He had longed for such an entreaty ever since their meeting.

They stood there for a lifetime, shuddering with each tremor, until the colonel once again sat her on the bed, this time sitting beside her with his arm around her shoulders.

It mattered not that her prompting had brought it about. He had, at long last, found a way to cut through her fear and all their pretense to accomplish that which he had unsuccessfully attempted so many times before. Now, with her in his arms, the colonel believed he could forget the rest of the world did ever exist. Nothing mattered but that which pertained to the woman he held. He dropped his head back against the wall and closed his eyes.

Aislin sat, resting within his arms, and soon stopped crying. The thunderous boom of the melee outside continued for hours. At each shot, Aislin shivered, but less and less under Garnett's secure hold. After a time, she scarcely heard the artillery at all. Her senses were otherwise occupied. She heard above all else the colonel's faint heartbeat beside her cheek. She was overwhelmed by the warmth of his strong yet tender support, and even his rough hands found a unique softness as they lay clasped over her own.

Aislin closed her eyes and tried to imagine they were sitting on their balcony, listening to the sounds of a thunderstorm rather than those of a battle.

The cannon fire slowed and eventually stopped. When things had quieted, the two emerged cautiously from the general's quarters. Soldiers were still running in every direction, carrying weapons and supplies, readying themselves in case of another attack. The smell of gunpowder hung heavily in the air.

Garnett found the general, but the men spoke for only a moment before the general insisted Garnett take Aislin home.

The colonel took off his jacket and wrapped it around her to ward off the cold mist that had arrived to battle the smoke-filled air of the harbour.

The pair walked the road in silence. Neither wanted to speak nor would they have had the words. It was nearly dawn.

James met them at the door, worried sick that something had happened to them. The colonel glanced over an explanation, and keeping Aislin in arm, walked her to her chamber. They stopped at her door.

"Will you be all right?" he quietly asked.

Aislin only nodded and gave back his jacket.

The colonel forced a smile. "Good night."

"Good night," she sighed.

Aislin walked into the room, leaving Garnett behind. She looked around, and realized that, somehow, she wasn't tired. She wanted to see William.

Aislin picked up a blanket and turned for the door leading to the balcony. She stepped into the cool, early morning arranging the blanket around her but looked up sharply, surprised to see the colonel leaning against the railing.

He turned upon hearing her approach. "Miss Aislin, why aren't you in bed?"

"I don't-" she choked on the words.

"What's wrong?" He gently reached out and pulled the fallen blanket back around her shoulders.

"Why are you so good to me?" she asked mournfully.

Garnett was taken aback, completely unprepared for such an inquiry.

"What reason have I given you," she went on, "to do all you've done for me?"

"I needed no reason, Miss Aislin," was his hushed reply.

"I was so horrible. You risked your life for me, and I was so ungrateful. I sat silently by while you took the blame for all of our troubles, when I'm the reason any of this happened in the first place." She paused. "I had done everything in my power to distance myself from you–to push you away. I," she swallowed and then chuckled a little, "I don't know how this happened–you and I."

Garnett's gaze softened, and he jokingly answered, "Perhaps I'm not quite the beast you thought I was."

Aislin smiled and looked at her feet; but the happier expression vanished from her face as quickly as it had appeared, tears returning to take its place.

"'Things aren't always what they seem,' you said. I'm beginning to think they never are."

Concern utterly engulfed Garnett. It pained him to see her in such a state. He searched urgently for the true cause behind her torment, all the while terrified of what he might find.

Aislin caught her breath. "In spite of my best intensions to hate you, I think… I've fallen in love with you. I know it's improper for me to say such things, but I won't apologize." Her voice trailed off as she fought the urge to look away.

The colonel stared straight into her stunning, black eyes, absolutely astonished by her confession.

Though momentary, Aislin couldn't stand his silence. "William, please say something."

He sighed, and he smiled. "Marry me," he softly blurted.

"What?" Aislin rose with a hint of laughter.

"Please, Aislin." He took her in his arms. "I know I'm not the sort of husband you had hoped for or expected, but I do love you. And I promise I always will. Please, will you marry me?"

Aislin giggled through her tears. "Yes, I will."

Garnett gave a heavy sigh, as if he'd been holding his breath for years. "Have you any idea how happy you've made me?" he murmured, resting his head against hers. "I've wanted for ages to tell you how much I love you. I thought this day would never come."

Aislin reached up and tenderly touched his face. "I think you and I should be more careful when speaking in such absolute terms, given our history. Or else *never* doesn't mean what we think it does."

The two smiled at each other, and William lightly kissed her on the forehead. He pulled her to himself and laid his cheek against her soft, dark hair. Eyes shut, they both drank in the moment, committing to memory every detail of one another in the waning darkness.

They stayed on the balcony together as long as their fatigue would allow. It was the colonel who remorsefully suggested that they depart for their quarters just as the night sky was beginning to grow lighter.

"I wish I could stand here and hold you all night."

Aislin answered with a laugh. "I think you have."

The sun had not yet taken the horizon, but the rays already cast over the water added to the beautiful colours painted across the sky.

She paused as he opened the door for her. "You're right, by the way," she whispered.

"About what?" he asked, with a crooked grin.

She answered slowly and sweetly, "A life with you was the last thing I expected, and far more than I'd hoped for."

Garnett's blue eyes settled directly on her as he broadly smiled his response.

"How do you suppose we ought to tell James?" she raised more light-heartedly.

Both laughed.

"I think perhaps I'd better take care of that." Garnett said, with a wink. "Get some rest."

He kissed her cheek and closed the door.

Aislin slept for only a few hours but woke wholly rejuvenated. She rushed downstairs and found James and Garnett in the parlour. William's expression brightened immediately as she entered, but it was James who approached.

He took Aislin under his arm and whispered, "It's not too late to change your mind."

Aislin snickered, "You're horrible."

James laid his kiss on her forehead and gave her shoulders a squeeze. "Congratulations, Miss. I'm happy for you both, though your judgment is in question," he jested.

They all shared a laugh, and a bit more ribbing, as Aislin joined them for tea and toast.

*　　*　　*

The next few days were a blur as preparations were made and all the arrangements finished. In such uncertain times, William and Aislin could think of no reason to put things off. They were to be married at week's end.

Aislin's dress for the occasion was one that had been in the wardrobe since her arrival at Newburgh. It was the most elaborate she'd ever owned, and until now, she'd had no opportunity to wear it. Pale blue silk was overlaid with a beautiful, intricate lace and accented with a soft, yellow sash. Rebecca commented over and over again on the dress's elegance and repeatedly told Aislin that she looked like royalty. Aislin just smiled.

Friday evening, James carefully placed the lady and her attendant into the carriage and drove them to the fort. The colonel had just concluded his duties and had borrowed the general's quarters to square his appearance, exchanging his green uniform for a dark, blue jacket as the finishing touch.

The couple was to be wed in the fort's chapel. Aislin whispered to Rebecca how silly she felt walking amongst all the soldiers, dressed as she was. The laughter helped to calm her nerves.

William was already in the chapel when Aislin and her escorts arrived. The small room was brilliantly lit with dozens of candles, bringing to life all of the ordinary objects set thereabout. The subtle illumination highlighted the colonel's shaded appearance against a wall of leaping shadows. He smiled softly as Aislin made her way to where he stood. The riotous luminaries cast a radiant incandescence about her pale figure that danced with each stride. He took her hands as the reverend stepped forward.

The ceremony was anything but ceremonious. It was all very simple and sweet. Aislin and William exchanged vows before a very meagre audience. The general and his wife had made a point of attending, by which the colonel and Aislin alike were more than flattered. A few other officers, most of them alone, along with James and Rebecca filled a handful of seats. Anna Russell and her attendant were the only other guests. The bride and groom didn't notice.

Aislin could hardly believe it was happening. She stared straight at the colonel, a torrent of memories racing through her mind:

Their first dance at the ball in Trenton. His daring plan to rescue her from imprisonment. The long, hard road to her freedom, strewn with a hundred queries of *are you all right* and that familiar, clear gaze.

The day he reappeared in the garden at the Newburgh estate. Countless rides through every kind of weather. Yet another rescue the day she fell. How he laughed at her charade for Mr. Drake.

The way her heart nearly broke at his prolonged absence, and its immediate healing the morning he returned from battle.

A walk on the beach. A dance at the general's party.

His unwavering protection and provision.

The kind touch of a steady hand.

A strong, comforting embrace.

A revelation suddenly presented itself. All this time, Aislin had felt it was the colonel who'd changed. She now realized he'd been just the same all along: looking after her, taking care of her. He had loved her from the beginning, maybe ever since Trenton. A delightful smile crossed her lips, answered by her groom.

The small gathering briefly visited the Garnett home after the service. Cakes and wine were enjoyed by everyone as the happy couple accepted the well-wishes of their guests. Anna clung to

Aislin all night, and Aislin gladly endured her teasing and *I told you so's*, all the while very pleased her friend had been right.

Aislin grinned until her face hurt, and all the more every time she caught her husband's gaze. His fine, blue eyes had taken on new life and glimmered with excitement at each glance.

The Garnetts were relieved when their guests began to make their excuses and disperse. Anna was the last to leave, congratulating Aislin again as they saw their way to the door. Aislin thanked her and repeatedly offered herself, should Anna need anything while Colonel Russell was away.

As the doors were closed, James and Rebecca slipped away to leave the pair alone. The colonel met Aislin at the foot of the stairs.

"Do you like the ring?" he asked, taking her outstretched hand and leading the way upstairs.

"Oh, it's beautiful," she answered wistfully. "This all seems like some sort of dream."

"A pleasant dream, I hope."

"The very best," she smiled.

Until they reached the top of the landing, it seemed like any other night; but there, rather than turn to her door, they stayed on–heading for the colonel's chamber. The servants had just finished moving all of Aislin's things that morning. She entered very timidly, unsure of where to alight. Though she saw her things about the room, it did not yet feel like her own.

Ever perceptive, the colonel caught her unease immediately. He gently brushed her hair beside her face, kissed her forehead, and wrapped her in his embrace. He stood, calmly holding his bride.

16

The ladies sat round the parlour, each with some article of their husband's clothing that needed mending. Aislin, Anna, Maggie Lawrence, and June Matthews-they assembled now every week to keep one another company, as it seemed one of their gentlemen was always away. This time, it was Captain Matthews.

"The rumour mill is running a bit slow this week, is it ladies?" Aislin broke the silence.

"Well," Maggie softly began, "I suppose, I have a bit of news."

"Out with it then," Anna insisted.

"I spoke to Martha Fisher yesterday-the new lieutenant's wife. She's expecting," Maggie nearly whispered.

The ladies all *hm*ed and *oh*ed to themselves.

"And when can we expect a new addition to the Garnett family?" Anna prodded Aislin, though none of them had children.

Rebecca, sitting nearest the hallway, laughed a little under her breath as she patched a pair of James's trousers. Aislin turned and gave her a look, but with a hint of a smile.

James had been bothering Aislin incessantly about her and William having children. Of course, he'd done so very passively, mentioning how refreshing it was to be in a house filled with the sounds of children or how fun it would be for the colonel to teach his son to ride. Apparently, James was not only convinced that they should have children, but also that they ought to have sons.

"Well?" Anna asked, impatiently.

"I think I liked it better when we had nothing to talk about," Aislin answered, turning back to her sewing.

The others giggled.

"Ha, ha. You started it, Miss Aislin," June pointed out.

"Yes, and I suppose there's no hope of my finishing it," she smiled.

The ocean breeze floated in through the open windows, spilling the fresh spring air over the whole house. It was April. No one was looking forward to the warmer months ahead, but more than that, they nervously awaited reports from the north. With the winter hiatus over, things would be picking up, and men would be moving out.

Aislin looked out toward the bay. It had been two years since she'd left home and eight months since they'd left New England.

She grinned. *What will Father and Madam say when they find out about our marriage?* she thought.

"Aislin!" Anna called.

She came out of her day dream.

"Where is your head, girl? June asked you a question."

"Forgive me, ladies. What was it, June?"

"How did you and the colonel meet?"

"Yes. You've never told us, Aislin," Maggie added.

Aislin chuckled a little under her breath. "Ah, we're old family friends." She felt bad about lying, but the truth was out of the question. She continued with a touch of honesty to ease her conscience: "We met for the first time at a ball."

"Was it love at first sight?" the romantic Maggie asked.

Aislin laughed out loud. "Hardly!"

"Well, now you've peeked our interest. Tell us what happened," Anna demanded.

"Oh, nothing really." Aislin would not divulge the details. "It's just that he seemed awfully arrogant. And we didn't get along very well."

"So what changed?" June inquired.

"I got to know him and found he wasn't as bad as I'd thought." It was a vast understatement.

"I knew all along they'd marry," Anna boasted.

"Oh really," Aislin retorted. "You only met us six months ago."

"Seven," Anna replied, mockingly indignant.

Everyone laughed.

Just then, an interruption arrived at the door, home early from his duties at the fort and accompanied by a few guests.

"Will, why do I feel like we've just walked right into the middle of something?" Colonel Russell joked at the women's laughter.

"I've found that some questions are best left unanswered, my friend," Garnett responded.

He reached around Aislin's shoulder and kissed her cheek.

"And look who we've found," he announced, turning toward the men.

"George!" June shouted as she ran to the door.

Aislin stood and put her arm around William, he around her shoulders, as the Matthews reunited.

Overcome with emotion, June clung to the husband she'd missed for almost a month. "I thought you were staying until next week."

"I could go back," he joked. "I'm sure they'd be glad to see me."

"Oh, no, you don't," she smiled.

The other women began to gather their things, but Colonel Garnett interrupted.

"Ladies, your men have already agreed to stay and have dinner to celebrate, so I'm afraid you're trapped."

"Splendid!" Anna exclaimed, in her ever-outspokenness.

"Shall we eat on the terrace?" Aislin requested, from under William's arm.

"A brilliant idea, my dear."

James had stepped up beside the colonel. "I'll have drinks ready in a moment, sir," he offered, with a wink at Aislin.

"Yes. Thank you, James." William addressed the party, "Shall we?"

Such was the charmed life of Mrs. Garnett. Aislin found herself constantly surrounded by friends and loved ones. There was always a party or an afternoon tea to attend or host, and the colonel found every excuse to dote on his wife. They continued their rides as often as they could and made frequent trips to the shoreline throughout the summer.

The one discomfort was the heat. Aislin found it difficult to sleep at night and was often wakeful.

One particularly sticky night, William awoke from a dead sleep. He couldn't recall what had stirred him, whether a dream or some external force. He sat up and rubbed his head.

Aislin, sleeping so light as she did, woke at his movement. Without getting up, she touched his back. "What's wrong?"

"Nothing, dear. Go back to sleep," he quietly smiled.

The colonel got up and walked to the window. Aislin, now wide awake, stepped behind him and ran a hand over his shoulders. William turned to face her and took her in his arms.

"I'm sorry I woke you."

"It's all right, darling," she whispered.

The colonel's sweet smile quickly turned a bit roguish. "What do you say we make the most of a sleepless night?"

"What did you have in mind?"

A midnight ride had crossed the colonel's mind briefly, but he thought better of it. Pirate or Indian attacks had been rare as of late but were never out of the realm of possibility. Besides, the city gates had been long since closed and barred for the night.

"Gather those blankets and come out to the balcony," was all he said before he set about the room.

Aislin, though puzzled, promptly threw on a robe. A few moments later, William met her outdoors, dragging the mattress from what used to be her room. He arranged it on the balcony deck and then took the blankets to complete the assembly. The pair soon settled in, lying where they could just see the stars out from under the roof. The winds from the inlands were just what the restless couple needed.

Aislin sighed, "Why have we never tried this before?"

William hummed a little laugh to himself. "When the war is over, would you like to stay here in St. Augustine?"

"I think that would be wonderful."

"Warm weather and all?" he jested, rolling to his side. He laid his head on his hand, looking at Aislin.

She giggled, "Warmer weather and all."

"What if our friends moved away?" he said, more seriously.

Aislin reached up and caressed his cheek. "We'd make new friends. And even if we didn't, it wouldn't matter as long as you're here."

The colonel smiled broadly.

"But I thought you wanted to go home to England after the war?" Aislin inquired.

"My home is where you are," he said, pushing her wind-blown hair from her face.

Aislin grinned up at him.

"Besides, I thought you'd want to be able to visit your family," he added.

"Well, that's awfully thoughtful of you."

With this, William kissed her, and their conversations ended.

*　　*　　*

Aislin paced around the terrace nervously. She was going to have to tell him. She had no choice. The problem was, she didn't know how. More than that, she didn't know how he'd take it. In talking with William, she had insisted on being the one to do it. Now she wondered why; but it was too late to back down.

She smiled as she thought of her conversation with the colonel just moments ago.

She had found William in the study but had been far more nervous about telling him. Aislin knew it wasn't fair to distrust him, but she couldn't help but fear his reaction. The timing was all wrong. She worried he'd be angry.

She entered the study cautiously and knelt down beside his chair.

"What is it, darling?"

"I have something very important to tell you."

The colonel said nothing. He put one hand on her shoulder and held her hands with the other.

"Do you remember-about a month ago-the night on the balcony?"

His brow furrowed as he nodded. Then his expression changed suddenly as he realized what she was trying so hard to say. "A baby?" the colonel asked breathlessly.

Aislin bit her lip and nodded anxiously. A smile crept across William's face. He took her hands and, standing, brought her to her feet.

He gasped as he embraced her, "That's–that's wonderful!"

"You're happy then?" she sighed.

"Of course," he pulled back to look at her, still smiling. "Aren't you?"

"Oh, yes! It's just–I was afraid you'd think... Oh, I don't know." A smirk finally found her.

"Aislin, the woman I love more than anything in this world is going to give me a child. What's to be unhappy about?"

"I know it was silly. William, I'm sorry."

"It's all right," he laughed. "When will..."

"Next spring. March, if I'm counting correctly."

"Well, I know a certain member of this household who should be just as excited to hear as I."

"I'd like to tell him, if you don't mind."

"Are you sure? You know how he can get," the colonel teased.

"I think I can handle it," Aislin answered, trying to look conniving.

With that, they left the study. Aislin went to the terrace while William went to find James. Her pacing ensued, and soon she was joined by the two men, with Rebecca in pursuit.

"What is this?" James's curiosity was rapidly growing. "The colonel said you have very important news."

"I'm afraid," Aislin dragged out her words as a smile escaped, "you're going to get your wish come spring."

James looked quizzically at Aislin, then the colonel, who was grinning from ear to ear. It hit him all at once.

"Well, you don't say. Congratulations, sir." He shook the colonel's hand then walked to Aislin's side.

Rebecca had grown a bit flustered. "Well, isn't anyone going to let me in on your little secret?"

Everyone chuckled quietly.

From under James's arm, Aislin softly answered, "We're going to have a baby, Rebecca."

"Oh!" she exclaimed, instantly turning red from embarrassment. She covered her face feeling very foolish.

James left Aislin's side to comfort Rebecca as they all shared a laugh.

Plans in the Garnett home turned instantly to accommodations and necessities for the expected arrival, and their excitement was contagious. The other officers' wives were practically beside themselves at Aislin's news. Anna, of course, couldn't refrain from making constant comments.

The ladies began showing up almost right away with bundles of tiny clothes and other gifts. The colonel, however, was the most visibly enthused. It seemed he was coming home every day with some new idea or proposal: names, schooling, and the like. Aislin was just glad to find he was equally thrilled at the idea of a daughter as he was a son.

She had only one disappointment through the whole affair, and it was over the one thing that William denied her. He had forbidden her to ride unless in a carriage, for fear of a fall. He trusted Aislin's skill but repeatedly argued that accidents still happened, to the skilled and novice alike. Aislin didn't fight him, given the fall she'd had in Newburgh, even though it felt more like punishment as the beautiful fall days approached.

17

The colonel came home one evening, a numbing look of shock dulling his usually bright, blue eyes. He avoided Aislin at first, going straight to his study. He didn't know how to break it to her. Unfortunately, it never took her long to find him. He was bent over in his chair, wringing his hands, when she quietly came through the door.

"William?"

He looked up at her soft call.

"What is it?" she asked.

The colonel reached out for her hands and sat her in the chair across from him. He struggled to look at her as he spoke.

"We have orders," he slowly began. "I'm being sent to South Carolina in two weeks." He hated to be so blunt but didn't know any other way to tell her.

"For how long?" She mumbled, as her emotions got the best of her.

He shrugged his shoulders and shook his head with a groan.

Aislin took a deep breath to try to calm herself. "Then we'll move?"

Again the colonel shook his head. "You can't come." The words nearly strangled him.

"I don't—what does this mean?"

William sighed, "We're preparing a series of attacks throughout the south, in the hopes of capturing Charles Town and a few other cities. We'll be constantly on the move. There's no where for you to stay that you'd be safe."

"With you. I'd be safe with you!" She grasped at any chance to stay with him.

"Aislin, this isn't going to be like the last time. These battles won't be short and sporadic. It's going to be vicious and incessant, and the enemy won't care if you get in the way. Darling, I'm so sorry. If there was any way, I–" he stopped.

The colonel reached out and brushed her cheek. He knew there was nothing he could say to make her understand or to ease her distress.

"Can't you ask for an exception? Do they know about the baby?" Aislin already knew the answer but couldn't help asking.

"They've granted exceptions already, and I can't ask for anything more." His voice trailed off as he spoke.

The tears Aislin fought so hard to keep back, now won out as they rolled down her cheeks. William's heart broke.

"I do hate to see you cry," he whispered. He got out of his seat and onto one knee in front of her. "As soon as I can, I'll bring you to me. I promise, we won't be apart any longer than absolutely necessary."

Aislin sniffed at her tears and nodded.

The colonel, still knelt before her, wrapped his arms round her tightly and laid his head on her lap. Aislin embraced her husband, leaned over, and kissed his face.

"We have two weeks," she said gently, trying to comfort both William and herself. "We'll make the best of it."

The colonel sat up. He stroked her tear-stained face and, smiling, kissed his wife.

*   *   *

"Make the best of it." It didn't take Aislin long to realize this was impossible. The two weeks she had hoped would be the longest in her life, raced by in a blur.

It was a clear, crisp autumn morning when she saw William to his ship. It was the sort of day that usually brought a wonderfully jovial atmosphere to the Garnetts' home, but now, no amount of sunshine or spirited surroundings could overcome the sorrow and torment that hovered in the air.

Aislin scarcely tried at all to withhold her emotions as she painfully waited to say her last good-bye. She was never out of Garnett's grasp as supplies were loaded and everything finalized.

"I'll write as often as I can–every day if possible," he said, pulling her in close to him.

Aislin nodded through her tears and trembling. She draped her arms around his neck, and the two held one another, closing their eyes in hopes that when they opened them again they'd find all of this was just a bad dream.

"I love you, William," were the only words she could manage to speak.

The colonel swallowed hard. "Darling, I love you, too."

His eyes began to well and turn red. He kissed Aislin on the cheek, forced a smile, and turned to board the ship.

The only thing that stopped Aislin from chasing after him was James's secure hold around her shoulders.

The ship moved mercifully fast out of the harbour. Aislin would have stayed to watch it disappear over the horizon, were it not for James, continually insisting that all this stress wasn't good for her or the baby. With him on one side and Rebecca on the other, they trudged slowly home, pausing every now and then as Aislin stopped to look back.

A few months later, Aislin couldn't remember what it felt like to fall asleep without crying. Her only comfort was the steady flow of letters that trickled in from William. He did indeed write almost every day. Though he warned occasionally that he may not be able to write again for a while, due to their movement, still the letters came (but some in greater intervals than others).

Rather than get better, things got worse. The strain made Aislin very sick. By November, the doctor had restricted Aislin to the house with orders that she remain in bed as much as possible. For once, she was glad there was no way to get word to William. She would have hated to add any other worry to his already overly-taxing environment.

On days when the weather was dry and warm enough, James made a point of bringing Aislin downstairs to the terrace. He was adamant that she be out in the fresh air at any available opportunity.

Anna, Maggie, and June came by to visit each day. One by one, their husbands, too, had been sent away. The first of December, Anna moved into the Garnett home, and June moved in with Maggie.

There would be no hope this year of having the men home through the winter. The war had moved south. With a less formidable climate, the fighting would carry on without pause.

Christmas passed as any other day. The ladies all gathered together and enjoyed a wonderful meal, but this was the only variance from their regular routine.

The soldiers continued dutifully in their correspondence, careful to leave out most of the goings-on of the war. Captain Matthews had come under Colonel Russell's command which, for some reason, brought a great deal of relief to Anna and June. They supposed it was the idea that the two men would look after one another that gave such consolation. Such good news was hard to come by in the dark winter months.

One January afternoon, James came to collect Aislin for lunch on the terrace, cheerfully helping her to her feet. Yet, no sooner had she stood than Aislin doubled over with a moan.

"Miss Aislin?" James quickly sat her back on the bed.

"Send for the doctor. Something's wrong." The words had to be forced from her lips. She struggled to breathe, sitting hunched over the edge of the bed.

James couldn't leave her. "Rebecca!" he called. "Rebecca, come quickly!"

She burst through the door the very next second.

"Send Henry for the doctor. And hurry, please!"

Anna came running in at the commotion. Seeing Aislin's crumpled form, wrought with distress, she knew it was serious.

"What can I do?" she asked, helping James sit Aislin back in the bed.

"I don't know, ma'am," he muttered.

By the time the doctor arrived, Aislin's condition had grown much worse. She was feverish and had broken into a cold sweat, shuddering and crying from the pain. The doctor was visibly concerned. He gave Rebecca a few instructions, and she quickly left the room.

Aislin didn't ask. She knew what was happening. Though she'd never been through childbirth, somehow she knew. It was too soon–much too soon. Her tears were unrelenting.

James and Anna wiped the beads from her forehead and her cheeks in turn, futilely trying to calm the poor shaking girl–doing everything they could to make her comfortable. Aislin held tight to Anna's hand.

Rebecca returned with the young man who had fetched the doctor. They were carrying a collection of cloth and basins of water.

"All right, if the lady will stay," the doctor addressed Rebecca, "the rest of you will please clear the room."

The lad gladly left, and James began to rise from his seat beside the bed.

Aislin clung to James's arm. "No. Please let them stay."

They all looked at the doctor.

"Very well," he answered quietly.

The fact that he didn't fight her made Aislin's heart sink. Additional comforts were often given only to the ill-fated.

Hours passed and nothing happened. The pain continued in waves as though it would never end. Aislin sobbed uncontrollably in between agonizing groans.

Rebecca stood, tearfully quiet, in the corner when she wasn't assisting the doctor. James sat in a chair beside the bed, facing Aislin. He spoke calmly to her, words she never heard. Anna, sitting on her other side, just kept gently smoothing back Aislin's dark, damp hair.

At last, nightfall brought the frightful conclusion. A few torturous moments delivered a tiny creature who never took her first breath.

Aislin wasn't sure if she should, but at the doctor's query, she held her lifeless daughter in her shivering arms. She held her for only a minute, kissed her face, and returned her to the doctor, who silently carried her from the room.

Anna was beginning to lose her composure; so to keep from further upsetting Aislin, she stood and walked to the window.

Aislin's emotions completely overcame her. James wrapped his arms around her, all the while knowing there was nothing he could do to console her.

*   *   *

"It's a crippling blow, to be sure. Do you think she'll be all right?" Anna asked James, after breakfast the next morning.

"Given time, I'm sure she'll come around. Though I do wish the colonel were here," James added, looking out the window.

At sunrise that morning, he along with Henry, saw to the baby's burial. The only words Aislin had spoken after the birth were to give her daughter a name. She called her Williamina, after the colonel, saying it wouldn't be right to bury her unnamed or in an unmarked grave.

Aislin refused to eat all day and wouldn't talk to anyone. Still, Maggie and June continued to visit with Anna at Aislin's bedside. In truth, their presence was much more uplifting than Aislin was willing, or able, to let on. She wanted to feel better, and she wanted to enjoy her friends. She just didn't know how.

Of course, James was absolutely right. Time was the cure to Aislin's illness. She ate a little more each day and gradually came to converse more openly with her daily visitors. After two week's time, she was having meals in the dining room again and meeting the ladies in the parlour. On the other hand, it took her over a month to go beyond the house and grounds. Having Anna in the house along with James and Rebecca was her greatest encouragement through her voluntary confinement.

Aislin continued to receive letters from William, but now this small solace was stained with question. How would she tell him about the baby? What would he say? She knew he wouldn't be angry, but she could no sooner withstand his disappointment than she could his wrath.

The weather stayed cold through February and even though the chill could be biting and cruel, Aislin began riding again as soon as she felt up to it. Anna went with her on warmer days, and despite a few ridiculing remarks, the ladies cared less and less about their missing an escort.

It was mid-March when the fog of melancholy and disappointment finally lifted from the Garnett house.

Aislin, Anna, and Rebecca had spent the morning in the market, admiring the return of life and colour to their formerly bleak world. James met them at the door with a smile-the sort Aislin hadn't seen in months.

"James, what is it?" she asked, catching his infectious enthusiasm.

"Letters, Miss Aislin." He handed both her and Anna their correspondence.

"I don't believe I've ever seen you so happy to hand out a few simple pieces of paper," she teased, as she began to open hers.

"No," he grinned slyly, "but the colonel doesn't usually include me in the delivery of news as he has these tidings."

Aislin paused and looked sharply at James, eyes wide open. Aghast at his comment, she raced through her letter.

"Ha!" She felt her heart would burst as the words leapt off the page.

She finished her reading and threw her arms around James's neck. He kept his arm around her shoulders as she returned to read the letter once more.

"Oh, thank heavens! This must mean they're doing very well-to move us all like this. Oh, thank heavens," she continued to repeat.

All of their letters detailed the same effect. James would have all four households packed and aboard ship before the end of the month. They were headed to Port Royal, South Carolina.

The letters also asked the ladies to send ahead any correspondence they'd like. The men were greatly looking forward to hearing from their wives and were finally in a position that allowed for it.

Everyone set to writing their letters after a celebratory dinner that night. Aislin saw a small opportunity. She timidly approached James as he sat writing in the study. She paused just inside the door.

"Miss Aislin?"

"James, would you do me a favour?" she asked quietly.

"Of course, Miss."

Aislin sat down across from him. "In your letter, would you tell William about… about what happened?"

"You're sure, Miss?" He looked at her over his spectacles.

"I can't tell him. I know I probably ought to be the one to do it, but I can't. It would be like reliving it all over again. Perhaps one day I'll have the courage to talk to him about it, but…" her voice just trailed off.

"I understand, Miss. And I'm sure the memory will become a little bit less painful with time." James patted her hands with a wink.

"Thank you," Aislin replied, returning his smile.

18

Major Lawrence, alone, met the ship when the ladies arrived at Port Royal.

"Well, I must say. This certainly is the most handsome cargo we've had yet to arrive here."

Maggie out ran everyone else to meet her husband on the dock. The others smiled, following behind, happy for Maggie but silently disappointed at the absence of their own husbands.

After the couple had concluded their greeting, the major began to address the group.

"I hope everyone had a pleasant trip."

"As well as can be expected," Anna answered, still a little green from the rocky voyage.

"Now then, to answer the question on everyone's mind: Miss Anna, Miss June, your men reported in for new orders just last week. I'm afraid I don't know exactly when we expect them back, but they did leave letters for you both," he stated, reaching into his coat pocket. "Miss Aislin, the colonel is here, and he wanted to meet the ship but couldn't get away from a meeting with the general. He wanted me to tell you that he'll meet you later at your residence."

Aislin smiled and sighed a little to herself.

"On that note," the major continued, "try to keep in mind the arrangements we've made here are only temporary. We're all staying very close to the port. I'd be lying to tell you there's no danger here, but it gets worse toward the interior. Also, the housing is scarce. Miss June, you and George (when he returns) will be staying with Maggie and me. And Miss Anna, you and David will be staying with the Garnetts."

"Sounds all right to me," June answered, with a nod from Anna.

"Business as usual," Aislin added.

"Very good," Major Lawrence replied. "Shall we?"

There were soldiers everywhere, and they watched the women as one might suspiciously eye an untamed animal. Aislin was very glad to have James by her side and Major Lawrence leading the way. Maggie's husband wasn't an overly large man, but he was quite tall and carried himself as though the world were at his feet. He could indeed be very intimidating.

Their new homes looked as though they had once been one or two room houses that had been recently modified to accommodate. The two houses that the troupe would be using stood right next to one another in a small grouping of these structures. The servants' quarters were included among them, and instead of stables, temporary lean-tos had been constructed.

The quarters themselves were small and sparsely furnished. There were no balconies or gardens to speak of, but the assembly had no trouble settling in and soon felt right at home. The ladies, with one exception, were so happy to be nearer their husbands—and not on a swaying ship–they couldn't have cared where they stayed, whether a palace or a soldier's tent.

"Well, we can be certain of one thing," Anna sighed, standing at the doorway to the Garnetts' bedchamber.

Aislin was straightening a few things in the chest and smiled as she answered. "And what, pray tell, is that?"

"Our husbands truly love us and must have desperately wanted us here."

"What makes you think so?" Aislin chuckled.

"To bring us to a place like this, knowing what we must think of it; some place so obviously dangerous."

"Oh come now, it's not that bad. And what danger? We're surrounded by soldiers."

"That's what worries me," Anna retorted a little sarcastically.

"Bah. William will be home soon, and until then, we have James to look after us."

He gave her a wink as he delivered another trunk to the room.

"Nothing is going to happen," she said decidedly.

William's homecoming was unmistakable. The door flew open with a thud against the wall and was immediately followed by his call.

"Aislin? Aislin," he repeated, until she appeared.

Without saying a word, she rushed into his arms. Both of them laughed and made over each other, in between William's impetuous kisses.

The colonel rested his forehead against Aislin's. "Oh Darling, I'm so happy you're here."

"So am I. I missed you terribly!"

Garnett pulled carefully away so as to clearly see her face. "Before you even begin to wonder... James told me about the baby. Aislin, I'm so sorry I wasn't there. If there was any way, I–"

Aislin gently put a finger to his lips. "I know, William. It's all right."

"And you? Are you all right?" his cool, blue eyes dashed with a touch of concern.

Aislin chuckled to herself at the familiar inquiry. "I'm much better, especially now that I'm here."

The colonel returned her smile.

Their life in Port Royal was unlike any Aislin had yet experienced. There were the soldiers of course, but within their company, Aislin was surprised to see dozens of women and children. It didn't take her long to realize these were not the sort of women with whom she ought to socialize. They called themselves camp wives, but they were not the families of the soldiers. Aislin heard the officers call them "trulls" and "doxies." Their business among them was far more than inappropriate.

When Aislin asked, William dismissed them as a "necessary evil." He reasoned that they served a purpose in the camps: doing laundry, sewing, and cooking, as well as acting as nurses and improving the overall morale of the men. Then again, they certainly had their drawbacks, which went without saying. The colonel insisted that he'd never participate in such activities.

The happy reunions soon became an uneasy imprisonment. The women rarely went beyond their homes or connecting yards. When they did venture out, it was all four together, often with

Rebecca or one of the other lady's servants, and never without one of the men.

Colonel Russell and Captain Matthews did indeed return, but their departure a few days later required the absence of Colonel Garnett and Major Lawrence as well. They were gone for about a week, and all four came home together. It was after this last brief visit, however, that the men left their home in Port Royal for good.

The women received very few letters and knew little about what was going on. Most of the soldiers had left the settlement, changing their once lively surroundings to a ghostly silence.

*   *   *

The British had made their move on Charles Town. Over the last couple of months, they'd made a roundabout way north overland and reached the Neck, between the Ashley and Cooper Rivers. They were hard at work preparing for the siege and defending their position; while the awaiting ships, though under heavy fire, began to force their way into the harbour.

It was during this time that Garnett was sent north along the Santee River to capture a crucial crossroads. A force of Continentals had stationed there, providing their comrades in Charles Town with needed supplies and keeping open central lines of communication. If the colonel was successful in the effort, it would expedite the siege (and more quickly get him home to Aislin).

Garnett, together with Colonel Russell, was joined along the way by Major Lawrence and his infantrymen. The three friends were a valued support.

The plan they devised was simple: Colonels Garnett and Russell would go on ahead, hoping to catch the enemy by surprise in a night attack. Major Lawrence would remain behind, as the rear guard.

They began their march long after the sun had set, borrowing cover from the darkness, silently taking their positions. The Continentals had given them most every advantage. There were no scouts or patrols barring the way of the British, and upon arrival at the encampment, Garnett and Russell found the rebel commander had put his cavalry in the way of his infantry.

The colonels drove their men right into the heart of the camp. The Continentals were completely caught off-guard. Most were able to escape through the swamp, including the commanders, but they were forced to leave behind wagons full of supplies and a great deal of the cavalry horses. These, the British happily commandeered. The strike was a success.

This small accomplishment left the besieged rebels in Charles Town suddenly and completely without any lines of communication. From there, Garnett and his forces fanned out across the region, cutting off Charles Town from any outside support.

British negotiations for the total surrender of the Continental forces continued through the end of the month, and little by little, they gained ground as the rebel grasp slowly slipped. In the end, the negotiations demanded that the whole of the enemy force be taken as prisoners of war, most to then be paroled within the city.

The three friends and their men were thrilled to learn of the victory. The surrender left no Continental Army in the south, imparting the British with full control.

"With such a fine city as Charles Town in our possession, I see no reason to keep the women where they are any longer than necessary," Major Lawrence opened, refilling Russell's cup.

Garnett nodded in agreement, propping his feet on the desk and settling into his chair. "I imagine they'll be more than willing to leave Port Royal behind."

There had been a few light rain showers throughout the evening, but inside the tent, the officers paid it no mind.

"Best give the men a few weeks to get quarters established, though," Russell answered.

"Leave it to David to rationalize the fun out of a victory." Lawrence nudged the back of Russell's seat as he took his own. He continued with a chuckle, "That's why he and the mistress make such a good pair. Miss Anna keeps him from boring himself to death."

Garnett laughed at his friends and began thinking of his own wife. Russell and Lawrence could nearly read his thoughts as they wandered toward their obvious conclusion.

"Don't worry, Will," the major drew him back in, "it won't be long now."

"Well we've lost him," Russell prodded, at the colonel's pensive state. "He'll be like that for the rest of the night."

"Nah, he just needs more to drink," Lawrence said, reaching for the bottle, "as do I."

"Oh yes," Garnett snickered, "that's just what we need–a tent full of drunken officers, when the general comes by. Or even better, three hung-over officers trying to fight off the rebels in the morning. I can just see Ed rolling right off the top of his horse in the heat of battle."

The men all laughed.

"Knowing him, he'd fall mid-shot and end up hitting one of us!" Russell added.

"Well, I'm glad to know you both have such faith in my abilities as a soldier. And how did this get turned on me anyway?"

"You are the one holding the bottle," Garnett pointed, with a smile.

"Yes, well I'm not the one who nearly shot Captain Lewis, during the hunt last fall."

"He walked into the shot!" Garnett tried to defend himself. "I almost had that buck, too."

"You'd have had a fine time explaining that one to Miss Aislin. 'Darling, I've been kicked out of the army, and I might be arrested for murder; but we'll have a splendid pelt when I've finished!'"

"My, my, my, David made a joke!" Lawrence raised his glass in a mocking toast.

"Not a very good one, mind you," Garnett retorted. "But maybe the old boy does have a sense of humour."

A shrinking shadow appeared in the doorway. "Excuse me, sir?"

"Yes, Lieutenant," Garnett answered.

"I've a message, sir." The young man was clearly uncomfortable with his task.

The colonel took his feet off the desk and leaned forward. "And...," he said, annoyed at their interruption.

"Uh, the command has changed hands, sir. General Lord Cornwallis has been left in charge of the army here. The messenger said the general will be through day after tomorrow."

Garnett raised his eyebrows, gesturing his interest to his friends. "Very good, Lieutenant. Thank you."

"Sir," he nodded and left.

"I imagine that means we won't be here much longer," the major sighed, and leaned back in his chair.

"Safe to say," Garnett muttered, thoughtfully.

The general did make an appearance as promised. He was very pleased with the outfit presented upon arrival, which, of course, reflected well on the colonel.

The general was merely passing through, but he did leave Garnett with a new task. His friends sought to hear the news after the general's departure.

"What's it to be then, Colonel?" Major Lawrence asked.

"The governor who escaped from Charles Town is with the Continentals retreating to the north. The general wants us to go after them."

"But they've had more than a week's head-start. How can we possibly catch them?" Colonel Russell sceptically inquired.

"He's left the matter in my hands. We're to do the best we can and then decide if it's worth the pursuing." The colonel stood looking over his maps.

"That seems an awfully heavy burden to place on your shoulders," Russell stated, a little indignantly. "Not to mention, you haven't seen your family in two months. To send you on such a wild goose chase–well it seems a bit of poor judgment, if you ask me."

"Then it's a good thing we didn't ask you," Garnett smiled. He patted his friend's shoulder as he turned to cross the room. "Rest easy, David. We'll catch them."

"You sound awfully certain," Lawrence posed.

"The general's given us two hundred and thirty odd men, all mounted, in addition to the Legion. We'll catch them. And we'll have our families moved by the end of next month."

"While I don't share your enthusiasm, I sure hope you're right." Russell ended the conversation as the men dispersed to collect their effects.

The troupe arrived in Camden (a sixty mile trek) the next day, only to set out again in the middle of the night. By the following morning, Colonel Garnett's sanguine appraisal seemed to be anything but. Rather it seemed he had glimpsed their future. Through their midnight ride, they had closed the gap on the retreating Continentals, and suddenly found themselves separated by little more than twenty miles.

But the British advance guard was exhausted. Horses bore two riders because so many mounts had collapsed along the way, and the soldiers themselves weren't much better off.

By late afternoon, the two forces met. The Redcoats gained an advantage as the rebel rear guard struggled to buy time for their commander. Garnett didn't wait for the rest of his forces to catch up. Instead, he formed ranks and led the charge straight at the Continental line.

He and the British Legion were on top of the rebels before they finally began to take fire. The rival commander had let them get too close. The Redcoats seemed impenetrable as they road down the opposition. The rout was horrific–Patriot soldiers trying to defend themselves against their mounted foes. Muskets and pistols were useless within the fray–impossible to reload. They made a more ready defence as substitute swords against those of the British. The only fire taken by either side was from the lucky few who had escaped the centre of the mob, but it was enough.

It looked as though the rebel leader meant to surrender, but in a moment of confusion, his troops fired once again on the Redcoats. Garnett clenched his jaw, gritting his teeth, as the enemy drew him into their sights. His mount nearly somersaulted as it fell, bringing it's rider to the ground in an entangled mess. He was pinned–barely able to reach his weapon.

His troops seemed to stutter for a moment. It looked as though their commander had been killed. Outraged by such blatant treachery, the officers rallied the men and renewed the charge.

The whole bloody affair lasted not even half an hour. Upon seeing the colonel fall, the soldiers lashed out like wild animals, ruthlessly attacking the Continentals.

It was Colonel Russell who ultimately brought order to the rampage as Major Lawrence freed Garnett. The result was just less than one hundred captured rebels, but twice that many injured, and more than one hundred killed; while the British suffered only a handful of casualties and about a dozen wounded.

Everyone was glad for the ease of their win, but Garnett and his friends knew it was no battle for which they would receive accolade. They quickly made arrangements to get the rebel wounded and prisoners off to hospitals just to the north, and then began the march back to their headquarters. Word of the fray spread quickly, travelling faster than the cavalry.

19

The outcome, as well as the reaction of their superiors wasn't nearly so bad as the men had thought it would be. It was merely stressed that the officers ought to take more seriously the control of their men, but no one could overlook the fact that their primary goal had not been achieved. The rebel governor had escaped.

The worst part of the affair was the news reaching them from reconnaissance-things being said within rebel camps. Colonel Garnett's name was being spoken almost as a curse. The rumour was massacre, butchered patriots, and murder of the surrendered.

The colonel's commanders paid little attention to the "gossip," as they called it, and his friends were mostly successful in their attempts to encourage him. Though angered and frustrated over the situation, Garnett could only maintain his dismal guise as long as it took to receive word from Aislin.

He and the others (including Captain Matthews, who'd been stationed at Charles Town since the siege) had already sent letters to their wives. At the end of the following week, Garnett would be meeting the women back in Port Royal to see to their transport. They were to caravan along with the troops, who were moving the last of their supplies from their southern camp to Charles Town.

"I'm glad to be leaving this dreadful place, and even more so that we're not going by ship." Anna didn't like being on the sea for any length of time.

"It should be a short trip, going by wagon, even over this marshy territory," Aislin amiably agreed.

"Aren't you ladies finished packing yet?"

No one had noticed William's arrival, and Aislin almost came out of her skin as he spoke. She threw her arms around her husband's neck.

"Good heavens, William! You nearly scared me to death!"

He kissed her forehead and smiled, "I'm sorry, my dear. I only meant to surprise you."

"Well you succeeded," she laughed.

"Hello, Anna," he addressed their housemate.

"How are you, Colonel?" she returned, with a giggle.

"Quite well," he sighed, looking back at Aislin. "How have things been here?"

"Oh," Anna moaned, but Aislin interrupted.

"We've been fine," she said, eyeing Anna, "but we are happy to be putting Port Royal behind us."

"I'm sure," William answered. "And I think you'll be pleased with our new arrangements in Charles Town."

"Anywhere's better than here," Anna replied.

"Well, how about a break from packing for tea?" Aislin suggested.

"Sounds wonderful," William said, ushering the ladies from the room.

After dinner that night, the colonel entered their chamber nearly dragging his feet. He sat down on the bed and then let himself collapse backward onto the welcoming surface. Aislin smiled. She knew how tired the ride that day, along with all his recent excursions, must have left him. She walked over and carefully removed his boots. William laughed under his breath as he raised his head off the bed to look at his wife.

"I suppose this is the part where you tell me how much you've missed me," Aislin joked, at her state of servitude.

The colonel chuckled again. "Indeed."

In one swift move he reached up, wrapped his arms around her waist, and flung both of them back onto the bed. Aislin giggled as she settled in beside him. She was so completely consumed with both relief and delight at having her husband with her again, she barely knew how best to express her sentiments.

William's arms around her, Aislin returned the embrace resting her head against his chest and the soft white shirt he wore.

She sighed in her deep contentment.

"William, tell me about Charles Town. What's our new home like?"

"I believe you'll like it there. It's similar to St. Augustine in many ways. We can't see the harbour from our house, but it isn't far–just a short walk. I've already found a couple of roads outside the city that ought to be fit for riding. And you'll have your balcony and your gardens again."

"Tell me about the gardens."

Aislin felt him move as he huffed another laugh. She propped herself up to see her husband's face, and was met by a casual grin, those two silver pools nearly drowning her in their gaze.

"They are smaller, like in Florida, and with much the same colour; and the lilies are already in bloom. I can already see you sitting in the middle of it all–reading, surrounded by all your flowers," he said, gently brushing her cheek and running his fingers through her long hair.

Aislin smiled. "It sounds perfect," she whispered.

William gave her shoulders a squeeze and kissed the top of her head.

The company was packed and loading the last of their belongings into the wagons the next morning. William, Aislin, Anna, James, and one other soldier were the last to find their places. Aislin and Anna watched, very amused, as the men tried to calm a skittish horse who refused to be hitched.

The colonel had just finished telling everyone else to get to the wagons, that he'd take care of the horse, when a shot suddenly erupted from the tree line about one hundred yards away. The misfired shot gave the party all the warning they needed. But Aislin, rather than run for the cover of the supply train as the others did, instinctively ran to William.

"What is it?" a soldier yelled from the front of the line.

"Rebel militia, I'd wager. Are we ready to get under way?" The colonel immediately began to evaluate their position as he watched the trees.

"At your word, sir," the soldier shouted back.

"Then get moving," he hollered.

Garnett wrestled the animal into its rigging as Aislin and James helped him fasten the hitch. Musket fire rang in their ears all the while. James then got into the wagon and turned, taking Aislin by the hand to help her in.

The colonel made for his own horse, pausing only to ready the few weapons at his disposal. Once mounted, he looked in on Aislin.

"I'm not letting you out of my sight." He kissed her cheek and commanded, "Just keep your head down."

He, along with the few soldiers free to fight, put themselves between the enemy and the wagons. The colonel's orders were to fire only at visible marks, since reloading would be difficult.

The woods were thin, and as the militia moved closer, they made easy targets. They were also on foot, and with the soldiers all mounted (or at least mobilized by wagon) the party was able to quickly put a safe distance between them.

The weapons soon silenced, with the final worthless shot fired from the lagging rebels. The colonel turned up beside the wagon that carried his wife. He had only to look inside, and Aislin answered his unspoken question.

"We're all right," she huffed.

Though no one was injured, Aislin sat with her arm around Maggie's quivering shoulders. The fray was nothing new to Aislin as she'd been through so many before, but the major's wife had never been caught up in such conditions. The other women looked shaken and nervous as well.

"You're safe now, ladies," the colonel reassured them. "Those must have been a few stragglers from the rebel camps. I doubt we'll encounter any more trouble."

Garnett smiled at Aislin, who smiled right back, and then headed for the front of the line.

"I don't know how you can stay so calm," June said with a shudder in her voice.

Aislin's gaze shifted, "Unfortunately, I've had practice."

"Why do I think it wasn't a ball that brought you and the colonel together?" Anna raised, only partly joking.

Aislin didn't answer.

*   *   *

The accommodations in Charles Town brought comfort as well as new restriction. There had been many a shake-up in the British Army, and the soldiers' presence forced a sense of caution on the Garnetts. William repeatedly warned Aislin against being seen more than necessary, for there was no way to tell who in the town was a stranger and who a former captor.

Aislin, nonetheless, had to go out and maintain an appearance to keep her friends from becoming suspicious; but each time they passed a group of soldiers in the street, she couldn't help looking over her shoulder.

Their new homes were lovely–everything they could have asked for. They were settled right in the heart of the city, with every convenience at their fingertips, and Aislin found her husband's descriptions to have drastically underestimated the house's finer features.

When the colonel was home, he made a point of spending nearly every moment with Aislin: taking her on rides outside the city, going for walks in the markets or along the port, or just spending a quiet evening on the balcony watching the bustle of the city below. He worried less about her being recognized when he was there to escort her. William and Aislin were both confident in his ability to protect her.

Most often, the pair chose to walk through the city's busiest rows of shops. Aislin loved the lively atmosphere, and the colonel saw it as a good opportunity to continue to make his presence known, among his men as well as the other officers.

They were there on a sunny summer day, walking arm in arm, when a familiar face quickly (and absently) passed by them in the street.

Aislin nearly spun around as she turned to confirm the woman's identity.

"What is it?" William responded to the jerk at his arm.

"Wait a moment," she replied, her voice trailing as she began to walk toward the mysterious figure.

Garnett stayed a few steps behind, puzzled over what had caught his wife's attention.

Aislin's heart leapt straight to her throat as she realized. "Madam Andrews?" she cried.

Madam paused for a moment, afraid if she moved too quickly, the caller might disappear. Then she turned toward the address.

"Aislin? It can't be," she gasped. "Oh, my dear girl!"

The two women embraced there in the streets, and for once, Madam thought nothing of decorum.

"My word, look at you!" Madam fawned over her. "How are you? Are you all right?"

"I'm fine, Madam," she smiled broadly, "but what on earth are you doing here?"

"Oh, I moved out of New England to get away from all the fighting, but out of the frying pan and into the fire, as they say," she answered sarcastically.

The two shared a laugh just as Madam caught sight of the colonel, who had cautiously made his approach.

"Oh dear," she muttered, unsure of his presence.

The colonel walked right up beside Aislin, who bit her lip and began to fumble her words searching for a proper explanation.

"Ah, Madam, you remember Colonel Garnett?"

"It's 'Colonel' now, is it?" she asked, a little forcefully.

Aislin started to giggle nervously.

"Yes, ma'am, it is," he answered, trying to subdue a smile.

Madam Andrews eyed them both. "Clearly I've missed something."

Aislin could barely contain herself. "Well, you yourself said we made a lovely couple."

"No. You two?" She didn't know what to say. "Now how did that happen?"

Everyone laughed.

"It's a long story," Aislin replied.

"And one we would do well not to share with all of Charles Town," the colonel added.

"Indeed." Madam's tone of voice changed to a far more upbeat tune, "Well, how would you two like to join me for dinner tonight? I would love to hear all about it."

Aislin looked to her husband as he readily accepted the invitation. "We'd love to, Mrs. Andrews."

"Wonderful. It'll be five o'clock. My home is just around that corner there–second on the left."

"We'll be there," Garnett cheerfully responded.

The two ladies parted with another embrace.

"I'll see you shortly, dear," Madam smiled, as she went her way.

"Yes, Madam," was Aislin's courteous riposte.

The couple arrived as scheduled, but this time, Madam greeted them quite formally, as though they hadn't been parted for those three years. Her consistency and solidarity were always a great comfort to Aislin.

The trio stayed together trading stories well into the night. Aislin told her mentor about the colonel's plan: how he'd freed her and protected her over the last several years. She told about their stay in St. Augustine, and how she and the colonel had come to be married. She spoke briefly about the conflict and the battles they'd seen; and Aislin even mentioned, though barely, the baby she'd lost earlier in the year.

Madam expressed her feelings and opinions on all such matters, and then told of her move from New Jersey, in hopes of escaping the worst of the war. She had been in North Carolina until recently. When she'd heard of the British victory in Charles Town, she decided to take residence there, sure that under British control it would be more peaceful than the countryside. Being the widow of General Andrews helped to secure her residence.

"If nothing else," she'd said, "the winters couldn't be so bad as in New England."

The colonel told no stories, only answered Madam Andrews's questions and added to Aislin's tales the bits she'd left out. There was, however, an unavoidable query about the rumours regarding the Waxhaw Massacre, as it had come to be called. Garnett gave as strong and clear an explanation as he could, (of course, leaving out most details) but was still left uncomfortable and almost offended by the conversation. Had it been anyone other than Mrs. Andrews, it might have been quite ugly.

At evening's end, the ladies made plans to have tea together the following afternoon and promised the three of them would gather for dinner at least once a week, as long as the colonel wasn't away.

Throughout the ride home, Garnett couldn't help but notice the smile that remained on Aislin's delicate face.

"You're happy Mrs. Andrews is here?" he posed.

"Very," she answered softly.

"I must admit, it will be a great comfort to me knowing she's here with you when I have to be away."

"And I imagine she'll have more than a little advice in regard to being a soldier's wife."

Both huffed a laugh as Aislin rested her head against the colonel's shoulder. It was but a short ride home.

20

The colonel stayed home and their small family remained in tact for more than a month after the move. Garnett's only absences were brief, yet frequent visits with the general. He almost always returned home by nightfall, and Aislin got very used to having him around.

In fact, he was home for almost all of July-bedridden with malaria. The illness was hard and took quite a toll on the whole household.

William always awoke with a frightful headache and always asked for Aislin. She would sit beside him and rub his head or wipe his face and neck with cloths of cool water. When he slept, Aislin tried to sleep, although it didn't usually work.

When the colonel had at last regained enough strength to get up, he found he didn't want to remain so for any length of time. His joints were stiff, and his muscles were sore. Getting used to being up and about again took William longer than he had anticipated, but by the time he did make a full recovery, Aislin realized he'd done so much sooner than she would have liked.

He was off to battle again. In her mind, he couldn't possibly be strong enough, and she worried about him all the more.

The lone conflict she heard about while her husband was away took place in Camden, just to their north. It was a swift victory for General Lord Cornwallis and his men; and it was a badly managed mess on the part of the Continentals and their militia. Aislin wondered what was keeping the Continental commanders from surrendering.

The colonel didn't return after the battle, as did the other officers and their men. Aislin later found out that he had been pursuing one of the rebel militia groups and their leader. Though Garnett was unable to capture the commander, he was quite successful in defeating and scattering the rebel troops and also managed to rescue a large contingent of British prisoners. The command in Charles Town was rather pleased with the overall venture.

For several weeks, Aislin heard nothing at all. Then in September, a visitor arrived: a uniformed rider.

James stuttered as he called for Aislin and invited in their guest. The servant stood only a breath away from his mistress as the soldier spoke.

"Mrs. Garnett?" the young man inquired.

"Yes." Aislin choked on the word.

"Mrs. Garnett, Corporal John Galloway. The colonel has asked me to bring you to him: you, James, and Miss Rebecca. He asks that you come immediately. I'm to escort you myself."

While Aislin was excited to hear from her husband (and even more so to be invited to join him), she couldn't help noticing that the boy wouldn't look her in the eye.

"Sir, why the urgency? Is something the matter?"

She hated to ask. At the moment, part of her felt it would be easier not to know.

The corporal sighed, "He's sick, ma'am."

"Is it malaria again?" she asked, breathlessly.

"I'm afraid it's worse, ma'am. It seems we've had an outbreak of yellow fever."

Aislin nearly collapsed back onto James. He held tightly to her shoulders, fighting his own dismay.

"I'm very sorry to bear such ill tidings, ma'am." He paused, but continued when Aislin didn't respond. "If we leave tomorrow, we could make the camp in just a couple of days."

No one spoke for a few minutes. James sat Aislin on the sofa and went to get her something to drink. She tried to put her concern aside and think rationally, but her head felt foggy.

She took the glass from James and then addressed their visitor.

"What if you and I rode ahead and had James and Rebecca to follow behind?"

"Miss Aislin–" James began but wasn't allowed to finish.

"We could move twice as fast without wagons and baggage. Couldn't we?" she turned back to the soldier.

"Well, yes, I'm sure we could. But it would be a hard ride, ma'am. And to maintain speed, we couldn't carry much more than ourselves. Are you sure you'd be up for it?" he asked, hoping to discourage her.

"I'm certain," Aislin confidently replied. "How long would it take?"

"I left this morning to arrive at sundown."

"So if we left before sun up?"

"We'd arrive around dinner time tomorrow, or at least a soldier on a cavalry horse could."

"The lady can ride, sir," James interjected, "able to keep up with most, I'd say."

"Very well. You wish to leave in the morning then?" the soldier obediently complied.

"Yes. That will give enough time to make arrangements here before we go."

Aislin found that putting her mind to the logistical matters made her feel much better, even if only for the moment.

"Shall I show the gentleman to his quarters for the night, Miss?" James asked.

"Yes, thank you, James." Her thoughts began to turn.

He patted Aislin's shoulder as he showed the way.

"I'll be right back," he whispered.

Aislin leaned over and dropped her head in her hands. That was how James found her upon his return a few moments later.

"Miss Aislin?"

There were tears on her reddened cheeks when she looked up.

"This is bad," she muttered.

"Oh, Miss Aislin." James sat down beside her.

"He wouldn't send for me if it wasn't."

"Here now," he said, handing her a handkerchief, "maybe it's not as bad as it sounds. Maybe he just misses you."

Aisin huffed, "You can't do any better than that?"

James smiled, "Keep your chin up, Miss. No sense in getting all worked up, and the colonel wouldn't want to see you so upset."

"I know," she nodded.

"Don't worry about a thing. Rebecca and I will take care of everything before we leave tomorrow."

"Thank you," she finally smiled.

Aislin went to Madam Andrews' for dinner. Madam, of course, did the best she could to console and encourage her bereaved guest, but her words fell on deaf ears. Aislin's mind was a world away, thinking about William.

Madam promised her she would speak with Anna and the other officers' wives to let them know what was happening, and implored her young friend to reconsider her plans to ride. In the end, the ladies solemnly parted ways, and Aislin went home to make the last of her preparations.

With shaking hands, she worked beside Rebecca, setting aside the things she wanted to make sure were brought after her. Rebecca hummed softly as they went about their task, which went lengths to calm Aislin's nerves.

All were gratefully tired upon evening's end; else none of them would have slept.

*   *   *

It was still very dark outside when James softly knocked at Aislin's door. She answered, gathering her robe and the wherewithal to begin the difficult chore ahead of her.

She dressed simply, wearing the linen dress and apron she'd worn the day she and the colonel first went to the beaches in St. Augustine. She packed a similar change of clothes, water, and a few light provisions. Then she had her breakfast, gathered her coat, and joined the corporal in the street where one of the stable hands waited with their horses.

James walked her out, a lantern in one hand and the other around Aislin's shoulders. He helped her into the saddle and spoke as he handed her the reins.

"Be careful, Miss Aislin."

"I will." Her smile was half-hearted.

"We're right behind you," he said, patting the horse's neck.

Aislin nodded, "See you in a couple of days."

The pair disappeared quickly into the early morning fog. They held the horses to a trot until they were out of the city. Neither spoke as they went, and after they'd let the horses loose, conversation was out of the question.

They took their first break a little more than an hour after sunrise, their second around noon. Each time, they let the horses rest and tried to eat. Very little was said.

By that afternoon, Aislin was dreadfully tired and getting sore. Her rides with the colonel were never so long, but remembering her husband, her strength was renewed.

The sun was only just beginning to set when they arrived at the camp. The scene that met them was all too familiar. Aislin was surprised at how rapidly her memory refreshed. The fear she'd felt as a prisoner of the British unexpectedly fell over her, and she began to guardedly watch those closest to her.

Galloway led them right to the colonel's tent. There was one young soldier at the entrance, but Aislin didn't wait for his assistance to dismount. She was off the horse and inside the tent the moment after the lad had taken hold of the reins. The corporal followed her.

There was a curtain drawn through the middle of the room, and before she had rounded the corner, she was met by a young boy about twelve or thirteen years of age. She surmised that he was there to look after her husband.

"'Scuse me, ma'am," was all he said, leaving with a pale full of some fluid Aislin mercifully didn't recognize.

On the other side of the curtain was a table full of rags and unfamiliar utensils. William lay in his cot near the back of the tent facing the makeshift wall. The ground beside the bed was stained a terrible reddish, brown.

Aislin swallowed hard, trying to suppress her emotions before she approached. She reached out and touched his arm but flinched, immediately drawing her hand back, as if she'd just touched a hot kettle on the fire.

The colonel didn't move.

She sat on the edge of the bed and gently ran her hand over his shoulder. This time, William turned gingerly to see who was there.

"Aislin?" he murmured.

"It's all right, darling," she said softly, brushing back his dark hair. "I'm here."

He winced as he turned a little farther to see her more clearly.

"How did you get here so fast? I only sent Galloway night before last. Or have I been sleeping?"

"The corporal and I left this morning and rode straight through. James and Rebecca are coming behind us," she answered.

"You made the whole ride in one day?" There was amazement behind the colonel's question.

Aislin laughed, "One very long day."

The corporal had stopped at the edge of the curtain and spoke up at the last comment.

"If I may say, sir, should we give the lady a sword and a pistol, she'd make a fine Dragoon."

William looked at his wife and smiled through tired eyes.

"I imagine she would," he jokingly replied. "Thank you for your help, Corporal."

The boy answered with a polite, "You're welcome, sir," then nodded and left.

Garnett laid his arm across Aislin's lap and held on to her waist as if he were trying to keep her from going.

"How are you feeling?" she asked, noting a light behind his pale blue eyes.

"I'm fine. I'm sure it looks worse than it is," he said, trying to be dismissive. "I should've known better than to think it would take you days to get here, once you'd heard."

"You certainly should. I would have left yesterday when the corporal arrived, if I could have."

William started to laugh, but it became a cough. He turned away from Aislin, who had averted her gaze, startled by the sound.

The colonel caught his breath. "I'm sorry."

"It's all right," she replied calmly. "Is there anything I can do?"

"Just–just stay with me."

William was clearly exhausted. Aisin took a deep breath and tried to steady herself. She wasn't accustomed to seeing the colonel in such a vulnerable state.

"Why don't you rest, dear. I'll be here when you wake."

He didn't answer. He just quietly closed his eyes and lay still.

Aislin kept her place for a few minutes more. She felt so much better just sitting beside him, watching him sleep.

Leaving her husband to rest peacefully, she walked outside to get the pack from her horse. The corporal stood waiting for her at the entrance.

"They're bringing a bed and a few other things for you, ma'am."

"Thank you, Corporal. I'm obliged for your help." The day had finally caught up with Aislin, evidenced in her tone.

"Not at all, ma'am. I had been assigned to the colonel when he became ill. I'll be available for anything you need, day or night."

"Can you tell me, has the doctor been around?"

"He usually comes after he's finished with the others for the night. I'd expect him soon."

Aislin thanked Galloway once more and collected her things. She was still settling in when the doctor arrived, just as predicted.

"Mrs. Garnett? I'm Dr. Riley."

"I'm pleased to meet you, sir." She paused, trying not to be rude but then requested of him, "How's he been...really?"

Riley sighed, "Today was a good day. He was awake for a good while and seems to have slept better."

"*Better* is a good word," Aislin smiled.

"Now don't get me wrong, ma'am. The colonel is very sick. I'd say he's in the worst of it now. Do you faint at the sight of blood?"

"No, sir."

Aislin thought it was a strange question.

"Well, I'll be blunt. There'll be a lot of blood and a lot of vomiting. And there won't be much you can do to make him comfortable. The fever is pretty relentless, and he's very weak. You'll need to watch him, even when he sleeps. If he starts coughing and can't roll to his side, he could choke. When you need to rest, call Corporal Galloway, and he'll assist you."

"I have help coming in a day or two," Aislin added, meekly.

"Good. I'm sure you'll be glad for it by then. I won't be available much during the day. I have others to attend."

The doctor's words weren't unkind, just flatly honest.

"I understand," she quietly replied.

"Very well. I'll check on you tomorrow. Good night, ma'am."

Dr. Riley put on his hat and left.

"Good night."

Aislin suddenly felt very out of place. She appreciated the doctor's candour and that he didn't patronized her, as most would have done. On the other hand, she was so taken aback by some of the things he'd said, a part of her wished he had softened the blow a bit.

21

Aislin stirred at a noise she couldn't place. From her space beside William, she felt herself sit up and look to her husband. He was coughing–so violently that the bed shook beneath him. Then it stopped. The noise stopped, and so did William's breathing.

Aislin sprang to her feet, shouting as loudly as she could. Only there was no sound–not her screaming nor the moving of the soldiers. She was terrified and seemed frozen where she stood. Though she tried desperately to get to William, she couldn't take even one step.

Out of nowhere, the noise came again–distant at first, then somehow right beside her.

Aislin was jarred awake. She sat up feeling very out of breath. She'd been dreaming.

She looked to William, who was coughing though not as hard as she'd dreamt. Aislin got up to sit at his bedside. She gently shook the colonel from the last remaining grips of the sleep that held him. He woke as she called his name.

"William, are you all right?" she whispered.

He forgot to whom he was speaking–forgot even that Aislin was there.

"My stomach–it's hard to breathe."

Aislin barely heard him as he struggled to speak.

"What can I do?" she asked.

"Help me sit up," he said, already labouring to do so.

"Here, now. Take your time," she smoothly commanded.

They managed to get him sitting as William gathered his wits about him. Aislin reached for a candle sitting on the table and lit a second. The light seemed to pull the colonel back to his senses.

"Aislin," he stated, though with question.

"What is it, darling?"

"I thought I dreamt you. You're really here."

Aislin softly smiled, but a lump found its way to her throat. She realized all at once how sick he really was. He didn't remember anything of their earlier reunion, except as one remembers a hazy reverie.

"I'm so happy to see you," he sighed.

Aislin was at a complete loss. She could think of nothing to say to her husband. Instead, she just continued to force her smile.

"I remember this." William absently ran his fingers over the material of the linen dress she still had on. "You wore this the day I first took you to the seashore."

Fighting her tears was beginning to feel impossible.

"That's right," she said, almost under her breath. "You should try to rest, dear. It's very late."

"I've missed you," was the last thing he said before he closed his eyes once more. Aislin thought he looked as if he were resting far more peacefully.

She began to sing–though barely above a whisper–a soft, sweet lullaby that she recalled from her childhood. Her memory failed her as to where she'd learned it, but she did remember loving the tune. Aislin became aware that it was she and not William who was benefiting most from her serenade, as she finally felt her sleepiness again overtake her.

The next few days were very trying. The corporal helped where he could, or more specifically, where Aislin allowed. She stubbornly cared for the colonel doing most of the work herself, especially at night. She was terrified of what might happen if she left him.

Even after James and Rebecca arrived, Aislin pushed herself to the point of being dangerously fatigued. It took James's pleading, and often his gently pushing her from the room, to get her to break from her self-appointed chore. At first, she insisted on sleeping in the bed beside the colonel (jolted awake each time he coughed or made any big movements) and ate every meal, when she ate at all, at William's bedside.

As she too progressively worsened, James began to politely force her from the tent for at least a few hours each day.

The colonel slipped in and out for weeks, until Aislin's memories of her strong, healthy husband seemed more like distant daydreams. While it had crossed her mind, with some small measure of relief, that the illness could keep him from the rest of the war, the same concept gave her pause. Even if William did recover (which was no guarantee, she knew) Aislin just couldn't imagine him being the man he once was.

Finally, James instituted–and enforced–a schedule upon Aislin, Corporal Galloway, and himself. Galloway would take the morning watch each day, when Aislin would sleep; James would have the afternoons and part of the early evening; and Aislin would stay the nights. Rebecca was put to work running errands, taking care of meals, and doing the other chores the three couldn't manage.

Though Aislin wondered at first if they'd keep their word, James and the corporal called for her each time the colonel awoke to the point of being alert (as he usually asked for her). It worked out much better for everyone.

Two weeks into their stay, Aislin had visitors. Colonel Russell and Major Lawrence had come by to see how Garnett was doing, and she was very grateful for their company.

"We're doing the best we can, Miss Aislin, but I'm afraid there's no man in this army equal to your husband," Russell told Aislin, intending a compliment. "I seem to be falling rather short as his replacement." He laughed at his own remark, trying to keep the conversation a little more light-hearted.

"It's amazing, really," Lawrence commented, "as if the whole war hinged on his involvement–his presence."

"We certainly could use his guidance," Colonel Russell added, somewhat sadly. Then his tone turned serious. "I suppose you've heard about George."

Aislin nodded, "I've written June–promised we'd look in on him."

Captain Matthews had taken up with the illness as well. Mrs. Matthews would have come herself, but she was expecting.

Lawrence interjected, "I had heard he's not as bad off as some of the others. A bit of good news, I suppose."

"Tell me," Aislin spoke softly, as if telling a secret, "is it true what they say? That the general is in a hurry to get to North Carolina and intends on leaving the sick behind, if they don't improve soon."

"No, quite the opposite. The general is eager to get on with things, but seems to be even more so to see his men recover," Russell consoled her. "In fact, I've heard him speak specifically about Will. And I can say for certain, though he may plan small manoeuvres in an effort to get things under way, the general will put off as long as possible any major move without our colonel here. He knows better than anyone the benefit of Will's experience and leadership in the field."

Aislin smiled and felt herself relax.

Things at last began to look up toward the end of the month. William began to come around as the bleeding and fits of fever finally subsided. He rested better when he slept, and with her husband out of the woods, Aislin also found sleep more easily.

The colonel stayed in bed recuperating into October, and the recovery was much more difficult than it had been after the bout with malaria. When he did begin to move around, it was with the assistance of one of his three keepers.

Though still fairly weak, he was in the saddle again a couple of weeks later. Knowing how limited he would be, the general's first assignment was one believed to be considerably safer than most. Garnett was sent to meet a fellow officer and grant requested assistance. However, the general was uninformed of the tragedy that had already befallen his men.

22

The road-weary group solemnly trudged up the hill after the colonel. They walked very carefully around and over their fallen comrades, each of the climbers aghast at the devastation. To come upon such a chilling sight, when they had expected to arrive as reinforcements–it left the men dumbfounded.

A few paused beside the bodies of friends in a trifling attempt to pay their last respects. The colonel himself stayed steadily on his ascent, secretly hoping he would not find his aim: the group's commander. He hoped he'd been taken prisoner or somehow got away. His target, however, met him near the summit.

Garnett knelt down beside Major Lawrence and immediately began trying to figure out how he would tell Maggie.

Captain Matthews stopped as he approached. "Oh no," he sighed.

He hadn't meant to disturb Garnett, but the colonel rose to his feet anyway, his eyes never leaving the ground.

"How could this happen?" he said, under his breath.

The captain answered, "I don't understand. He said matters were in hand, didn't he? He only asked for reinforcements to finish the campaign."

"He sent that correspondence weeks ago," Garnett muttered. "We waited too long."

"Look at what those animals have done." Another soldier crouched nearby was pointing to a woman lying lifeless in the dirt. "Those rags in her hand–she was tending the wounded. These rebels aren't soldiers. They're monsters!"

"Lieutenant, please contain yourself," Garnett gently rebuked the officer, knowing it would be important to the men that their leaders maintain their composure.

"Forgive me, Colonel."

Garnett set his mind to business. "Arrange a detail. See that all of them are properly buried."

The lieutenant nodded his compliance and went off to accomplish his task.

In near silence, the men reluctantly concluded their business on the battlefield. Afterward, the troupe received their much deserved rest at the camp outside of Charlotte.

Garnett had intended to confine himself to his quarters for the evening, but Matthews managed to convince him to join Colonel Russell and the other officers in town for a drink. The captain made a persuasive argument in stating it would raise the men's spirits to see their commander.

The soldiers settled in a pub near the edge of town. Garnett was relieved at the presence of a few other garrisons, fresh from far less discouraging endeavours. They enlivened the small, dark room as well as the colonel's disheartened troops.

Garnett spoke very little, though Matthews, Russell and the others in his company continued to dig away at his brooding disposition.

"Come on, Will," the colonel continued to push, "try to lighten up a little. We have time enough ahead of us to be miserable."

"I'm sorry, David." Garnett didn't even attempt to sound cheerful. "I just," he sighed, "I just want to get home and see Aislin."

From out of nowhere, the man behind him turned and spoke up. "What did you say?"

Supposing him to be a soldier out of uniform, the colonel begrudgingly replied to the stranger, "My wife. I want to see my wife."

"No, her name. What did you say it was?"

The eagerness in the man's voice startled Garnett and he answered in spite of himself. "Aislin. Why?" He didn't know what had compelled him to give up the name.

"Her last name–what was it?"

The stranger was sitting on the edge of his seat, and the wild look in his eyes made Garnett wonder if the man would strangle him or break down in tears.

"Garnett, of course."

"No, before she married. What was her name?"

The colonel had grown tired of the invasive questioning. "I can't see any reason why I should tell you."

By now, they had the attention of the men around them. So the stranger leaned in and spoke in very hushed tones.

"Was it Laraway?"

The colonel was stunned. He couldn't find the words to answer him.

"Was it Laraway?" the man insisted, still keeping his voice low.

"I don't know what you're talking about," the colonel growled, nervously.

"Please, she's my sister."

Garnett squinted at the inquirer. He looked familiar, but the colonel knew this was not the Laraway he'd met previously. "Clayton?"

"No. I'm Thomas."

"That's not possible." The colonel was beginning to think he was part of some elaborate hoax-or worse, a trap. He remembered well the death of Aislin's eldest brother years ago.

"Uh," he groaned. "There was a horrible mix up. She thinks I'm dead, doesn't she."

"Something like that," replied Garnett, remaining evasive.

"Is she all right? I heard rumour that she'd been kidnapped."

The colonel turned around. Everything about the man seemed suspicious.

"Look," the stranger continued, "I know you can't trust me any more than I can trust you. I just want to know if she's safe."

Garnett took one last look around. He was literally surrounded by his own men. If there was any danger, they were more than prepared to handle it. His concern then would be explaining the incident to his friends and fellow officers.

The colonel turned back to the young man and only nodded. Then he looked away for the last time.

"Thank you," the stranger whispered.

The next morning, as the men busied themselves about the camp, a messenger arrived. He approached Garnett with his letter and rendered his explanation.

"Sir, this is addressed to Mrs. Garnett. I was instructed to deliver it to you and to inform you that it's from her family."

Quickly the lad nodded and left. A cold shiver ran through the colonel as he looked down at the piece of paper in his hand. He couldn't imagine any member of Aislin's family to be so audacious as to send correspondence to her through him, especially after the stern warning he'd given her brother in Trenton. He was immediately consumed with the fear they'd been discovered-perhaps while Aislin had been tending to him in camp. Garnett was already blaming himself as he opened the letter.

He searched the signature line. It was signed, *I Remain, Your Devoted Brother, Thomas Laraway.*

Though he wasn't sure what he was searching for, the colonel looked up to study his surroundings before returning to read the body of the letter.

It read like the letters Aislin had received from her father and brothers while still in Newburgh. Thomas outlined his meeting of the colonel and expressed, in jest, his interest as to her marrying a British officer, if she had in fact done so. The rest of the letter regarded his recent ventures and the goings on of the troop he was with.

Garnett paused. While the letter gave no pertinent military information-whereabouts or movements of any companies or the like-the colonel temporarily replaced the husband as he began deliberating whether or not to turn the correspondence over to his superiors, and thereby possibly turn Laraway over as well.

He shook his head and quickly pocketed the letter. If this man were caught, the likelihood of exposing his affair with Aislin increased exponentially. He couldn't relinquish the letter, nor could he let it be found by another. Garnett wondered if they'd all be better off if he simply burned it.

He next thought of Aislin. The colonel knew she'd try to understand such action, but knew also that she'd struggle to forgive him for destroying evidence that her brother was alive.

He determined at last, the correspondence would reach its intended. Garnett kept the paper on his person the whole trip home.

*   *   *

The colonel began his report of what he'd found at King's Mountain. Remorsefully, he sent word to the general, who upon receiving the correspondence, recalled the colonel and his men to have them take up winter quarters.

Much to Aislin's relief, William arrived back in Charles Town only just after her own return. Captain Matthews stayed behind with Colonel Russell. There were a few things to get in order before they would leave camp for the winter.

Normally, the colonel could practically take the door from its hinges by reason of anticipation at seeing his wife. But upon this return, Aislin could have missed his quiet entrance all together, were she not looking for him.

William very softly embraced her and held to her while he spoke, knowing she'd immediately recognize the malady in his eyes otherwise.

"I've missed you terribly," he murmured.

"I've missed you, too, darling." Her response was coated in concern.

Aislin pulled away to see his face.

"William, what's wrong?"

He took a deep breath, deliberating which to tell her first: of Edward or Thomas. He resolved hearing the latter might bring some measure of reprieve after hearing the first.

"Is Maggie here?"

It was the colonel's unpleasant duty to tell her as well.

"No, but I was expecting her and Anna at any moment."

Aislin could hardly stand knowing he was keeping something from her.

"William, what is it?"

"Aislin, I must ask you not to get emotional. I'm counting on you to be strong for Maggie," he gently instructed.

She choked back the lump that was already rising in her throat, expecting the news would be the worst. Still holding her, William looked straight into her eyes as he spoke.

"Edward's been killed."

Aislin lowered her head, closing her eyes. "God, no," she sighed. "Do you think I ought to be the one to tell her?"

"No. I think I'd better," he answered tenderly.

A long moment later, James answered the soft rapping at the door. Anna entered, immediately spouting off about a lunatic carriage driver who'd nearly run over a woman across the street. Maggie followed behind, shaking her head at her exasperated friend.

Aislin met them with a smile and quietly led them to the parlour.

"Maggie," she awkwardly began, "we have something to talk over with you, dear."

She caught the seriousness in Aislin's wavering voice.

"And what is that?" she asked cheerfully, though falsely so.

"Why don't you have a seat?" William kindly offered.

Maggie did as she was asked, but Garnett's formality alarmed her.

"Colonel, I'd be very grateful if you'd just be out with it."

Her happy demeanour had vanished, replaced by oncoming distress. Anna sat next to her holding her hands.

Garnett folded his arms and looked at the floor. He had planned on trying to break it to her gently, but now realized it would only prolong her unease. Emotion flooded his voice as he looked up and spoke.

"Maggie, Edward was killed in North Carolina."

He felt there was more to say but couldn't find the words.

Maggie didn't seem to react–almost as if she didn't hear him. Then, in a shaky voice, she responded. "There must have been a mistake."

William sat down beside her.

"I'm so sorry, my dear. I found him myself."

Maggie sank. She closed her eyes and bit her lip to keep it from quivering. The colonel put an arm around her shoulders, and she buried her face in his chest as the tears forced their way out. She didn't say another word, only slowly allowed the sadness to overcome her until she was a shaking, sobbing mess.

As they stayed there in the parlour consoling their friend, William continually glanced up at Aislin, who stood beside the group on the sofa. Aislin had tried to be brave, and while she was quiet, still had to allow a few tears of her own to escape. She had imagined herself in Maggie's place so many times before. Although she never lingered long on the thought, she dreaded such news of William every time he went away.

After the worst of Maggie's crying was ended, the Garnetts offered her food, drink, and every other comfort they could think of. Maggie politely refused them all.

"Well, we can't let you go home like this," William gently insisted.

"If it's all right with you, Colonel–and you of course, dearest," Anna addressed Maggie, "she can come and stay with me. I certainly wouldn't mind the company."

"I'd be grateful for the accommodation," Maggie whimpered. "I do hate to be rude, but I'd like to lie down."

"I'll have James see you home," Garnett began.

Anna nodded, "Thank you, Colonel."

After seeing the women out, Colonel and Mrs. Garnett again took their seats in the parlour, Aislin wrapped in her husband's arms, leaning back against him. She quietly brushed away her tears as William spoke.

"I know the thoughts that must be running through your mind. Is there anything I could say or do?"

"Not unless you're ready to leave your post."

Aislin meant it, but she said it in jest. She felt the colonel's laugh beneath her.

"*Ready* is quite different from *willing* or *able*. There've been many days when I was more than ready to leave the whole messy ordeal behind for good."

"What stopped you?"

Aislin almost never asked about anything involving his career, and William very rarely tendered any such information. Yet something compelled them both.

He sighed, "Most often a sense of duty–of commitment–and you, since the day you came under my charge."

"Me? How's that?" she asked softly.

"Well, at first it was making sure we weren't suspected or caught. Then it became my way of providing a comfortable life for you. Not to sound as if I'm blaming you. I would have stayed even if you hadn't come along."

He kissed the top of her head as if to say he was very glad she had.

"So then I suppose we blame your overwhelming sense of responsibility," she teased.

William squeezed her tightly in his arms and laughed a little to himself. "I'm glad to see your sarcasm is in tact."

He paused and seemed to sense that Aislin had slipped into some sort of daydream. He leaned around and spoke softly in her ear.

"Where have you gone to?"

"Hm?" she broke from her trance.

"You left me for a moment. What were you thinking about?"

He gently pulled the hair back from her shoulder.

"I was wondering how much longer this war will last," she answered, thoughtfully.

"I'm afraid that's one answer I can't give you, my love."

"I know. It's just," she paused, shaking her head, "I've already lost too many people I care about to this blasted war. And though it's only temporarily, I regularly lose you as well."

"Good heavens!" he exclaimed, with a chuckle. "I almost forgot."

"What?" Aislin turned, startled at the outburst.

"I have something for you," he said with a smart grin.

"Well?"

Garnett pulled the letter from his coat pocket. "A man, claiming to be your brother, sent this to me."

"My brother?" Aislin was puzzled at the how as well as the why of her brother's presence so far south. "Clayton or John?"

"Thomas," he answered with his own measure of doubt.

"William–" she began, not wanting to speak on the subject.

The colonel plodded right along. "Aislin, he certainly did favour your brothers in appearance, and the writing seemed familiar."

A withheld breath escaped her. "Uh-but...How?"

He shook his head. "I met him in Charlotte. I didn't believe it myself, at first, but I've run out of reasons not to believe him. If it had been a joke or a trap, I'm sure it would have to have come to fruition by now."

His smirk widened as he watched Aislin's reaction to the news. She poured into the letter, a smile winning out over her expression. Aislin knew her brother, and she knew his writing. This was Thomas. She was sure of it.

"I can't believe it," she stammered.

"He reminded me of you-his mannerisms mostly-the way he spoke."

"Thomas was my eldest brother," she said wistfully. "From the time I was a small child, he was always looking after me and always able to do things even my other brothers couldn't. He ran my father's office for him-drew in most of the business himself actually. He was well thought of by most, and I had greatly admired him. I wanted to be just as well thought of as he," she said nattily and slipped back into William's embrace.

"His only concern was for your safety. A concern I was happy to lay to rest. I suppose he knows now of our marriage."

"Which means the rest of my family soon will," she said, mostly to herself.

"I've not heard you speak much about your family."

"No. But I could say the same of you," she said, pointedly.

"Hm. Perhaps some things are best left unsaid."

Aislin turned again to look at her husband.

"How have you been feeling since you left?" She searched his features for any telltale signs of the lingering illness.

The colonel let out a burst of laughter. "You have mastered the change of subject, my dear."

"Oh stop," she retorted, trying to quell her grin. "I was being serious."

"I'm fine, darling. I promise, there's absolutely nothing for you to worry about." Then he tilted his head and added cheerfully, "Speaking of change in subject, let's go for a ride."

"But it'll be dark soon, and it's getting cold."

"You don't want to go?" he asked in amazement.

"Of course I do," she answered flatly, "I just wanted to see if my saying it out loud made it seem any less ridiculous."

"And?" he smirked.

"It still seems like a rather foolish thing to do, but that could be said about a lot of things we've done."

The colonel laughed as he squeezed her close once more, and followed with a push that lifted both Aislin and himself to their feet. He wrapped his arm around her as they made their way outside. Both tried, at least for the moment to restrain the saddening thoughts of their friends; choosing instead to focus on one another and their relished bit of good news.

23

The Garnetts' grand Christmas party was a little grander that year, and in spite of the hardships they'd recently faced, everyone was in rather good spirits. The general, (who'd not only come to respect Colonel Garnett but had also begun to look on him as a protégé) made an appearance which did even more to encourage the holiday crowd.

This was the first time in several years it actually felt like Christmas to Aislin. Too long had she missed her family and her friends, and even though their had been many a change to the members over the years, she found herself at last engulfed in a sea of smiling faces belonging to those she loved and cared for most in the world.

William was never far as they mingled among their guests, even though Anna and Maggie had Aislin cornered for most of the night. And while they couldn't stay long, due to her delicate state, June and Captain Matthews stopped by for a short visit as well. Madam Andrews, on the other hand, was present for the entire evening, and Aislin couldn't help but note that she'd never seen her teacher enjoy herself so well.

Several other officers and their wives attended as well, many of whom Aislin was meeting for the first time; but as the night progressed, even they started to feel like family. Everyone had a wonderful time at the party, and all benefited greatly from the momentary escape of the war's harsh reality.

Along with all of the other joys that had surrounded her, Aislin had to add yet another. Just days before, the post had delivered what would be Aislin's favourite Christmas gift: a second letter from Thomas (though he promised it would also be his last, knowing the danger a Continental letter could cause when present in a British home). He had addressed it to Colonel

Garnett to avoid suspicion, who turned it over with one of his signature, mischievous smiles.

This confirmation of her husband's story, however unneeded, renewed a hope within the young Mrs. Garnett she was sure she'd lost. Each time it seemed impossible for her to tolerate the war and the whole of her circumstances any longer, such small, beautiful moments brought a strength to her faith that she relished beyond all else. Although it was usually easier to blame God than to thank Him within the current state of affairs, He never failed to provide comfort in one form or another. Needless to say, the colonel's Bible maintained its permanent place at the Garnett bedside, an unfailing reminder of His grace more than their faith.

As the New Year approached, William, Aislin, and the others prepared to say their good-bye's to yet another friend. Maggie had decided to move back to her parents' home in Virginia and was leaving the week after Christmas.

When she'd written her mother about Edward, her father immediately began asking Maggie to come home; and as she had little other choice (even though her friends would have gladly kept her on), she accepted the invitation. She was her parents' only child, much loved by both her mother and father, and knew she'd feel more comfortable with them and less like an imposition.

Her friends, though sad to lose Maggie, were happy to know she was moving to what would have to be more familiar and uplifting settings.

On the day before Maggie was to leave, the Garnetts rode with Captain and Mrs. Matthews to the Russells' home on the outskirts of the city, to say their final farewell. As they made their approach, however, the group noticed heavy, black smoke billowing from the direction of the Russells' house.

"Oh my," June muttered.

At the reins, Captain Matthews was ready to charge off to the house but was stopped by his friend who'd fortunately kept his wits about him.

"George, wait. The ones who set it might still be there," Garnett warned, already reaching for his arms.

"That's what I'm afraid of." Matthews' gaze was fixed on the rising cloud.

"What's happening?" Aislin asked from the back of the carriage, as the men left their seats and began unhitching the horses.

William turned his attention to his wife. "Aislin, keep to the other side of the tree line. Hide as best you can, but wait where you can see. If something should happen, run and get help. Here." He handed her a pistol as he collected another from under a seat in the carriage. "Just in case."

The men were off before the women had a chance to respond. Aislin and June, in obedience, got off the road and into the trees as deep as they could go without encountering too much resistance. Garnett and Matthews, on horseback, had soon outrun them, and Aislin recalled hearing the first shots long before she saw their target.

Anna and Maggie had been brought into the yard, held by fewer than a dozen rebels. From the short distance allotted them, the colonel surmised that the group was militia or perhaps only local troublemakers. They weren't Continentals and carried only a couple of muskets between them. Clearly, they hadn't counted on running into much, if any, trouble.

Garnett and Matthews road down the bandits, firing a pair of shots each. The few left standing after all of the weapons had been triggered were quickly put to the sword by the cavalrymen. Two so proficient in battle were able to easily dispatch the rebel crew.

Aislin, though she witnessed the outcome, was glad to have missed the bulk of the clash. Watching William about his business was always difficult.

She was ready to leave her hiding place but stayed as she heard Anna begin to yell at Garnett. He turned suddenly and ran into the house. Aislin then realized that Colonel Russell was not with the rest of the group. She was sure that was where her husband was headed: to find his friend.

Still crouched in the brush, Aislin watched in horror as a strange man carrying a loose bayonet entered the house from the opposite side. The others hadn't seen him. There was no one to call for help and hardly a moment to think. She dashed toward the house, paying no heed to the calls from her companion.

Hoping to sneak up on the assailant, she went in through the same door she'd seen him enter. She walked as quickly and silently as she could, holding firmly to the pistol in her hand. As she loomed closer to the hall leading toward the parlour, she heard low, gruff voices and knew William had already been met with surprise.

She turned and peered around the corner. She couldn't see her husband or Colonel Russell, but she could see the invader. He almost had his back to her, but she knew if she moved he'd see her. She had to be fast and bold. She wanted desperately to avoid pulling the trigger.

She held the gun in her left hand as she wiped the sweat from the palm of her right, took a moment to steady herself, and then in one fluid movement, turned the corner and raised the gun to threaten the aggressor.

He turned at the intrusion, and when he did, Garnett made his move, taking advantage of the momentary distraction. Aislin lowered the weapon and watched as William wrestled the man to the ground. Before losing his grip on the bayonet, the foe made one attempt for the colonel's throat. Narrowly missing, he dropped the weapon which Garnett recovered and, reaching for the man's throat, succeeded where his enemy had failed.

Aislin closed her eyes as tightly as she could and turned away but for only a moment.

"Aislin, help me," William said, in a voice she thought much too calm.

She marched into the parlour after Garnett. There, Colonel Russell lay facedown in middle of the floor, bound at the hands and feet, beaten so severely Aislin nearly broke into tears at the sight.

"Darling," William gently called.

She knelt down and began working the ropes to untie Russell's feet.

"What do we do?" she asked, a little unsteadily.

"Go and fetch some water–sheets whatever you can find. We need to try and clean him up before Anna sees," he answered.

He rolled the wounded soldier onto his back. The whole affair was almost routine to Garnett. Aislin, on the other hand, had only ever observed their fighting from a distance. She'd never seen much of the carnage left behind.

William carefully tore away Russell's blood-stained shirt, so as to get a better idea of the damage and began trying to wake him.

"David," he called the name again and again until Russell opened his eyes.

"Will." His tone was breathy and laboured. "Where's Anna?"

"She's fine. She and Maggie are outside with George," Garnett reassured his friend. "Everything's all right."

"Ugh," David moaned, "I don't even know what happened."

"I'd say you had the sense beaten out of you."

"Ah, don't make me laugh," David winced.

"Mm, you may have a broken rib," William grumbled.

Aislin returned with the supplies she'd gone after, once more stepping over the body of the rebel attacker.

"Glad to see you awake, Colonel." She smiled weakly as she stooped to tend his wounds.

"Miss Aislin, you poor dear, how do you always end up in the middle of these things?" he said, cringing as she began her task.

"Rest yourself, Colonel. You'll need your strength if you're going to put on a convincing show for Anna." Aislin didn't want to answer his question.

"I suppose I'd better take care of this mess." Garnett gestured with a nod at their fallen adversary.

As he rose to his feet, Aislin moved so she couldn't see what was to follow. She'd had more than enough of the whole event.

Captain Matthews entered cautiously and addressed Aislin, as she was the only available party.

"Miss Anna's a bit upset. She wants to see David."

He looked over his injured friend and knew it was no time to bring in the colonel's wife.

Aislin groaned and pushed her hair from her face. "Tell her he's helping William, and they'll be out in a few minutes."

"She'll realize it's a lie when she sees him," he said, almost to himself.

"Well you can tell her the truth if you like, Captain, but I doubt it'd do any of us much good."

She normally wouldn't be so short and sarcastic with a gentleman, especially a friend, but the incident was getting the better of her.

"You're right," he said, not at all phased by her disrespectful manner. "I'll see to her."

Aislin was ashamed of the way she'd spoken to him.

She called as he reached the door, "Captain."

"Yes, Miss Aislin?" he turned.

"I'm sorry."

"Think nothing of it," he smiled and stepped out the door.

Aislin finished her chore and helped the colonel sit up against the legs of the sofa. He grimaced as the new position stretched sore muscles and put pressure on vulnerable abrasions. William returned the next moment carrying a clean shirt and aided Russell in dressing and getting to his feet. It took Garnett's constant support to keep his fellow officer standing, but both were putting in the best effort they could.

They made it to the stoop outside, where Russell stopped and had to be seated on the stairs. Anna rushed toward them and only paused when she saw the condition of her husband.

"I'll be fine, dear. Don't worry," he managed, in a very smooth manner. "You're not hurt, are you?"

Anna shook her head. "They stole the slaves and the horses," she muttered.

"I don't care about the horses, Anna. Are you all right?"

"I'm fine," Anna replied, trying to sound calm but still wiping tears from her reddened face.

It wasn't like Mrs. Russell to lose her composure. The colonel sat her on the stoop and pulled her close to him.

Aislin had no trouble imagining what they'd been through (remembering plainly the rescue Colonel Garnett had led at her

172

family's home), but still found it hard to believe all that had taken place.

"All right," the usual position of ranking officer came out in William, "David, you and Anna can stay with us until all of this is sorted out. In the meantime, why don't the rest of you come back with us for dinner. I think a little company would be good for us all."

What he left unsaid to the group (and what his officers mutely understood) was his intention to ascertain the particulars of what had happened that evening. If there were others responsible for the goings on at the Russells' house, he wouldn't let them go with impunity.

"What about the fire?" June asked, pointing to the barn at the other side of the yard.

"Just going to have to let it burn itself out," Russell mumbled.

"We don't have the men to put it out, dear," Captain Matthews added.

"George and I can come back later with Henry and a few others–make sure it doesn't take the house," Garnett directed, and then quietly mentioned to the captain, "And we can straighten up the rest while we're at it."

The rest, they both knew, referring to the dead rebels in the yard.

"Let's get the horses and get everyone out of here," he concluded.

Maggie timidly spoke out, "Colonel, what about my wagon?"

She looked out beside the house where the wagon stood loaded with her few possessions.

"I'm surprised they left it," she murmured.

"Well," Garnett thought out loud, "I suppose we'll hitch one horse to the carriage and one to the wagon. George?" he questioned the Captain.

"If you and Miss Aislin would like to take the wagon, I'll drive everyone else," he offered.

The look Matthews cast in Aislin's direction caught Garnett's attention. As the colonel turned to his wife, he noticed for the first time how pale and distressed she seemed to be.

"Very well," Garnett replied.

Once aboard, William put his arm around his wife and kissed the top of her head as she leaned into him.

"I'm sorry you had to see all that," he said, gently.

Aislin didn't respond.

"Darling, what's wrong?"

He could tell she was crying by the way her hands brushed against her cheeks.

"I just-I don't know what to make of all this," she said, quietly. "Anna and Maggie aren't soldiers. Even if they were only after Colonel Russell, why would they attack their home?"

"Local justice, I guess. They think that *Tory* families are just as deserving of punishment as the Loyalists fighting for us." His tone was almost complacent.

"It isn't fair," Aislin whispered. "People shouldn't have to fear for their homes. Soldiers shouldn't have to worry about their families while they're away. Isn't the war enough on its own?"

Garnett squeezed her shoulders taking a deep breath. "I've asked so much of you and never realized the toll it must be taking. You've been with me through so much; it's been easy at times to treat you like one of the soldiers."

"I like that you trust me with such things. I was fearful at first that maybe you'd try to shut me out rather than include me."

"Perhaps I should have," he said, under his breath.

Aislin wrapped her arm around William's waist. "That would have been worse."

"Just the same, it's all right for you to pull back if things get to be too much. I would never want to put you in a position you weren't prepared to handle. Today, for instance-seeing all of that had to be shocking at best."

"I suppose I knew what was coming. I just wasn't ready for it," she sighed.

"You could've fooled me," Garnett said, with a chuckle. "When you came round that corner, I was so surprised I almost forgot myself. What on earth possessed you to do such a thing?"

Aislin smiled, thinking of how the scene must have looked–her wielding a gun aimed at the back of the rebel brigand–but looking back, she couldn't question her reasoning.

She spoke as rationally as she could, but her smile could be heard throughout. "I saw him going in the back door, and I knew no one else did. If I hadn't, what would you have done?"

"Honestly, I'd rather not say," he replied, with less humour.

"Well, I did the only thing I could think to do. I couldn't very well let him just go and…" She didn't finish her thought.

"I know," he said, resting his cheek against her. "And thank you, by the way."

Aislin wiped away the last stray tear and held snugly to her husband right the way through the ride home.

24

The colonel met with the general at year's end to begin discussing their next manoeuvres and what battles might be brought by the onset of spring. The meeting went exactly as predicted; instead, it was at home the colonel would encounter the unexpected.

James was waiting at the door when Garnett arrived, and it was all the colonel could do to calm his usually well-composed servant.

"I didn't know what to do, sir. I'd have come and told you, but I was afraid to leave." James wrung his hands, looking more worried than the colonel had ever seen him.

"Get hold of yourself, man," Garnett instructed, trying to quiet his nervous friend. "What's happened?" He was trying not to jump to any conclusions but was quickly losing his patience.

"It's Miss Aislin, sir–"

"Where is she?" Garnett shortly interrupted.

"Upstairs," was all Garnett heard before he charged toward their room.

James followed, continuing his explanation. "I could hear her crying, but she wouldn't open the door–wouldn't answer me. It's been almost an hour."

Garnett's attention fell on the door he now faced.

"Aislin? Darling, please open the door." He could hear her crying as well. "Aislin please," he continued to call. "Aislin, you're scaring us."

The colonel knocked one last time and turned to James. "Get an axe, hammer, whatever you can find."

James could only nod as he left on his assignment.

"And send Henry for the doctor!" Garnett shouted after him.

Upon James's return, both men set to breaking down the door. It didn't take long.

"Go and get some water," the colonel directed, as he entered the room.

Aislin lay in a crumpled heap on the bed, shaking but otherwise unable to move. William rushed to her side kneeling on the floor next to the bed. He was visibly mortified.

"Oh, darling, what's wrong?"

"I don't know," she breathed, barely able to speak.

"The doctor's on his way," he said, soothingly.

Aislin lay with her arms pulled in tightly and wrapped around her stomach. William held firmly to her hand as he gently began brushing the fallen hair back from her face. He tried to make her more comfortable but was beginning to realize his efforts were in vain. Aislin turned her face into the pillow, still shuddering.

The doctor did arrive soon after, and dismissing the colonel from the room, began his work. Garnett had nothing to do except pace the hall and wonder what had come over his wife. James kept a seat nearby, hunched over with his head in his hands wishing he had sent for the doctor sooner. He couldn't help but blame himself for Aislin's state, even though the colonel had insisted it was no one's fault (except perhaps his own, he had noted).

Though it felt like hours to everyone else, the doctor's visit was brief. Garnett nearly fell over himself as he bolted to meet him at the door. The doctor held up his hand before the colonel could say a word.

"She's going to be fine."

Garnett's shoulders fell as he sighed in relief. "What happened?"

"I'm not exactly sure," the doctor said, very nonchalant. "It seems to have been some severe muscle cramping in her abdomen. Normally, I would say it might have been some spoiled food she came into contact with, but it could also be related to the pregnancy."

William's eyes widened. "Pregnancy?"

"Yes," he continued haphazardly. "It's very early-possible she didn't even know yet. Anyway, congratulations, Colonel." The doctor donned his hat and headed toward the door. "Keep an eye on her. She'll be fine."

Garnett glared at James. Both looked as though they were trying to think of what to say, but neither ever came up with anything more than huffing half a syllable. The colonel shook his head and went to be with Aislin.

Still lying on the bed, she smiled at him as he entered. William took a seat alongside her and leaned over to kiss her forehead.

"How are you feeling?"

"I'm all right. The doctor gave me some wretched medicine that's starting to help." Her voice was still weak and her eyes were very red. Looking toward the hall, she continued, "Why did you break the door?"

"It was locked," he said bluntly. "You didn't lock it?"

Aislin shrugged, "I must have, I suppose. I just don't remember."

The colonel brushed her cheek and raised an eyebrow as he spoke again.

"The doctor says you're expecting?" he posed.

"I knew there was a chance, but I wasn't sure until he said." Her speech had begun to break.

William's brow furrowed. "What's wrong?"

"Nothing," she said, attempting to force a smile. "It's just I…" Aislin sighed heavily and began to tear, "I'm afraid."

"Because of what happened last time?"

She nodded.

"Darling, everything's going to be fine," he reassured her. "You'll see."

"I know it's silly, but I can't help it," she cried.

"No one could blame you for being afraid."

William's heart broke as he thought of what she'd gone through, and it only made things worse to know he was soon to leave her once again.

"Everything will be all right. I'm certain of it."

Even though nothing could have been farther from the truth, William was unable to regret his lie as Aislin leaned into him and rested within his arms. He silently prayed that his prediction wasn't all together false.

Later that evening, James brought to the colonel's attention a supply of fruit in the kitchen that had gone rotten. When Garnett asked his servant why the fruit hadn't been thrown out, James had no answer to give, nor did he have anyone to ask. The cook had vanished.

The colonel charged his friend to carefully watch his wife, and also to keep a close eye on the rest of the house.

*   *   *

It was only a few short days later when Garnett was again called away to the Carolina backcountry in pursuit of the rebel forces. He had his friends to accompany him, but it did little to raise his spirits as they trudged endlessly through the torrent of winter rains.

The now Major Matthews (having been promoted to the post of the fallen Major Lawrence) joined Colonel's Garnett and Russell as they sat one evening around the fire on a rare dry evening.

"I still think it's a bad idea," Russell was saying, as Matthews took his seat.

"Ah, the replacement Legionnaires?" the Major guessed.

"They're nothing but filthy, treasonous rebels. I don't care what sort of oath they've made. They can't be trusted."

Colonel Russell made comment on the recent alignment of rebel prisoners of war and the addition of such to the ranks of the Legion. These prisoners, rather than resign themselves to the prisons floating in the Charles Town harbour, swore an oath of allegiance to the king and were dispersed to the Loyalist regime.

"We have our orders, David." Garnett tried less to reassure and more to admonish his friend. "We're bound to meet this band we're chasing sooner or later. And we can either do so with or without that half of the Legion. Personally, I'd rather have the help."

Matthews tried to change the subject. "June told me there's to be an addition to the Garnett house this summer."

"How is she?" David's concern stemmed from what Anna had told him of the last.

"She's worried, understandably so. We're hoping, because she knows better what to expect, that it won't be so hard on her this time," Garnett replied, trying to veil the apprehension in his voice.

They followed the enemy commander for a couple of weeks, through flooded marshlands and muddied trails, steadily gaining ground until mid-January. It was then Garnett found he'd nearly caught their rivals. The colonel knew the distance that separated them was meagre; and in an effort to take them by surprise, he moved his men in the middle of the night. The tactic had worked for him before.

The two forces met at dawn. The colonel was pleased to find militia again made up the core of the rebel brigade. It looked to be a reprise of so many previous battles, and Garnett expected the task wouldn't take long.

He wasted no time, sending the Legion to storm right through the middle of the field. Yet, the moment they approached striking distance, enemy sharpshooters began emptying the British saddles. The colonel quickly recalled the attack and followed with an order to send in the infantry for a bayonet charge.

He watched as the militia fired only two volleys and then retreated. Elated at the quick success of the endeavour, Garnett gave the order for the men to push forward and finish the Continental mainline, moving reserves in to flank their opponents and aid in the conclusion. As they charged in, the Continentals' right side collapsed. The British broke their lines and began the rout.

Suddenly, the Redcoats found themselves surrounded as the Continental lines caved in on them. Garnett watched in horror as his men were rapidly engulfed. The British fought as fast and as hard as they could but to no avail.

The colonel tried to rally the Legion, hoping they could still break through and save some of their comrades, but the Legion refused to follow. Some surrendered to their friends in the rebel ranks. Most fled the field. Garnett immediately began gathering as many of the other cavalrymen as he could and led the rescue attempt through the heart of the battle. They waded through the relentless mire of soldiers, pulling out those they could reach, barely escaping with their own skins in tact.

They were followed as they fled the field–chased for miles before they were finally able to lose the assailants. The whole ordeal was a disaster, and Colonel Garnett would be the one responsible.

25

My Dearest Aislin,

I thank God for each passing day, as it is one more that must surely draw me closer to home and to my Darling. I miss you terribly, and now more than ever.

The trials recently faced afford no description here, though I would mention that we have suffered a bitter loss, the first of such by my own hand. My fellow officers have offered only criticism, some seemingly pleased to have seen me fail.

Before word should reach you otherwise, I am compelled to inform you that I had tendered my resignation and requested a court-martial to prove myself in the matter. Both have been refused by the General. I am currently to carry out my duties just as I would, had the trouble not occurred.

I realize the breadth of emotion such news must invoke, and though I am uncertain of the ultimate outcome, please be assured that everything will be all right.

I have no doubt there are many questions you would wish to ask, and I am sorry that I cannot speak at length on the issue. I must ask you to remember me and all that you know to be true of me, no matter what you may hear, as I am sure the rumours will soon spread beyond our camp.

I hope this letter finds you well and in good spirits. Know that I think of you often and long desperately to see you. It is my sincerest hope that I will be home with you before the rains end.

Yours In Deepest Affection,
William

Aislin stood on the balcony with the letter in her hand. She'd read it a half a dozen times and still felt unsettled. She wondered what horrible things could have happened to make William think he ought to resign. Why would the general refuse the resignation? What if he changed his mind?

She knew she'd find no answers until the colonel returned home, so she tried to put the news from her mind. Her friends, as always, were at her side to help. Anna and June were both staying with Aislin while their husbands were away, and both were quick to reassure her that their own men would certainly look after Colonel Garnett's best interest in the affair.

The general indeed had no intention of allowing Garnett to resign his post. He was completely unwilling to lose one of his strongest leaders at present, or at all for that matter, and still maintained a great deal of respect for the colonel and his abilities. The general also knew of the trouble Garnett had encountered with the Legion and was convinced they had more to do with the loss than the colonel himself. So Garnett continued in his efforts, though he did so under the scrutiny and spite of the other ranking officers.

*　　*　　*

Russell and Matthews plodded their way to Garnett's tent, arriving just as the general was leaving. They kept their distance at first, so as not to appear too eager, and then rushed in to find Garnett bent over in his chair, staring at the floor.

Colonel Russell began breathlessly, "Will, what's happened? The whole camp is rumouring there's been a massacre."

"Are we going after them?" the major quickly asked.

"Sit down, both of you," he answered, quietly.

Both did as they were ordered and listened intently to what the colonel had to tell them.

"The Loyalists on their way to meet us were attacked. The ones who made it through say they came across a group they mistook for our dragoons–a group in green coats. It was Light-Horse Lee," Garnett said, with no lack of disgust. "The colonel saluted the group, and Lee's men cut them to ribbons. There are nearly one hundred dead and half again as many wounded. The men are still clearing the woods."

Garnett knew the men wanted action-retribution-but the general had just left, giving orders that they would stay put and keep to the original directive, being to catch up to the whole of the southern Continental force.

So he added, "Now is not the time for revenge. But as we must surely encounter the rebels on this present course, I believe such a time is not far off."

The colonel's smooth and assertive tone left no room for argument. His friends knew he was as angry and frustrated as they, and both knew if there was anything could be done, Garnett would lead the way.

They waited for three weeks, as patiently as they knew how, until their opportunity finally came.

*   *   *

Garnett sat in his tent, strapping on his boots, murmuring under his breath as he worked: reminding himself of a few last details, running over strategies once more, imaging what the day ahead might hold, whispering a prayer for his wife and himself.

The sun had not yet begun to rise, but the camp was already alive as soldiers prepared for the day ahead. There was a hushed din of those speaking just above a whisper and the occasional clanking of metals against one another. It seemed everyone was trying their best to remain quiet, even though there was no cause.

The colonel stepped out into the heavy morning mist and, setting down his shako, began the work of saddling his horse. Even though others did, he never trusted anyone else with the task, not before an event of such importance. The animal stomped the ground impatiently, as if he too knew what lay ahead of them.

Garnett firmly patted the horse's shoulder. "Easy, old man. It won't be long now."

He picked up the black shako and was soon joined by his friends. There was no pleasant greeting, only a few nods as they mounted and headed to where they would meet the general and the other commanders.

Cover was all removed once more as the men took their places, standing solemnly around the table. The meeting merely reminded them of what they already knew: they were vastly outnumbered and the enemy held the high ground, as well as the most invulnerable points on the field. The tactics were covered at length, each man receiving and acknowledging his assignments. Dawn broke just as they were finishing. The three Dragoons left, feeling very confident about their orders, more than happy to carry them out.

Garnett and his men detached from the rest of the British force and headed out to meet the Continental advance guard–led by Colonel Lee. The British Dragoons struck in full force, driving back the rebel division.

Colonel Garnett road through, continuing the attack. He was resolved to gain satisfaction only after they'd sent the enemy into a retreat. So engaged was he in the chore that he didn't notice the pistol drawn and aimed from off to his right side.

The sharp pain overtook him so suddenly, he almost dropped his sword (and probably would have, had it not caught around his hand). He pulled his right arm in closely to him, carrying his sword in his left. Determined not to lose their place, he persisted in the onslaught defending himself as best he could.

The reinforcements from the 23rd Regiment of Foot arrived shortly thereafter and effectively ran Lee and his men back to the Continental mainline. Garnett promptly ordered his own troops to hold the line and await the advancing infantry.

"Colonel," Major Matthews called from behind him. "What are you doing?" His question was meant to address Garnett's sword being carried in the wrong hand.

The colonel instinctively turned over his right hand to appraise the damage, not meaning to reveal the injury to his friend. Nevertheless, the major caught sight of the wound.

"Send the surgeon!" Matthews began to shout.

"No, Major," Garnett returned. "It's not that bad."

Matthews pulled up alongside him to see for himself.

"The ball's passed through. It just needs dressing," the colonel insisted, even though the hand was virtually useless.

"Sir, I really do think a doctor ought to have a look at that," the major respectfully maintained.

"It's fine. We have work to do."

With that, the colonel sheathed his sword and began to head his horse toward the frontline, but as he did, the call came for his Legion to fall back. The general had ordered them in reserve until the infantry could bring the fight to a level playing field.

The major still kept to Garnett's side as they began to move.

"I'll have it bound while we await our next orders, all right?" he sighed, a little exasperated.

The Legion had only a short adjournment of their duties and were soon competing against another division of the rebel Dragoons, Garnett leading them right through the thick of things. They kept the road cleared and defended the British flank as they continued to advance on the rival lines.

Still wielding his sword in his left hand, the colonel found that as such, the fighting became even more tiring and laborious. He and his men fought valiantly and pressed relentlessly against the foe, even after most of the Continentals and their militia had retreated from the battlefield, chased by British infantry.

Atop his horse, Garnett began to feel disoriented. He struggled through the fog, still doing all he could to guard himself against the present onslaught; but he was beginning to realize the harder he fought, the worse it became. The colonel was ultimately forced to retire himself after having sustained yet another injury, which nearly lost him his seat. Under escort to the surgeon, he left the command in the hands of Colonel Russell.

The conflict soon ended, as Garnett gradually succumbed to the exhaustion that had threatened to overtake him. He last remembered the awful sounds of screaming and moaning that surrounded him inside the surgeon's tent.

26

Garnett rode slowly down the way that would lead him home, wondering how he would explain everything to Aislin, and how she would react to the news. He looked sullenly down at his right hand, bandaged over the place where his first two fingers should have been. He hadn't written her about the amputation, afraid it would worry her needlessly (and all the more when Aislin saw another's handwriting, instead of his own).

He knew there would be a barrage of questions he was neither prepared nor inclined to answer, and he was already rehearsing his intended responses.

Aislin and June had just retreated to their rooms to rest before dinner, leaving Anna to silently mind the window they'd watched all afternoon. When the men did arrive, it was to such little to-do, the women upstairs did not stir. Anna was again left downstairs, but then with her husband, while the other officers saw to their own.

William quietly entered the room and sat carefully on the edge of the bed. He leaned himself on his left arm reached over Aislin, and gently leaned down to kiss her forehead.

She opened her eyes and greeted him with a soft smile.

"You're back," she sighed and began to push herself to sit upright.

The two sat silently holding one another for several minutes. Aislin was consumed by all the things she craved to ask him, but even more overpowering was her desire not to ruin the first few perfect moments she had with her husband. She determined to put it all aside until William tendered the answers himself.

As he drew away, he absentmindedly raised his right hand to brush the hair from Aislin's shoulder. She didn't see the injury, and might not have noticed, if it hadn't been that the colonel flinched as the dressing violently reminded him of what he'd meant to hide.

"What's wrong?" she asked, as he tried to collect himself.

"I suppose it's foolish to try to keep it from you," he muttered. "You're bound to notice."

William thought to brace her for the sight of it, but realizing it would be futile, attempted to brace himself instead for her response. He slowly pulled his hand forward and held it out for her.

"William," she gasped.

Aislin tenderly took his hand and lightly ran her fingers over the binding. She was left utterly speechless as she finally looked up at him.

"I took a ball in the hand. The fingers were ruined," he whispered. "It wouldn't be so bad," he went on, with a hint of mischief, "if it didn't make my gloves feel so odd."

Aislin couldn't help but laugh at his self-imposed mockery.

"I've missed that sound," he said, with a grin.

She had to ask, "Are you all right otherwise?"

"I'm fine," he nodded. "But aren't I supposed to be the one worried about you? How have you been feeling?"

"All right, really," she answered, seeming surprised at the truth of it. "Some days are harder than others, but that's to be expected."

"I'm glad to hear it." He turned, "We'd better get downstairs. We have company."

"Colonel Russell and Major Matthews are back as well?" Aislin enquired, more cheerfully.

"Safe and sound," William replied.

The two soon joined the other couples downstairs, and the scene began to reflect so many they had lived before.

Major Matthews made the first address as the Garnetts joined the crowd.

"I'm sorry about the hand, Miss Aislin," he said, sounding awfully sincere. "I suppose the colonel got away from us for a moment."

She could tell the men had already informed Anna and June of the incident by the way the women tried to glimpse the damage, without looking as if they were staring. Aislin decided to take the opportunity to bring some levity to the situation.

"Yes, well, he can be rather difficult to keep track of at times," she jokingly retorted.

All stayed for dinner, throughout which the conversations were enormously energetic. The men told stories (about everything except the battles), at which the women in turn were obliged to laugh or fuss over, depending on the subject.

Anna had suspended one particular question until after they'd retired to the parlour, but having eventually overcome her, she asked it at first opportunity.

"Have you found it difficult getting on without the use of that hand, Colonel?"

She knew it was too outspoken, and were they in different company, she never would have asked. Everyone knowing Anna as well as they did, however, thought nothing of it.

"I've done well enough," he answered politely. "The difficult part has been practicing my writing and sword exercises with my left hand."

"I would think you could lay down the sword for a while after this," June interjected.

The colonel chuckled a little to himself. "Not just yet, Miss June."

"You're going back," Anna exclaimed, "even with such an injury?"

She spoke the words on Aislin's mind, and Garnett knew it. He caught the glare in her eyes. The look he returned was apologetic and a little insecure. Aislin, herself, wasn't sure why she had expected he'd stay, knowing him as she did; but she was still startled to hear it. She knew she'd have to wait until later to gain any sort of resolution.

"Believe me," Russell spoke more light-heartedly, "we're all wondering at this point what exactly it would take for the general to release him from duty."

Aislin tried to keep up her spirits, but as the evening wore on, it became progressively more arduous. William had reached over to hold her hand, which she gladly accepted. This brought him some measure of comfort in believing she wasn't angry with him, even though she was obviously upset.

It was getting late when their friends at last departed for their own homes. The colonel closed the door after them, and then turned to his wife.

"Come and sit down," he calmly instructed.

Aislin returned to her place in the parlour as William took a seat just opposite her.

"I don't have a choice, darling," he began in his explanation.

"I know," she timidly replied.

"You do?" he questioned humbly.

"I know if you did have a choice, it wouldn't be to leave–that you're doing what you must."

Her supportive tones only seemed to frustrate him all the more. He stood up and paced beside his chair.

"Aislin, I did try," he groaned.

She was sufficiently taken aback by his statement to then keep silent.

"I went to the general with a request to retire from my duties, and he flatly rejected it before I had even finished the proposal." He added, under his breath, "David wasn't joking when he said that everyone's wondering what it will take to earn my release."

William sat down beside her and gently took her hands.

"For what it's worth," he continued, "I am sorry about all this."

She closed her eyes and shook her head. "You have nothing for which to apologize. In fact, I was just thinking," she said softly, "how proud I am to be your wife and how I ought to find more opportunities to tell you so. You're a good man and a fine soldier, and I appreciate how difficult it must have been to even approach the general with such a request."

William couldn't find the words to respond; but the smile that crossed his lips and the gleam in his handsome, blue eyes were all the return she needed.

Breakfast the next morning brought with it a welcomed familiarity. The normally empty seat to Aislin's left was now filled, and she found her heart skipped a beat each time she looked up and saw William beside her.

The first day of the colonel's return passed quickly, as did the week following. The rains had subsided, giving way to the beautiful southern spring weather, which frequently brought the Garnetts on leisurely walks through the city streets or the nearby harbour.

Aislin had grown particularly fond of walking in the parks, alongside the rivers, a little farther inland. There were more trees to shade the paths which, accented by the recently bloomed flowers, provided for beautiful scenery as well as a bit more privacy.

Among the few sharing the pathways one afternoon, two soldiers walking toward the couple began to draw their attention. William and Aislin recognized the one as being the boorish Major Allen who had invaded their circle at the General's Christmas party in St. Augustine. His assignments had, unfortunately, put him close to Charles Town throughout the previous year and still required his frequent interaction with Garnett.

The other soldier, both thought, seemed familiar; but neither could place him. The stranger in turn had fixed his sights directly on Aislin as if he were thinking the same of her.

Each man tipped his hat to the others as they passed uneasily beside one another, but there were glaring looks from all parties. Aislin glanced over her shoulder only to catch the stranger whispering to his cohort, still staring back at her as they moved on.

"William, who was that?" she asked, after they were beyond range of being heard.

"The man on the left was Major Allen." He tilted his head and squinted, trying very hard to recall the person she'd actually queried.

"No, the other," she persisted.

"I don't remember," he answered, sounding noticeably bothered. "I think we'd better be getting home."

Aislin could practically read his thoughts: he was worried they'd been discovered. If the man did recognize her, his being a soldier put them at considerable risk.

James was surprised at the couple's early return and was immediately aware of the colonel's anxious demeanour. Garnett dismissed Aislin and then quietly called James to the study.

"I think Aislin may have been recognized," he abruptly began. "I can't place the man who saw us, but the look he gave her really makes me wonder."

"What will we do, sir, if she has been discovered?"

"For now, I'm going to have her lie low–stay close to the house. She's not to answer the door, and she's not to leave the house without either myself, Colonel Russell or Major Matthews."

"Understood, sir."

The colonel sighed, "I suppose I'll break the news to Aislin."

"Good luck, sir," James quipped.

Garnett couldn't help but smile as he shook his head and left the room.

Aislin didn't protest the new restrictions, knowing full well they were for her own protection. She followed her orders, going so far as to make sure to be out of sight when someone knocked at the door. Under the present circumstances, she was even more grateful William had his leave of regular duties while he recovered, believing the probability of danger was greatly reduced in his company.

The colonel, on the other hand, had just begun in the attempted defence of his family. He met one afternoon with a few of the commanders still stationed in the area, at the conclusion of which he was unexpectedly approached by the soldier they'd encountered just days earlier.

"Colonel Garnett," the man called.

Garnett turned, but didn't offer any sort of amicable deportment.

"Sir, I don't know if you remember me, but I was part of your regiment in New Jersey a few years ago. Sergeant Davis," he introduced himself, seeming pleased to be reacquainted with the colonel.

Garnett remembered: the outspoken soldier across the fire. He'd been there when Aislin was in transport.

"Sergeant Davis, I do remember," the colonel replied coolly, all the while worried as to what the man's next comment might be.

"Hopefully for something other than my blunt behaviour among your ranks," he said, a little diffidently. "I'd like to think I'm not the man I was."

"People do change," Garnett returned politely.

The two men were suddenly faced with Major Allen, whose advance they'd both missed.

"Colonel Garnett, sir," he addressed his superior. "Sergeant. How are you gentlemen this afternoon?"

They nodded in courteous response, but the major's upbeat deportment was already irritating Garnett.

Allen wasted no time. "So how are you and the mistress getting on, Colonel?"

"Quite well, as always," was his grated riposte.

"I'm glad to hear it." The man chuckled a little to himself, "I have to tell you the funniest thing."

Garnett silently prayed for some miracle that would somehow force them to part ways.

"The sergeant here, God bless him, said the other day that he thought your wife looked like some woman you had *arrested* several years ago."

The sergeant, evidently embarrassed at the revelation, hung his head and looked as though he was preparing a statement in his defence. The major afforded him no opportunity.

"Oh, don't fret yourself, Sergeant. The way I heard it told, that woman was quite attractive. I suppose the colonel could even take it as a compliment."

The colonel was anything but complimented.

Allen went on, "By the by, what ever happened to that girl? Someone said she'd made some sort of escape near the outskirts of New York."

The sergeant turned to hear the answer as well.

Garnett spoke steadily and very authoritatively. "The last I'd heard, it was suspected local militia had aided her in the escape. The whole mess was rather inconvenient. My own home was searched as a result."

"Your home, sir?" Davis enquired. "That seems a bit heavy-handed."

"Not at all," the colonel confidently continued, "I was eager to help in any way possible."

The sergeant smiled, somewhat proud of his commander's patriotic answer.

"And you were still unmarried then, in New York," the major resumed his invasive questioning. "How on earth did you find time to court a girl and marry in the busy state of things?"

He tried to sound jocular, but Garnett saw through him.

"I'd met her several years before, and you yourself know our post in St. Augustine was far more peaceful than most. It was then we were afforded the opportunity to marry," he easily explained, as it was mostly truth.

Allen smiled. The colonel had no difficulty determining the nature of the questions, and he'd had his fill.

"Speaking of whom, I should be getting home. Pleasure seeing you again, Sergeant. Major," he added curtly.

"Have a good evening, Colonel," Allen replied.

Garnett practically dragged himself through the front door. He wasn't sure what he was going to do or what he was going to tell Aislin. He wasn't sure if there was anything to tell. If he was wrong and the major's questions were only meant to annoy or make fun, then there was absolutely no cause for alarm. On the other hand, if he knew or even suspected Aislin was the missing prisoner, there would be trouble to say the least.

The colonel couldn't take the chance–not where his wife was concerned. He immediately began to formulate a plan to protect her and their unborn child.

27

"I'm going to send Aislin back to St. Augustine," Garnett addressed his friends.

The men had gathered on the porch, watching over the women sitting a little farther away in the garden. The colonel poured drinks for Russell and Matthews as he spoke.

"I much favour the political climate there over that of Charles Town. James is moving the household at the end of the month, before we redeploy to the north. I wanted to let you know in case you were considering similar arrangements."

He couldn't reveal the real reason for the move, even to his friends, for fear of their reactions.

The major sighed, "June's grown quite attached to Charles Town and the people here. I think we've decided to stay, so long as duty permits."

"Of course," Garnett nodded kindly.

David stood a moment in silence, evidently giving the matter serious consideration. When he did speak, his voice was very solemn.

"I'd like to send Anna along with Miss Aislin. We had planned on moving back to St. Augustine anyway, and I know she'd rather not stay on the plantation alone–not after what happened at Christmas."

The colonel nodded again. "Mrs. Andrews will be going along as well, which I was glad to find, especially in view of Aislin's condition."

The conversation took a swift change with that of the speaker.

"Is everything else all right?" Matthews posed. "Forgive me, but you've seemed a might distracted lately."

"He's right, Will. Is there something wrong?" Russell asked further.

Garnett was grateful for the men's solicitude but was resolved to keep the affair a secret.

"I expect I'm a bit worried about Aislin. Her health was a concern to begin with. Now to add such a lengthy trip–I just hope it's not too much for her."

He wasn't nearly as apprehensive as he led them to believe, but he had to give them something to put to rest their misgivings.

The week they were to leave, everyone struggled to keep their spirits up, but they each did their part in the effort. Aislin, having pleaded to be given some chore in the packing, carefully stowed away each of her books, and a few other more delicate articles, into one of the smaller trunks. Rebecca was packing the tea service and other such items, while James and the other men were carrying the heavier objects in and out of the rooms.

The weather had been particularly nice, and to make the work a little easier, every window and door in the house had been left open. The fresh air was enlivening.

As they worked, James continued to sing an old drinking song he said he'd learned as a boy in the pub where he washed floors. The strange and silly lyrics of the song made the women laugh. Aislin remarked to Rebecca, questioning whether James's knowledge of the song was as innocent as he'd said.

The colonel arrived home as the work was winding down for the evening, a smile forced across his face as he entered the unusually merry company.

"Where, in heaven's name, did you learn that awful tune?" he goaded James, removing his hat.

"It just so happens," James happily retorted, "the ladies like my singing and my tunes."

Garnett, still smiling, shook his head and patted his friend on the shoulder as he left to seek out his wife. Aislin had long since taken her leave of the packing and was sitting, sewing a small pair of socks that just filled the palm of her hand. This she set down beside her on the sofa and stood to greet William as he approached.

He softly kissed her cheek. "How are you feeling?"

"I'm fine," she said sweetly, then turned her attention as she glanced around the room. "I think we're nearly finished–maybe day after tomorrow." Her gaze resettled on the colonel.

"Well don't rush," he gently directed. "The ship won't be here until the end of the week."

Aislin turned to put away her sewing as a subtle knock came on the open door. Major Allen hardly waited for James to conclude his greeting before he charged right into the house, with Sergeant Davis in tow.

"That's all right, my good son," he was saying cheerily. "We'll see ourselves in."

Garnett stood facing Aislin and the door, but Allen had intentionally entered too quietly to be noticed at first. Upon hearing him at last, Aislin began to turn in his direction, but she was jolted suddenly as William grabbed a hold of her.

"Don't turn around," he whispered. "Go out the back and wait in the stables until I come for you."

She obeyed without hesitation or even so much as acknowledging the order. James, seeing her leave, sent Rebecca to follow her–staying behind with the colonel himself. Rebecca, though she didn't know the truth of the situation, knew enough to be aware of the colonel's feelings toward some of the men in the town; and she knew there were those whose presence he didn't want inflicted on Aislin.

"Sorry to intrude, Colonel," Allen began, "but I'm afraid we have a bit of news for you."

In actuality, the major had purposefully taken it upon himself to deliver the information, hoping for such an occasion to invade Garnett's home. He was not easily discouraged in his attempts to prove foul play.

"Did we miss the lady of the house?" he promptly continued.

"Yes, I'm afraid she's not feeling well," the colonel coldly responded.

"Oh," Allen dove right in, "well, the matter we came to speak to you about is one I believe will be of more personal interest than professional. Your wife was stricken ill this winter was she not?"

Garnett was surprised. He hadn't told many about what had happened, and he wondered what possible significance the incident could hold, especially to the major.

"Yes, she was," he replied broodingly. "Some bad fruit, we had deduced. Why?"

Colonel Russell and Major Matthews entered the room as Garnett was speaking. They both looked winded and quite angry. Allen, on the other hand, looked suddenly more conniving and a little pleased with himself.

"Major," Russell boomed, "I thought you understood that we'd be handling this inquiry."

"My apologies, Colonel," he replied flippantly. "The stop was on our way, and you and Major Matthews, I'm sure, have far more important matters to attend."

"You'll be lucky if I don't have you charged for disobeying orders."

Garnett stepped between them to stop the debate. "Gentlemen, could we please. None of you has yet to tell me what this is about."

The colonel was nervous. An inquiry were Aislin was concerned couldn't possibly be good news.

Russell began, still defiantly staring at Allen, but he shifted his focus to Garnett as he spoke. "We've uncovered something of a conspiracy, it seems."

"Conspiracy-what are you talking about?" Garnett queried.

"We've found the cook that ran out on you just after Miss Aislin's illness. It appears the woman was part of a larger organization whose goal was to reach loyalist families from within their homes."

Garnett was stunned. "You must be joking."

"I'm afraid not," Matthews continued. "If we're right, it's a good possibility these are also the ones responsible for the attack on the Russells' home around the same time."

"What's being done?"

"Executions, Colonel," Allen haughtily answered.

"Justice," Russell said flatly, returning his glare toward the major.

"You should have heard the cook," Sergeant Davis finally spoke out. "She confessed to the whole thing so proudly... It's the first time I've ever wanted to strike a woman."

Russell continued for him, "She even affirmed that it was she who locked the chamber door on Miss Aislin. Your wife escaped even more danger than we'd realized."

"It's unfathomable," Garnett muttered. "I had suspected some sort of trouble, but..."

Matthews put a hand on his friend's shoulder. "It's still hard to hear, especially that they were so close to both you and David."

"Look," Russell interjected again, "we know you and Miss Aislin still have your evening ahead of you, as do we. We'll keep you informed as things progress."

"Thank you, David. George." Garnett only nodded to the others.

"Good night, Will," Matthews concluded, as they moved toward the door.

"Good night, gentlemen."

The colonel turned to lean against the wall as they left. He wasn't angry. In fact, he was relieved. He knew well what they'd escaped.

He sighed, pushed himself away from the wall, and addressed James. "Shut the doors."

"Yes, sir," the servant softly replied.

Garnett collected Aislin from the stables, and the house went about the usual business. He elected not to worry her with the unsavoury news.

There were no gatherings on the evening before the families' departure. Each kept to their own houses, sitting in half-empty rooms missing furniture, trunks and other oddities they had packed aboard ship earlier that afternoon. They'd be leaving first thing in the morning.

William and Aislin sat alone on the balcony, listening as the sounds of the city streets beneath them began to die away. Those quiet moments alone together were the one thing they'd both desired, but been hard pressed to find, as of late. Aislin didn't even care to look at the scenery. She spent most of the time with her eyes shut, reclining back against her husband's shoulder. The colonel kept his arms wrapped tightly around her, breathing in the perfumed smells of her hair and skin.

Aislin didn't ask him about when he'd join her in Florida or where he'd be going on his deployment. She knew the limited answers he could give her would afford no satisfaction. She did her best to pretend it was any other night.

William was the first to break the silence. "Have you thought of any names for the baby?"

"No, none that I'm particularly fond of," she said, dismissively.

The truth was (and William knew it) she couldn't bring herself to think on the subject. Thus, he gently persuaded her into the conversation.

"I had thought John for a son, after your brother and my father. What do you think?"

"John Garnett. I think that would do just fine," she sighed.

"And I was thinking Elizabeth for a daughter," he continued, in a more playful tone. "I remember how well you liked that name, being that you used it for Mr. Drake."

Aislin laughed in spite of herself. "It was the only name I could think of," she recalled. "Elizabeth would be very nice." She noted, "Named for Madam Andrews."

The mentioning of their time spent in Newburgh reminded Aislin of a question she'd meant to ask. She hadn't until then, because the timing just never seemed right. She couldn't resist the opportunity and turned to face him.

"You never did tell me," she said faintly, "why did you save me? You rescued me and my family, and you didn't even know us. The first time I asked, you said that things aren't what they seem. Tell me the truth," she pleaded. "Why did you save me?"

The colonel resolved himself to telling her the truth, stifling a smile that hinted at a little embarrassment.

"Honestly," he awkwardly began, "I answered you the way I did, because it was the closest thing to the truth I was willing to admit. I saved you, because I couldn't bare the thought of never seeing you again. I saved you, because I loved you…love you," he quietly corrected himself.

She reached out and caressed his cheek, her lips turning a smile that highlighted her soft expression. William smiled back, turning to kiss the palm of her hand.

"In truth, Aislin, I believe I loved you the instant I saw you," he said, in almost a whisper. "You changed my life that very moment. I thought of you every minute of every day after the ball." His tone turned a little comical. "Didn't you ever wonder how I just happened to be coming by your house that day?"

Aislin muffled a small laugh. "Yes, I did."

"I was there to see you. I had wanted to apologize for my behaviour and attempt to earn your friendship, if nothing else. The circumstances that followed prevented me. After that, I had you with me and was afraid of ruining what relationship we had."

"That of captor and captive?" Aislin sarcastically retorted.

William laughed, "In point of fact. But I still remember," he said whimsically, "how it felt to see you every morning. Since then, any time I've had to spend away from you has left me feeling as if a part of my soul is missing. That's why I couldn't tell you all those years ago. That's why I said things aren't always what they seem. It's just what I tried to tell myself, believing you would never feel for me all that I did for you."

Aislin couldn't contain the smile that left her positively glowing. "I think that's the most romantic thing I've ever heard."

"Really?" the colonel chuckled. "I thought it seemed horribly selfish."

"Maybe a little," she returned "but awfully sweet."

She took a deep breath, trying to savour the moment, and nestled into William. He rubbed her shoulders and held her tighter to him. The couple allowed themselves to lapse into silence.

*   *   *

The women's voyage was mercifully uneventful, although the same could not be said for the fleets in the Gulf to their west. It was learned just shortly after their arrival, Pensacola and the British seat of West Florida had been lost to the Spanish, an enemy declared now two years previous.

Aislin and Anna settled into the house the Garnetts had occupied a little more than a year ago; and Madam Andrews took residence just a few doors down, as she was unaccustomed to sharing her dwelling with so many other people. The women met every afternoon at the Garnetts' for tea and stayed together until after dinner time, when James would see Madam Andrews home. It was a comfortable routine.

Being back in St. Augustine had a strange affect on Aislin. She felt more at home there than anywhere else she'd yet lived. It was the place where she and William had begun their relationship–the place where they'd been married. It was the first house where she'd filled the roll of mistress. And it was the only place she'd truly felt safe (when the colonel was away) since she'd been taken from her home in New Jersey.

But it was also the place of her greatest heartbreak; and as she lay down at night, the feel of the room and the memory of its past events disturbed her sleep more so than the relentlessly warm weather.

The colonel faired no better. They had deployed immediately to the north in lead of the general's main forces, and while his days were consumed with the planning and execution of manoeuvres, his nights left him with all too much time to let his mind wander. Garnett worried about the health of his wife; and he lived under the constant suspicion of Major Allen, wondering if or when the major would once again act on his implied accusations. Just a few weeks into the march, however, welcome distractions began to present themselves.

Early one particular evening, the general called Garnett to his quarters for a very furtive meeting. A letter from General Lafayette (ally to the Patriot Commander in Chief, General George Washington) had been intercepted after an encounter across the James River; thus it was Garnett's knowledge of the French language the commander sought. The correspondence was promptly interpreted, revealing a most convenient surprise.

The letter had been written by the general to Governor Thomas Jefferson in Virginia alluding to the whereabouts of the state legislature. The colonel had his orders.

Matthews met the colonels when they returned to Garnett's quarters.

"I had no idea you knew French," Russell was questioning upon their entrance.

"As you can imagine, it doesn't come up often," Garnett retorted.

"Why so surprised, David?" the major added. "We all know Colonel Garnett to be a man of hidden talents." Matthews eagerly began again as the men took their seats. "Now if you two are finished discussing the weather and the like, could we to business?"

"When was he promoted to general?" Garnett sarcastically inquired of his fellow colonel.

"Ha, ha," Matthews mocked. "Come now, let's have it."

With a shake of his head, Colonel Garnett conveyed the commanders' plans: "General Lafayette was good enough to inform us in his letter of the location of our missing Virginia General Assembly. It just so happens they've settled at the home of their Governor Jefferson near Charlottesville." Garnett's tone was light, almost jocular as he made his presentation. "Therefore," he continued, falsely pompous, "we are shortly to join them, though regretfully unannounced."

His companions laughed under their breath at the manner of his speech. The news was rare fortune, and they would take every liberty to bring some measure of enjoyment to their otherwise weighing circumstances.

"So," the colonel said, coming to his feet, "tonight will be no night for celebration or frivolity, but for rest. We leave at dawn," he concluded, mildly more serious.

Two hundred and fifty light cavalry and mounted infantry set out at sunrise on Sunday morning. They didn't break from the charge until nearly midnight. Garnett and his men rested at the Louisa County Courthouse until two o'clock in the morning, and then renewed the storm. Reaching Castle Hill at dawn on Monday, they stopped once more to collect themselves, should they encounter a resistance greater than they'd expected. Unbeknownst to them, however, the opposition was already, silently working against them.

As they'd crested the hill looking down into Louisa County, a rebel ally had seen and recognised the troops. The militiaman wasted no time. He gathered his horse and galloped off to warn the Assembly at Monticello.

Believing they still held the advantage of surprise, the British soldiers were sorely disappointed upon their arrival at the plantation. They were allotted but a very few captives, and the pursuit of the last escapees brought their total number of prisoners to just seven. Though they didn't know it, they'd missed their target by fewer than ten minutes.

The group set up camp at the governor's home, and it was all the colonel could do to prevent the rash actions of his men in setting the place to torch or ruining it in some other way. Garnett didn't know Governor Jefferson, except by hearsay; but he knew enough to believe Jefferson to be a man of integrity. The colonel saw no benefit to damaging the house and couldn't help but remember what Aislin had said after the attack on the Russells' home last winter; men shouldn't have to fear for their homes and families. Garnett was reminded of just how badly he missed his wife.

The troop met the British main body in Yorktown shortly thereafter. Though they'd missed capturing the governor and most of the assemblymen, the general was determined to see the raid as somewhat of an accomplishment, being that they'd captured the seven. He was also pleased with Garnett on account of the gentlemanly behaviour of his men while camped at Monticello. Overall, it was a success for the colonel, but one of the last he would enjoy.

The general had been corresponding with the outlying commanders and been directed to settle at Yorktown until the navy could remove them to realign with the forces in the north. Stay put–a nightmare for any soldier. Foraging became the order of the day (as they were still trying to replenish the supplies hurriedly burned earlier that year while pursuing the rebel forces), but at least Garnett and the other men were free to send and receive correspondence from their families. Advisably, the men neglected to tell their wives of the anticipated move to the north.

28

Aislin marvelled at the unusually cool August evening as she and Anna took a turn around the garden. Madam Andrews sat reading quietly on the terrace.

"If the weather here is so fine," Aislin posed, "I wonder how the men are fairing in the north? I do hope the snows don't come too early."

"I don't," Anna said candidly. "If it snows, maybe they'll abandon these northerly pursuits and come home."

Aislin replied thoughtfully, "Not likely. It would only serve to slow such pursuits."

"Well, thank you for the cheerful support," Anna dryly responded. "And how do you presume to know the mind of a soldier, least of all their commanders."

Aislin only smiled. She knew her friend wasn't seeking an answer, and she certainly wouldn't offer one.

"You're still feeling all right?" Anna cautiously asked her, noting how quiet she'd been.

Aislin was just about to comment as to how remarkably well she'd been feeling, but the question had forced her to notice an unsettling within her. Madam Andrews looked up from her reading when her friend didn't answer.

"What's wrong, dearest?" she gently called.

Aislin shook her head, and then came the pain. She was nearly brought to her knees and might have collapsed if Anna hadn't taken hold of her. James more dropped than set down the pot of tea he carried as he rushed down to where the women stood.

Moments later, Aislin had been whisked to her chamber as the pain was gradually becoming worse. The doctor arrived within the hour, and the scene that played out was all too familiar.

"Early again," Aislin said, unable to hide her fear.

"But by a much smaller margin," James attempted to console her. "The odds are in your favour and there's a very good chance…"

He was interrupted by the doctor's bidding everyone to leave the room. Aislin again pleaded for the doctor to let them stay, but this time, he allowed only Anna (Madam Andrews was already down stairs in the parlour as it wasn't fitting for her to be in the room).

Aislin had anticipated the agony, but somehow, it felt even worse this time. At the other end of the house and a floor beneath, her relentless cries were heard throughout. This time however, it didn't last the entire night. Aislin's torture was ended but a few hours after it began.

*   *   *

"Colonel Garnett." Sergeant Galloway reverently stepped into the small room, disrupting the friends' meeting. "A letter's just arrived for you, sir."

The recently promoted officer handed Garnett the letter, nodded and left.

"News from home?" Matthews queried.

"I'm not sure," Garnett answered, tearing it open. "This isn't in Aislin's hand."

Matthews and Russell sat solemnly still as Garnett began to study the article. Their leader didn't react to what he read at first, but slowly, a look of complete astonishment crossed his face.

"What is it, Will?" Russell impatiently questioned. "Has something happened?"

The colonel's hand had reached his mouth as he sank back into his chair.

"It's from Mrs. Andrews," he muttered.

Both men held their breath. They could only imagine what was to come next. But at last, Garnett's expression softened and a smile was revealed as his hand moved away.

"We have a son," he said quietly, trying to stifle the rising emotion. "Aislin's named him John."

"And they're both doing well?" Matthews asked.

"Quite well," the colonel said, with muffled laughter. "Mrs. Andrews writes, 'Your son arrived in the late evening of Twenty-One, August.   Aislin is still feeling poorly, and somewhat overwhelmed, else she would have written herself; but she was worried if she delayed, orders might prevent your receiving word.   Thus she insisted on our writing immediately.'" The colonel chuckled a little to himself. "'Rest assured her letter will follow shortly.'"

"Well, congratulations Will!" Russell exclaimed. "This calls for something special."

He pulled out a bottle that apparently he considered "special," though the others would never have known a difference.

"A son, now that's a right good wife you have there, Colonel," Matthews kidded. "General John Garnett–that'll do, eh?"

"There he goes," Russell rolled his eyes, already a little annoyed, as he poured the round.

"Now don't get carried away, David," Garnett said, referring to the full glasses. "We still have regular duties to perform in the morning."

"Ah yes," Matthews maintained his obnoxious exuberance, "foraging is awfully demanding on the mental as well as the physical faculties of any soldier."

"Come to think of it, don't give him any," Garnett jokingly directed Colonel Russell.

"Here now, that's not very neighbourly of you," Matthews retorted.

"Well, speaking of children," Russell diverted the subject, handing the major his drink, "how is young master Edward?"

June had delivered just after the men deployed and named her son after their friend, the fallen Major Lawrence. The Matthews' son was now some fourteen weeks old.

"Already a burden on his poor mother, I'm afraid," the major answered.

Garnett interjected, "Well then we know who he takes after, don't we."

Matthews went on, dismissing the colonel's remark, "June says he doesn't sleep at all at night, and she's already lost one nurse."

Russell continued to tease the major, "You'll be in for it when you get home, my friend." He elbowed Garnett, who was laughing easily with his colleagues.

"Just you wait. You'll see," the major said confidently.

The men took their ease of the evening, and continued their celebration probably a little too late. Major Matthews had a terrible headache in the morning, though he was the worst of them.

Aislin's letter trailed that of Madam Andrews by a week, but there was no trouble in its delivery to her husband. She reported their son to be the mirror image of the colonel with identical, miniature features and the same crystalline, blue eyes. The tone of the letter was bright and encouraged. Garnett knew Aislin was in good spirits and was thus comforted to know the worries that had plagued her for the last seasons were now over and gone.

*   *   *

Sergeant Galloway left his horse and blew into Colonel Garnett's quarters as if he'd been pushed. He immediately commanded the attention of everyone in the room.

"Colonel, the general has requested your presence," he huffed. "He asks that you come straight away–you also, Colonel Russell."

The two men leapt from their seats and gathered themselves as quickly as they could. They'd been posted to the outlying boundary of the camp and had a good distance to cover to reach the general's quarters.

They both deliberated the reason for the general's request. The navy had been steadily fighting off the newly arrived French fleet, but there was little with which to be concerned. It was the Royal Navy of Great Britain, after all. They'd not suffered a major defeat in over two centuries. There hadn't been much action otherwise, although reconnaissance had indicated that trouble was most definitely on the way.

The colonels couldn't have been more surprised. They found the general, standing very regally, looking out the window toward the bay. Upon hearing them enter, he offered Garnett the spyglass.

"Take a look," was the only thing he said.

The colonel stepped to the window and focused on the bay. It took him only a moment to see the object of the general's sombre gaze. The ships that occupied the harbour were flying French colours.

"Where's the fleet?" he asked breathlessly.

"Look just beneath the horizon," the general answered dully. "Reconnaissance has found they're already landing troops."

Garnett's mind raced. *We'll have to abandon the plans to remove to the north. We need to retreat from the coast. We'll be pinned down.* But he waited for the general to pronounce their orders.

"General Clinton will depart New York on the fifth of October. We will reinforce our defences and await his arrival."

The general was clear and authoritative. No one dared question the prescribed actions as he delivered the details of their instructions, and the colonel loyally acknowledged each command, never airing a single concern. On the way back to camp, however, Colonel Russell took every opportunity to convey his apprehensions.

"We should be breaking camp to take up a more defensible position–one that isn't threatened on the broad side by the French fleet," he stated, with no lack of emotion.

Garnett tried to ignore him. He was fighting his own doubts and didn't need any further contribution. Russell was unaware of his friend's frustrations.

"Wait out the month," he continued under his breath, "it's maddening. The navy is gone–miles away from being any sort of help. If we encounter conflict from anything stronger than a garrison, the position will be compromised."

"Stop," Garnett sighed. "You're exaggerating."

Russell had grown flustered and shaken, but his remarks came out sounding more angry and accusatory. "It wouldn't take much more to trap us, Will."

"Don't you think that's occurred to me?" Garnett jabbed back.

"I just wonder if it's occurred to the general," he replied, not phased at first by Garnett's outburst. Then he took a breath and settled back into his saddle. "I'm sorry."

It sounded as though he'd continue, but he never did. They quickened pace and returned to the camp in silence.

29

It was two weeks later when their nightmares came to fruition. On Friday evening, twenty-eight September, the rebel allied forces were standing at their doorstep. There were no more letters, no communiqués of any kind, and no supplies.

The flanking positions had all withdrawn, under inescapable pressure, into the main body for better defence. They were under siege and under fire from every direction. The walls they'd built were shattered under canon fire, and their defences on the river, having been exposed to the French fleet, were under constant bombardment. It would be five days before their aide from the north would even begin the long trek to their more than compromised position.

The cavalry units had been rendered nearly useless under the circumstances. They were constructed for speed and agility-warfare on open ground and swift battlefield routs. Garnett and his men did what they could to assist their besieged general and the infantrymen, but they were growing more and more discouraged the longer they were asked to wait. Discouragement was compounded by frustration, compounded by constant unease.

A garrison, detached across the river, was suffering harassment by a force of multiplying French and rebel militia. They were badly outnumbered and in need of just the sort of help Garnett and the dragoons could bring them. The colonel dutifully assumed the assignment but still with some measure of trepidation. Uncertainty shrouded every move they made.

"You know Lauzun is with them," Russell posed, alluding to the French Duke's presence among the forces across the river.

"Who's Lauzun?" Matthews asked, with great effort in an exaggerated French accent.

"Oh, just a friend of the colonel's," Russell answered casually.

Garnett stifled a smile as he finished buttoning his jacket.

"Uh huh," the major huffed, looking back at Russell for the real explanation.

"You're going to have to tell him now," Garnett said. "He'll drive you mad otherwise."

Russell shook his head. "The Duc de Lauzun has apparently heard rumours of our magnanimous Colonel Garnett and seems to be anticipating, if not eagerly, the opportunity for an encounter."

Matthews raised his eyebrows with a smart look. "Ah, well that's interesting."

"It is indeed," Garnett concluded. "And I must say I myself am 'most anxious to shake hands with the French duke.'"

The men laughed as they followed the colonel outside.

It was a Tuesday night when they silently crossed the York River to the entrenched troupe. They took very little time in settling–only long enough to be mildly comfortable for a short sleep through the rest of the night. Their duties were resumed at daybreak.

Garnett and his men were foraging through the countryside, and it wasn't long before they caught the attention of the enemy forces. The advance guards were soon engaged, drawing in the rest of their companies.

Garnett and his men set out to create a wall against the oncoming rebel cavalry, while the British infantry fell further back and reset in case the dragoons weren't enough to settle the row. Rebel militia led by the French volunteers inundated their forces.

The colonel rushed into the fray, riding down those members of the opposition who were so unfortunate to stand in his way. Looking across the field, he sighted the duke, who by then had espied Garnett as well.

The two officers drove straight for one another. The only waiver in Garnett's course was such as to keep Lauzun on his left. The colonel fought the still awkward feel of the pistol in this hand. He gathered his wits and searched a weakness in the duke's seat, all the while steadying himself. He gripped tight to the reins and drove his knees deep into the saddle to brace himself against the clash.

They were within only yards of each other as both prepared to strike. There was a garbled noise just off the colonel's flank, but he had hardly a moment to notice it. A wounded horse crashed into his own, pushing Garnett from the saddle and throwing him violently to the ground.

He couldn't catch his breath. For a moment he lay perfectly still, unable to think except in awareness of the incredible pain that shot through his body. The colonel thought he could see Lauzun smiling as he dismounted and persisted in closing the distance.

Garnett tried to move; then realized his leg was caught under his thrashing horse. There was a wrenching twist and intense pressure as the animal fell, failing yet again in his fighting attempt to get to his feet. The colonel then noticed the convergence of soldiers upon him. He fired his only shot and laboured to free his sword.

Suddenly there were arms reaching for his own, pulling and lifting him to a seat behind another soldier. Garnett recognized Galloway and Russell as two of those defending their retreat. As the colonel continued to regain his senses he heard Matthews shouting from ahead, asking if he was all right. Finally answering in the affirmative, the major seemed to be assuaged of his concern.

They reached the tree line that bordered the open battleground, dismounted, and began to appraise the damage inflicted on their leader. Garnett shook the fog from his head and still struggling to breathe, worked to pull himself together.

Matthews tried to think of something witty to say so as to gain a reaction from the colonel. "I can't imagine that was the sort of encounter either of you had in mind."

Garnett wheezed an attempted laugh. By this the major knew better the state of his friend.

Russell and Galloway joined them a moment later.

"You all right?" Russell asked, not taking time to dismount.

"Fine," the colonel said, still a bit winded. "My horse?"

Russell shook his head. "I'm afraid Lauzun will have it as a prize."

"S'pose I should be glad that's all he'll have," Garnett joked. He let them laugh then went on, "We have work to do."

Galloway dismounted and walked the animal to the colonel. "You'll need a mount, sir."

"Find another, Sergeant," Matthews called. "We'll need your help."

They barely heard Galloway's "yes, sir" as they galloped back into the campaign. The dragoons renewed the charge but were vastly outnumbered. Garnett finally rallied his men to fall back, relying on the protection of the infantry units.

The infantry did their job and held the enemy out of reach of their encampments, but for no lack of trying, the French and American forces were now settled right on top of them–less than a mile away.

30

"He hasn't answered the last three letters we've sent." Aislin was whispering, pacing back and forth beside the cradle that held her sleeping son.

"That's not so unusual, Miss," James replied, attempting to console her. "They might be on the move."

"I know," she groaned. "But with this news of the Continentals having moved into the same area, I just can't help but wonder. Do you think they might have engaged?"

"I suppose it's likely," he answered.

Aislin exhaled noisily and sat down beside the window. James knelt down in front of her.

"You know if anything had happened we'd have received word. Miss Anna hasn't heard from Colonel Russell either. Wherever they are, I think it's safe to assume they're together and doing well–just evading the messengers," he said, with a smile.

Aislin allowed a grin to escape her and then looked up as John let out a soft cry.

"Oh, there now," she cooed, lifting him up. "I was beginning to wonder how long you'd sleep."

"Would you like me to call Rebecca?" James offered in vain.

"No, that's all right." Her answer was more than distracted as her focus had settled directly on the boy.

"I'll pretend to be surprised."

Aislin caught his characteristic sarcasm and rolled her eyes. James laughed at her reaction.

"I'm sorry, Miss Aislin. You are a wonderful mother, and we'd be hard pressed to find anyone so devoted to and in love with her son."

"Not to mention so frugal as to save the wages of a nurse," she retorted.

"Indeed." His attention turned to the hallway as a knock came on the door downstairs. "That will be Mrs. Andrews. I'll see her in and make sure tea is ready."

"Thank you, James."

Aislin was downstairs a few minutes later, regretfully turning the baby over to Rebecca so as to better attend to her guest. John was always nearby and usually monopolizing his mother's attention, no matter the circumstances. Madam Andrews was still in a habit of correcting Aislin when her behaviour called for it, but where the child was concerned, she never said a word. Most often, she would just smile and shake her head.

James had just seen to Mrs. Andrews, and was about to shut the door, when a gentleman from the street steered quickly up the stairs and onto the porch. His arrival caught Aislin's attention.

"Can I help you, young man?" James offered the stranger.

"This is Colonel Garnett's house, is it not?" he inquired breathlessly.

"Yes. The colonel is unavailable."

James barely finished the sentence before the man began again.

"Please, pardon my intrusion. I'm trying to find someone who can confirm the rumours. They turned me away at the fort."

"I'm sorry. I don't know what you're talking about."

James's voice faded as Aislin's approach became evident. He wanted to turn and urge her to go, knowing anything this young man had to say would likely upset her; but the man hurried into his explanation.

"The word is the army's under siege-pinned in by the French in Virginia."

"Sir, you've misunderstood. The army can't be under siege. General Clinton himself is still in New York."

James's consolation was lost on the stranger.

"No, sir, not the whole army-General Lord Cornwallis' men."

"Well then, even if it is true, I'm sure you have nothing to worry about. The general and his escort account for less than a quarter of his forces. There will be reinforcements arriving soon to relieve them." James was growing frustrated with the man's irrational and seemingly unfounded worries.

"No, sir," the man practically shouted. "The entire southern force is trapped by the siege."

"That's not possible." James shook his head, staring suspiciously at the stranger.

"That's what I'm trying to confirm. It certainly does seem impossible, but no one can say for sure what's happened. There is no correspondence coming from the men in Virginia, but word has just reached us that General Clinton has uprooted his army in New York. Some say in readying to move south. Why would he surrender their foothold in the north unless under dyer circumstances?"

"Sir, I'm sorry," James slowly answered. "I'm sure you must have misunderstood."

"Then you've heard nothing of the sort?" The man's frustration fell to pure confusion.

"No, sir," was the only reply he tendered.

"Well, then," he sighed. "I'm terribly sorry for the imposition." He tipped his hat and backed down the stairs. "Excuse me."

James managed to force a smile as he turned to face his mistress. He casually ushered her into the parlour, trying desperately to pretend there was no need for concern. He was supremely relieved Aislin didn't ask any questions. She couldn't untangle her mind to think of them.

A courier arrived the next morning, unsure of what to do with the undeliverable letters Aislin and Anna had sent to the troops in Virginia.

*   *   *

"It's no use," Russell sighed, falling into a chair. "They have us pinned. We could probably get back across the river but..."

"Fat lot of good that would do us. They're in no better shape than we," Matthews finished the thought for him.

Garnett didn't answer them–didn't even acknowledge them. The state of things had him feeling overwhelmed and confused, not to mention the physical weakness he was battling in trying to recover from the injuries acquired from their brief skirmish. He quietly studied the latest reports from the outposts. Reviewing the information over and over again, he hoped he'd come across something he'd missed before–something that would enlighten him as to a way out of their present mess. He found nothing.

The men carried on in their bantering but were abruptly stopped by a quiet comment from the colonel. "We'll just have to wait for the men in the north and trust they'll be here in time."

They all tried to pretend his answer would suffice, but it was a sad show at best.

31

They had waited as long as they could and had taken more battery than they had believed possible. Garnett and his men were informed that Cornwallis had already concluded his negotiations for terms of surrender (or rather his subordinates had). The colonel put to use his knowledge of the French language once more in a requested parlay.

Fearing for his life, should he fall into the hands of the Americans, Garnett met privately with General de Choisy and his men to plead for any form of protection they could offer. Their meeting included the duke.

Though they fought on opposing sides, Lauzun and Garnett had a mutual respect for one another as military leaders. Each had been following the other's career in the colonies with interest, and Lauzun had been more than impressed by the colonel's strategic abilities, as well as his nerve in the field.

While General de Choisy did not hold Garnett to any great esteem, he agreed to the colonel's request out of intent on preventing any rash actions from the Patriot camp.

His friends, of course, inquired after the colonel once the assembly had dispersed.

Garnett explained. "The probability of someone seeking retribution just seems too likely, considering Waxhaw's and the other encounters. Since the general is willing to allow me to stay behind, I'd rather not chance it."

"Well it's very good of them to agree to such terms," Russell said, ponderously, "but I'd still be a little apprehensive being here alone with the rest of us so far away."

"And unarmed," Matthews added.

"De Choisy will be leaving behind a guard to make sure there are no stragglers and to protect the camp against any last, desperate attempts. I trust him. I'll be safe."

Though the threat to his life was real enough, the colonel's words were blanketed with a calm resolution. His friends wished they felt the same.

Thus on Friday, the nineteenth of October, Garnett's friends surrendered their arms without him. He remained behind at their entrenchments in Gloucester, waiting for his men to return. They would keep their place in the current camp until arrangements were finalized for their parole.

Alone, the colonel sat in his tent tallying in his head the string of mistakes that had been made, leading them to this moment. He thought of what this would mean for their cause in the colonies. Would General Clinton be able to make up for the loss of so many troops?

He thought about the torment of parole that awaited him—having to merely watch and wait for the outcome to be decided without him. The colonel tried to put his mind to returning home, choosing to look at the dismissal for what it was: an opportunity to be with his family.

Their parole agreement had been such as to let the officers return to those cities and territories still in possession (militarily) of the Crown. Thus, Garnett and his friends would face no opposition in their homecomings.

St. Augustine was still under total British control. The Spanish had been moving in on the territory, but so far, had been unable to come much farther than West Florida. Though the fort had seen little to no military action in the war, it was still quite active, both in training and regular exercises, and as a prison. It would be an optimal place to maintain their lives as well as the colonel's career.

Bent over in his seat, hanging his head, the colonel was relieved without measure at the sound of footsteps outside his tent. He expected it was his friends, back from their last humiliating task. He was wrong.

Lauzun carefully entered the doorway. "May I?" he asked, in thickly accented English.

"Please." Garnett gestured to a seat across from him. "I'm surprised to see you back so soon," he turned.

"Yes, well, I take no pleasure in breaking a man's spirit. One can only stomach so much."

"I gather the rebels have not been very gracious in their victory," the colonel posed, pouring a drink for his guest.

"That would be vastly understating the situation. Most of your men were trying to surrender their arms to our troupe- anything to keep them out of American hands."

"Americans," Garnett whispered to himself. "We've lost haven't we?"

"It doesn't look good," the duke answered facetiously.

The colonel had to chuckle at the repartee, but his expression fell more serious. "We won't recover from this loss. They've actually won." He huffed another laugh. "I never would have thought."

"I don't think anyone would. But it's not such a bad thing, after all," Lauzun said, a little flippantly.

Garnett looked up at him. "Now what would make you say that?"

"Come now, Colonel. Surely you realize it was only a matter of time."

The colonel had certainly not realized.

"That *Common Sense* fellow had a point. How do a government and a people confined to one tiny island suppose to run the lives of those covering a *continent*, being separated by an entire ocean? With every respect to you and your people, you don't really think your king and your government can have the interests of these colonials in mind, do you?"

The duke caught the look on Garnett's face as the colonel laughed to himself.

"What?" Lauzun questioned, thinking perhaps the colonel were laughing at what he'd said.

"Uh," Garnett sighed. "You and my wife would get on famously."

"Your wife is a sympathizer?" His voice shook as he spoke, revealing his amusement.

"The worst kind," the colonel moaned.

"And people say God has no sense of humour. Or else you're being punished."

"Oh, if Aislin is punishment, there is no treachery I could regret."

"In that case, I'm happy for you," Lauzun smiled. "You'll return to her now, yes?"

"As soon as humanly possible."

Garnett hardly had the words from his mouth, when his friends entered the small room. Lauzun immediately felt uncomfortable. While he and the colonel had managed something of a friendship, he imagined the hate and animosity that must be lingering in the hearts of the men he'd help to defeat.

"I think it's time I'm going," he said, getting to his feet. He handed his glass back to his host. "Thank you, Colonel."

"Likewise," Garnett answered with a smile.

Russell felt he should try to ease the duke's awkward exit. "I suppose we're not angry with *you*, sir."

"Really?" Lauzun asked. "I would be."

He winked, and with a sly grin, he left the trio behind.

"I see you've discovered a kindred spirit." The major's joke was delivered half-hearted as he took a seat. "Oh," he groaned, "I never thought I'd be glad to be back at camp."

"I'm sorry I wasn't there," Garnett offered.

"Huh, you wouldn't be, if you'd been there," Matthews continued.

Russell issued real forgiveness. "You know we don't think any less of you, Will; and we certainly couldn't be disappointed or angry with you."

"Do let's try," the major poked.

He knew Garnett was feeling the failure of the event as much as, if not more so than all the other men; and he knew the colonel hated the fact he'd let his men surrender without their commanding officer. Matthews teased to try to end their perpetual discouragement.

Garnett shook his head and smiled.

"Oh, you'll be interested to hear," Russell said complacently, "Major Allen was killed during the storming of Redoubt No. 9 across the river–along with several others, obviously."

"Really…I'm sorry to hear that."

The colonel tried to sound concerned, but in truth, the news brought to him a sudden feeling of utter liberation.

Russell grinned. "No one would blame you for being relieved. I know he was a bit of a thorn in your side."

Garnett didn't answer. There was nothing he could say that wouldn't be either a lie or some element that would give him away. Russell accepted his quiet refrain knowing the colonel would never speak ill of the dead.

32

It was very soon after that word reached St. Augustine about the surrender in Virginia. Everyone was dumbfounded–and worried. The tone of "what now?" held hostage every thought, and it seemed not a single question had an answer.

There were rumours concerning parole, release and the like; but no confirmation came until, in early November, Aislin at last received a letter. The colonel and the other officers were still in Yorktown, making their last reports to General Lord Cornwallis and the other commanders. They were shortly to sign for their paroles and be dismissed of their duties in the war against the colonies. Garnett expected to remain in Virginia for a few weeks and would then be returning home. Aislin hated to think it was formality alone that continued to prolong his absence, but she was thankful to find he was safe and soon to be released.

More than anything, she was looking forward to introducing the colonel to his son. The whole house marvelled at how quickly John was growing, but each passing day served to Aislin only a reminder of how much time she and William had missed.

Meanwhile, in Yorktown, the colonel was facing possibly the most difficult of all trials ahead. He and the rest of the officers were expected to attend dinners and other such events with their counterparts of the Continental and French militaries. Everyone pretended, for the sake of rapport, to be looking forward to these interactions in an effort to put the conflict behind them and begin working toward absolution and reconciliation.

Garnett, Russell and Matthews, having readied themselves as best they could, finally made their way to the house where the first of these affairs was to take place. They were barred, however, by the two Colonial guards minding the front door.

"You're not welcome here," the first said abruptly.

Russell stepped forward when Garnett did not.

"I beg your pardon," he replied forcefully. "We're officers in the King's Army."

"I'm sorry, sir," the second said, through gritted teeth. "The Butcher is not welcome." He was glaring at Garnett, his fists so tight around the musket his knuckles had gone white.

"You find fault in 'a faithful discharge of my duty to my king and my country'? For this, we're to be 'humiliated in the eyes of three armies?'"

"No, sir, I didn't mean to include these gentlemen in our refusal. You may go inside," he continued, addressing Russell and the major.

"We respectfully decline," Matthews sarcastically responded. He turned to the colonel, "Come on, Will."

Russell and Matthews muttered under their breath as they left, appalled at the treatment of their commander and telling each other how glad they were to be dismissed from the task of dining with "those treasonous dogs." They were stopped suddenly by a call coming from just behind them.

"Colonel!" the voice shouted after them. "What's going on? Where are you going?" It was Lauzun. He had seen them at the door and was surprised to see them leaving.

"It seems my reputation precedes me," Garnett answered, laughing a little in spite of himself.

The duke looked at the others. "I don't understand."

"They've turned the colonel away," Russell replied. No humour plagued his voice. It wouldn't have been heard over the anger and frustration.

Lauzun wanted to try to make some argument for the colonel, but he knew well the colonists' feelings toward Garnett. The soldiers the duke had fought alongside had been all too generous in sharing their opinions of the Butcher, as they'd come to call him.

Lauzun shook his head. "Certainly there must be a mistake. Why don't you gentlemen come with me, and we'll see if we can resolve the matter."

"I don't believe we'll find any resolution in that room tonight," Garnett smiled. "It's all right, friend. You go and enjoy yourself."

"I believe I'd rather accompany you gentlemen," Lauzun jested, feeling very much the same way Garnett and his friends did about the whole affair.

"You're welcome to join us," Matthews offered.

The three men turned, surprised to hear the major's invitation.

"What?" Matthews asked.

Lauzun laughed. "While I do appreciate the offer, I suppose the general wouldn't be very pleased with my absence."

"You sail for France tomorrow, yes?" the colonel said, changing the subject.

The duke nodded. "I'm to carry home the news for General Rochambeau."

The news was, of course, the French victories in the colonies.

"We wish you the very best," Garnett offered his hand, "for a safe journey and continued success."

"Likewise," Lauzun smiled, "And the very best of luck to you and your family."

"Thank you."

With the last exchange, Lauzun returned indoors, and the small company of British officers left to seek out a more hospitable crowd to join for the evening. Insult, however, was yet to be added to the colonel's injury.

The next evening, Garnett separated from his officers to attend a dinner with a friend of the duke. It wasn't a particularly long distance to travel, but the colonel was still mending from wounds incurred during the siege. Thus, he travelled by horse.

Not halfway to the Frenchman's home, however, Garnett was abruptly stopped in the street by the steward of a local gentleman. The steward recognized the colonel's borrowed mount as one taken from the gentleman's stable several months earlier.

He demanded Garnett dismount and surrender the horse immediately. The colonel, pleading sympathy for his injuries, requested the man let him continue upon Garnett's word the horse would be returned. The steward wouldn't hear him, refusing to trust the colonel with the mount.

There, in the middle of the street and before the citizens of Yorktown, further humiliation was heaped upon Garnett as he dismounted and abandoned the reigns. But the colonel quickly found he was not without his own supporters.

A French officer, with whom Garnett was not acquainted, had seen the trouble. He and his aide approached the disgraced Briton.

"Colonel Garnett," the officer enquired.

"Yes," he replied, as politely as his spirit would allow.

"Vous étés un ami du duc de Lauzun, oui?"

The officer's aide began to translate for Garnett, "You are a friend of the Duke of Lauzun, yes?"

The colonel smiled and extended his hand to both gentlemen.

"Oui, et je parle français," he replied.

("Yes, and I speak French")

"Le duc parle fortement de toi. S'il vous plait, nous permettre l'honneur de vous aider."

("The duke speaks highly of you. Please, allow us the honour of assisting you")

With this, the officer's aide dismounted and handed the reigns to Garnett.

"S'il vous plait," the aide offered.

("Please")

The colonel graciously accepted and thanked them both for their generosity. His promise to return the horse was quickly dismissed by the officer who, upon Lauzun's word, already believed Garnett to be an honourable man.

It was little more than a week later when the men were finally released and set out to return to their homes. Garnett and Russell wished Matthews the very best as he embarked on the journey back to Charles Town, travelling with the troops by land; and all gave their word they'd visit when the opportunity arose.

The colonels travelled their days aboard ship and arrived in Florida in early December. Everyone anticipated their arrival. Even Madam Andrews was on hand to welcome them home.

The whole house exploded as the men made their entrance. Aislin lost her shoes as William lifted her off the ground, swinging her in a circle around the room. Madam, James, and Rebecca-carrying John-all stood nearby, excitedly taking in the display. Nearly every laugh was accompanied by a tear.

"Where is he?" Garnett exuberantly enquired.

Rebecca approached with their son, whom William immediately gathered in his arms.

"So you're John," he sighed.

The boy smiled, staring right into his father's eyes.

The colonel kissed him on the forehead and looked up, grinning wildly at Aislin.

She reached a hand to her husband's face. "I'm so glad you're finally home."

William kissed her cheek. "Home to stay," he whispered.

The colonel and his family settled in comfortably having gotten used to the idea he wouldn't be recalled to the battlefront. Their lives became a wonderful routine, and the whole party revelled in their good fortune.

At Christmas, the Russells announced the expected arrival of a new family member. Colonel Russell wore a constant smile, but surrounded by so many, it seemed almost common place.

Everywhere they went in the city, men offered the colonels a drink or a slap on the back, with thanks for their service in the war. Garnett and Russell frequently had to endure the people's complaints and criticisms of the war along with their compliments, but they simply tried to ignore the former.

It was a calm evening in early March as the party sat gathered about the Garnetts' garden. Aislin, Anna, and Madam Andrews sat talking beneath the shade of the terrace, as the men-never sitting for any great length of time-hovered close by. John sat at his mother's feet, and though he had been content to quietly entertain himself, a sudden squeal followed by his small laugh demanded the attention of the group.

"Such a commanding presence," Anna said. "Have we a future Colonel Garnett on our hands?"

"According to George, he's to be a general," Garnett replied, not sounding as sarcastic as he'd intended.

"And why not," Aislin added.

Anna turned, thoughtfully, "We haven't heard from the Matthews in some time now."

"Mm," Aislin nodded. "But I'm sure they're doing well. I can't imagine how little Edward must have grown."

John squealed again, seeming to notice he no longer held their undivided interest. Aislin started to lean over, but the colonel was already making his way to the boy. William lifted him up, as John continued to giggle.

"Must you interrupt your mother?" he said, immediately overcome with a smile.

Lord North resigned as Prime Minister the same month, and in April, the Commons voted to end the war as the last remnants of the conflict left the colonies behind. Though there were still some uprisings, the warfare had become mostly the business of the Royal Navy. Now, Parliament sought to bring the whole affair to a close.

News of the concluding ordeal continued to filter through the military posts, and it wasn't long before the news began to take hold of the lives of those in the last British settlements.

As the colonels prepared to leave for home one afternoon, the general pulled Garnett and Russell aside to share with them an unsettling matter of which he'd just been apprised. For the time being, the general meant only to share the information with his officers so they could prepare.

Both men left, following the brief meeting, but as he rode slowly from the fort, Garnett stopped to overlook the bay. One thought gripped his mind: what a pity his son would never grow to remember this place.

Aislin cheerily welcomed him home as she always did, but her query of his day brought William's call for Rebecca. She came and removed John from the room.

"I have some news–about the pending treaty," he addressed his wife.

"That doesn't sound good," she replied, slowly sitting down.

Garnett paced, trying to find the right words.

"William, whatever it is, please just tell me."

He sighed. "The articles of the treaty seem to indicate we will be returning St. Augustine to the Spanish as part of the reparations." He continued almost under his breath, "I suppose I knew it was a possibility, being we have virtually no business here in the colonies any more; but I had hoped…"

"What will we do?"

Aislin felt surprisingly calm. She had never feared a move so much as she had feared her husband being away. While she regretted they'd have to leave such a perfect home, she was greatly comforted in knowing, whatever happened, her family would be together.

William shook his head. "The military still holds me in their employ. The general seems to think they'll have us sail back to New York first, to rejoin the rest of the army. Then I suppose it's back to England."

"Does Colonel Russell know?"

"Yes, I imagine he's telling Anna now."

"Oh poor Anna. Do you think they'll make her sail in her condition?"

Aislin knew well, a routine voyage on a calm sea could make Anna ill, let alone her being in the state she was.

"It will be some time before we sail–probably well after she's delivered. But I'm not sure which would be worse: to sail now or wait and sail with a newborn. I imagine John will have a rough go of it, as it is."

Aislin sank a little in the chair. England–she'd never made such a long trip, nor had she ever been to the place. William gathered her out the chair and took her in his arms. He held her for a moment without a word between them and was then struck with a thought that might actually raise his wife's spirits.

"I've just had a wonderful idea," he said, pulling away just far enough to see her face. "Since we'll be in New England anyway, I'm sure it wouldn't take much to arrange a short side-trip."

He smiled, but Aislin had no idea what he meant.

"To see your family before we sail," he continued.

Aislin's eyes lit up. With the war ending, she was certain her father and brothers would expect her home. She couldn't help but smile as she began to think of how she'd explain to them the last five years.

"Do you really think we could?" she asked excitedly.

"We'll still have to be careful–discreet, I mean–but I think we could manage."

"Oh William!"

She flung her arms around his neck, already looking forward to the trip.

33

Madam Andrews, at last, made the difficult decision to travel with the two young couples in their evacuation. Her ties with other British citizens left her with little other choice. Loyalists in general were being forced to leave their homes. Those who weren't headed back to England left for islands in the Caribbean or territories in Canada. A few braved the move west, but harassment from the Indians made it a rather unattractive option.

John was walking when Madam Andrews along with the Garnetts and Russells boarded the ship that would carry them to New York. Anna had delivered a daughter, Bridget, little more than a month before the departure; and though the delivery hadn't been particularly difficult, Mrs. Russell still wasn't feeling quite herself. Aislin, having left John primarily in Rebecca's care, took it upon herself to look after Anna and the baby when she could.

The sailing was smooth, which was rare fortune for the time of year, but Aislin wrestled constantly with her anxiety. She was nervous about seeing her family again, and she was worried at the idea of being engulfed by so many soldiers. She knew her only accuser was no longer a threat, and William reassured her, even if she was suspected (which at this stage would be unlikely), he was certain nothing would come of it. On the other hand, his cautious demeanour led her to believe otherwise.

Once they'd come ashore, the Garnetts left their friends in the city and travelled the roads into New Jersey, hoping to find the Laraways in Trenton where they'd last been seen. Aislin had expected the trek to take far longer than it did, remembering the journey from Camden. The conflict of the last time, of course, made the difference.

A bustling town met them on arrival. While James looked after the women, the colonel set out to find the Laraways. He had just enquired after them at the bank, knowing Mr. Laraway would have to have some dealings there, when he heard a call from down the street.

"Colonel!" the voice shouted.

Garnett turned to see Thomas Laraway running to meet him. He began to feel uneasy, of both the approaching young man and the town being alerted to his military affiliation (owing to his being intentionally out of uniform).

"Well you could likely be a welcomed sight," Laraway spoke lightly, extending his hand. "Is my sister with you?"

"She is. We've come to see your family."

"Wonderful! Everyone's just returned to the house." He pointed toward a street just a little farther down from where they stood. "I'll let them know you're on your way."

"Thank you," Garnett managed, as Thomas left in the other direction.

Aislin held her breath as James turned toward their destination. She stepped out of the carriage holding tightly to her husband's arm. They were followed closely behind by James and Rebecca, still holding tightly to a restless John.

The couple in lead entered tentatively, uncertain of what to expect. The colonel half-feared one or any number of the Laraway men might yet seek their revenge. Aislin however, smiled as she crossed the threshold. She stifled a laugh, watching her father and brothers (having obviously missed her entrance) continuing in a frantic effort to straighten their clothes and arguing over the proper way to knot a necktie.

All the men looked up sharply as the party finally caught their attention. Thomas was the only one who smiled, the others still unsure of their company. Daniel Laraway took two small steps and then rushed toward his daughter. Aislin's eyes began to tear as she wrapped her arms around her father's neck.

"I'm all right, Pa," she whispered. "I'm all right."

"I have missed you," he said, holding her face in his hands and kissing her forehead.

With one more embrace, his gaze shifted toward Garnett. Aislin watched nervously as her father made his approach. Within striking distance, Daniel quietly offered his hand to the colonel.

"I'm very grateful for all you've done for us." Overcome by his emotions, Laraway's voice broke as he spoke.

Garnett wanted to respond, but the surprise had robbed him of his words. Instead, he smiled, still shaking Laraway's hand.

With the friendly greeting from their father, John and Clayton jovially pulled the crowd from the doorway with their heralds of welcome to their sister and her family. Aislin quickly presented her son who was suddenly, and from then on, the focus of their interest.

At dinner that evening, the Garnetts were introduced to the lovely young women, sisters Susan and Ella, who had recently become Laraways themselves. John and Susan had married more than a year previous, and Clayton, having met Ella through the marriage, wasted little time in making her his bride. Ella was already expecting and very excited at suddenly becoming an Aunt. She and Susan impatiently relieved Rebecca of her small charge.

The two women greatly amused Aislin. They weren't much like her friends, and they spent most of the night exchanging whispers and glances, trying to hide their stares at the colonel. Aislin's brothers were handsome in their own right, with dusky features and the same dark eyes she had; but they did tend to look plain in comparison to the sharper, more dignified officer.

The men all questioned whether or not Aislin had received the letters they'd each sent in turn. She confirmed her acceptance of the correspondence and proceeded to answer all of their questions. They listened to her stories with sincerest fascination and laughed as they related their reaction to Thomas's news of her marrying the colonel.

Clayton stood from the table, retrieving the pitcher to refill their emptying glasses as he spoke. "So what's next for our adventurous Aislin?"

The others chuckled.

"On the move again, I'm afraid." She looked at her husband who gave a tight-lipped, sympathetic smile.

"You'll be leaving with the fleet for England," Daniel supposed, without looking up.

"Yes, sir," Aislin respectfully returned.

John looked anxiously around the table. "But you just got back. At least stay a month or two."

She tried to steady her voice. "We can't, John."

"I'm afraid it's my fault," Garnett began.

Thomas stopped him. "The colonel is too much of an asset to our British comrades–very efficient in his duties."

"Certainly too efficient to stay," William huffed, "then not efficient enough."

Thomas and Daniel both smiled at his self-criticism.

The colonel continued, "It won't be long before I'm reassigned. Even if we could stay, we'd only be delaying the inevitable." He turned to Aislin, "I'm sorry."

She smiled, as her father answered for her.

"There's no need for apologies. You have to do what's right by your family. I'm certain we all understand that."

His statement, though mostly meant for Garnett, was also a directive to his sons not to press them further.

Later, lying in bed, Aislin's mind wrestled with the idea of their leaving the colonies, knowing she would likely never set foot there again; nor would she see her family. She leaned over to rest her head on William's shoulder. She felt torn, and he knew it.

"I am sorry," he whispered and kissed her forehead. "I wish things had turned out differently. I wish we could stay."

Aislin looked up at him and smiled. She knew what he meant. "Have you considered how things would be if the circumstances were different–if you and your men had won?"

A tilt of his head was his answer of curiosity.

"It startles me to think of what my father's reaction to you might have been, for one thing. And for another, do you really think it would change our leaving? Wouldn't you be reassigned anyway?"

He sighed, "I suppose it's impossible to say."

William tightened his grip around her and propped his free arm under his head. He stared at the ceiling. There was a question to which he wanted an answer, but he wasn't sure he should risk the asking.

Aislin could feel the turbulence in his constant movement beside her.

"William, what is it?"

He didn't answer at first. Instead, he turned to his side looking over his wife. He laid his arm across her and began to find his words.

"Are you happy with me?"

The colonel's soft expression got the better of Aislin's emotions. She reached up and brushed his cheek.

"William," she muttered.

"After everything that's happened, everything you've been put through… I had hoped, in the end, to give you back the life you lost. Now it looks as though that will never be possible."

"This," she glanced around her, "is no longer my life. Things have changed. My life is loaded aboard ship, bound for England. Yes, I will miss my family. I wish there was a way to have it all, but life rarely affords such luxuries. William, I knew when I married you things would be different. I wondered if I'd ever be able to see my father and brothers again, but even knowing what I know now, I wouldn't have chosen any differently."

The colonel smiled, suppressing a small laugh.

"You're laughing at me," Aislin snickered.

"No, my dear," he said, pushing the hair from her shoulder, "at myself. I should have known better."

She grinned as William pulled her close and laid a kiss on her lips.

34

After two short days with her family, Aislin said her tearful goodbyes and returned with her husband to the ships awaiting them on the coast. The congregation there now included the Matthews, who had been obliged to leave their home in Charles Town and had arrived while the Garnetts were off on their excursion.

The troupe stayed one last night in New York, entertaining none other than the third son of King George III and Queen Charlotte: the Duke of Clarence. The young royal, having arrived with the navy several months earlier, had heard of Garnett's many exploits in the colonies and had sought out the colonel upon the party's return to port.

Aislin was particularly amused by the duke. He was seven years her junior, but his conversations with her husband immediately evidenced his intelligence and experience. Thus, Aislin's first interaction with a member of the monarchy was an interesting and pleasant one.

Nevertheless, the women were soon left to their own devices as the men retreated into discussions that lacked a lady's interest. June, like Aislin, had never been to England, and the two women listened eagerly to Anna's stories of the country. Mostly, Anna shared of her fascination with the cities. She loved the life and the beauty of the scenes held within each street, but even more so, she loved the shops and spending as much of Colonel Russell's money as he would allow.

What Aislin was looking forward to most of all was seeing the estate her husband had once described for her: the lake and the hills, and the handsome house overlooking the gardens. Focusing on what lay before them made it very difficult to feel any remorse about leaving.

Each of the women was promised a picturesque estate provided by the finest officers in service of the British military. The cities offered the best schooling and opportunities they could have wanted for their children; and of course, they would also have their friends. The families intended to stay close and visit every day, if occasion allowed.

New friends were guaranteed as well. The Garnetts had already received an invitation from the Duke of Lauzun to join him in France, at their earliest convenience. William was teaching Aislin to speak French, so she would be able to converse with the duke and the other members of his house; and Mrs. Garnett's companions were impressed at how quickly she was learning.

Overseas, the men would continue to advance their careers, and opportunities to do so were abundant in Europe. There was always a row to be settled with the French or the Spanish. The colonies to the east, in India and elsewhere, needed attending; and the trade routes in between had to be defended.

Gaining an acquaintance like the Duke of Clarence would certainly be a help in their pursuits.

After a lively evening and a short sleep, the outfit collected themselves and left for the docks. Not half way to their destination, however, the memorable visage of Lieutenant Danvers stopped Garnett cold in his tracks. The colonel took such a firm hold of Aislin's arm, she gasped.

Turning with a wince, she said, "William, you're hurting my…"

She saw the horror in his eyes and easily traced his gaze. It was too late. Danvers had seen them. Aislin thought to run, but Garnett's grasp wouldn't have allowed it. If they did run, it would unquestionably make things worse. So they steadily marched toward the certain collision. They had talked their way out of similarly hopeless situations. Garnett hoped for the same fortune this time.

As the lieutenant drew closer to them, William and Aislin began to make out the smile that crossed his all too familiar face.

"I say, Will," Colonel Russell queried, seeing the man approach, "do you know this gent?" When Garnett didn't answer, Russell turned. "What's wrong?"

There was no time to answer. Danvers had arrived.

"Colonel Garnett, sir," he began congenially, "I heard you were sailing today and hoped I would catch you before you left."

And caught them he had–by surprise, at any rate.

Garnett didn't answer. He was startled beyond words. Instead, he reacted instinctively to Danvers' outstretched hand, receiving it into his own.

The lieutenant's expression softened as he continued, his glance shifting to Aislin. "I'm glad to see you and your family are in good health, sir. And may I offer my congratulations on both your marriage and the safe arrival of your son, though I know I'm a bit late. I see the move from New England agreed with you."

Something in Danvers' eyes gave away his secret. Garnett finally found his words.

"You knew," he whispered.

Danvers winked. "Well, the disappearance, conveniently timed with the arrival of your cousin; your hurried exodus from the north after our search–when word reached us of your marriage, I had only to imagine..."

"The search–you knew I was in the house," Aislin murmured, "and you didn't turn us in?"

All three were careful of their tone. The Garnetts trusted their friends but didn't want to cause any trouble.

The lieutenant laughed under his breath. "I was so nervous; I thought for sure I'd give it away. I've never prayed so hard as I did–hoping the men wouldn't find you."

Garnett was dumbstruck. "I don't know what to say."

"I didn't mean to cause you any worry, sir. I meant what I said. I simply wanted to offer my congratulations and to see you off. I was sorry you had to leave the way you did. Serving in your company was an honour and a pleasure."

The colonel again shook the lieutenant's hand, finally recovering his composure and overcome with a smile of relief and gratitude.

"How can I ever thank you?"

"No need, sir. Our prayers go with you on the journey home."

"God speed in your duties here, Lieutenant," the colonel added confidently.

The two men nodded as they parted ways. To the curious officers, Garnett quickly explained Danvers' former post in his company while in New England.

Hearing Aislin's stifled laughter beside him, William had not but to shake his head and sigh.

Epilogue

He left the colonies, "the Butcher"–a hated man; but he would
return to England a hero. The encounters and the friendships
forged in America seemed only to foreshadow the fortune and
adventures which were just beginning. Awaiting them across
the sea were devastating storms and pirate attacks, homecomings
and headlines, meetings with the King and Queen, princes and
parties, military commendations and promotions, Knighthood,
and yet another Revolution.

References

Baskin, Marg, and Holley Calmes. Oatmeal for the Foxhounds: Banastre Tarleton and the British Legion. http://www. banastretarleton.org

Bass, Robert D. 1957. *The Green Dragoon*. Sandlapper Publishing Co., Inc.

Selig, Robert A. The Duc de Lauzun and his Legion: Rochambeau's Most Troublesome, colorful soldiers. http:// americanrevolution.org

Tarleton, Lieutenant-Colonel Banastre, Commandant of the Late British Legion. 1787. *A History of the Campaigns of 1780 and 1781, in the Southern Provinces of North America.* The Scholar's Bookshelf